LOGAN

By

George Donald

CHAPTER 1

The shrill ring of the telephone brought me to a rude awakening. As soon as I opened my eyes, I realised it was mistake. The dull throbbing pain that hammered a steady beat inside my skull was no stranger to me and I knew that any movement faster than a snails pace would simply provoke the rhythm to beat faster.

At first, I couldn't understand why the world, or rather my office wall and the old wooden clock, should be lying sideways?

But it wasn't the wall lying sideways - it was me. Head down, I'd simply fallen asleep across the top of my desk. Again.

Still the phone chirruped away. I tried to sit upright and almost succeeded in raising an arm, but of course that was another mistake. The room spun out of control and the bile rose in my throat. My mouth felt as though I'd stuffed a three-day old sock in it and I had difficulty swallowing.

I decided to let the answer machine kick in and, eyes closed tightly against the drum band in my head, very slowly settled my numb cheek once more onto the desk and listened to my recorded voice announce that Logan Investigations was temporarily unavailable and requesting the caller to leave a message, that someone - me, since I was the sole employee - would return their call. I almost chuckled at that promise, pleased that I sounded sincere, but the effort would only have provoked another beat of the bass drum inside my skull.

The machine beeped twice and after a short pause a woman's voice, hesitant at first, began to speak.

"Eh, I'm calling about...I mean I found your number in Yellow Pages. You do missing persons I assume? The thing is, my name is Kilbride, Missus Phyllis Kilbride. It's about..."

She paused and I could hear her hesitation, as if uncertain whether or not to continue. I almost reached for the phone then, but long experience had taught me that after the session I'd had last night, my lips wouldn't work properly and I'd end up burbling like a halfwit, so decided to listen instead.

"About my husband," she continued at last. Then, as if embarrassed, I heard her say, "Please call me back."

The line went dead and a few seconds later I listened as the tape whirled back to the beginning.

I'm not bad at accents and figured Missus Kilbride originated somewhere in the Home Counties, Essex perhaps.

Her number. The stupid sod hadn't left a contact number.

In times gone by I might dismissed the call and either waited on her ringing back or simply got on with something else. But that was then.

Nowadays work wasn't that plentiful and beggars, or more properly drunks like me, couldn't afford to pass up any opportunity that brought in a few quid.

Grimacing against the pain, I took a deep breath and sat upright, aware that the effort was likely to bring up the chips whose vinegary taste still lingered in my mouth. Almost without thinking, I reached for the bottle of Bells, only to find that I'd drained it the previous night and there was but a few drops lingering in the bottom. Still, a few drops was better than nothing and might just get rid of the chip taste, I thought. I upended it, licking at the rim with a furry tongue and wishing to God I'd the foresight to stow a half bottle in my desk.

I exhaled noisily, trying to muster the courage to stand and get over to the small sink in the corner where in the mirrored cabinet above, I knew deliverance from the headache lay in the large bottle of prescription painkillers. The tablets were actually prescribed for my leg, but what the hell. Pain was pain, I reckoned, whether in the leg or the head.

My wooden walking stick lay on the floor, but I resisted the urge to bend over and lift it. Too much movement and I'd throw up all over the already grimy office carpet. Using the desk to steady myself, I staggered unsteadily towards the sink, reaching out with both hands like one of those zombie creatures in an old black and white movie and determined to cross the ten feet of space without stumbling. I'd already decided if I fell over, I would just lie down and die.

The pain in my left hip now joined the ache in my head as I dragged the useless bloody leg behind me. Curiously, I had numbness in my face too, almost as if some palsy had me in its grip. At last I reached the sink and held onto the stained basin with shaking hands and exhaled loudly, finishing with a belch that stunk of whisky and almost caused me to throw up, right there and then. Turning my head carefully to ease the stitch in my neck I saw it was almost eight-thirty on the wall clock. I couldn't believe that I'd slept for almost eight hours, but then again the bottle of Bells had obviously helped.

The mirror was cracked at one edge, but still retained enough of its shape to reflect the wrecked face that stared into it. No wonder my jaw felt numb. I must have lain most of the night on my right cheek, which now bore the imprint of the corner of the desk blotter. Lazily, I slapped at it once, then again and worked my jaw, forcing the blood to flow back into my reddened face.

I stared with bleary eyes, once bright blue but now vein lined and watery. My skin was blotchy and I badly needed a shave. My hair, strawberry blonde I think is the term the barbers use, was overdue a trim and sticking out from one side of my head. The stain on my loosened tie looked like it had been there a couple of days.

Now why hadn't I noticed that before?

The bile again rose in my throat, but I swallowed hard and forced it down. The last time I'd vomited into the sink I'd been days trying to get the bloody thing cleared. No, I'd wait till I reached the WC, I decided, suddenly conscious I was carrying a full bladder round with me.

I pulled open the cabinet door and grabbed the medicine bottle. There were no more than half a dozen tablets left. Typical of me, I silently fumed, leaving it till the last minute for a refill. I knew the potency of the painkillers and was always being warned by my pharmacist not to overdose. But the way I was feeling called for extraordinary measures, particularly if I was to follow up the telephone lead that just might prove to be an earner.

Tipping the tablets into my palm, I turned on the cold-water tap. The glass was behind me, ten feet away on the desk, so rather than risk another stagger, I simply cupped my hand and swallowed the pills, one at a time; a sip of water between each pill till I had taken four. The other two I returned to the bottle and slipped it into my jacket pocket. They would do for my lunch.

Whether it was a physical or physiological thing, I don't know, but within a few minutes I felt better, or at least well enough to try and return the woman's call. Slowly I returned to the desk and even more slowly, rescued my stick from the floor before seating myself behind the desk.

I listened to the tape once more and scribbled her name on my desk pad.

Phyllis Kilbride. Sounds polite and educated, I thought to myself.

The bile still threatened to erupt from me, but right now it would have to take second place to what might prove to be a fee paying client and boy, did I need a fee paying client.

Pen in hand, I turned the reporters pad to a new page and taking a deep breath, lifted the receiver and pressed the recall button on the desk phone. After a few seconds, the call was answered by the same, almost hesitant voice.

"Hello?"

"Missus Kilbride," I replied, suppressing a smelly burp, "John Logan of Logan Investigations returning your call. Sorry I wasn't immediately available, but I was with another client," I glibly lied. "How might I be of service?"

I could almost feel her indecision, the wisdom of contacting an investigation agency, the uncertainty if it had been the right thing to do.

"Missus Kilbride?" I gently prompted her.

"Yes, of course Mister eh…Logan. Indeed. I called about my husband. He's missing, you see."

No I didn't see, but this was no time to quibble. She was on the hook. Time to start drawing her in.

"Perhaps we might start with your husband's name?"

"Yes, yes, of course. Sorry. It's Martin. Martin Kilbride."

I scrawled his name on my pad.

"And how long has Mister Kilbride been missing?"

"Three days. No. Four days I mean. Four days, as of this morning."

"And have you reported Mister Kilbride missing to the police?"

"Yes I did, on that same night, three days ago. No sorry, four days now. Sorry. I'm getting quite confused."

She sighed suddenly and I suspected she was holding back tears, imagining her dabbing at her eyes with a tissue.

"Yes. I did report Martin missing," she continued, "but to be frank, I don't believe that the officers I spoke with were too…..." she seemed to struggle for the right word, "helpful."

I waited silently till she composed herself.

"I'm not saying that they didn't listen and they certainly took Martin's details and a photograph, but apart from a couple of phone calls inquiring if he had returned home, I've heard nothing more."

I wasn't about to start castigating the local cops, but I knew the system, overloaded as it was. Some young uniformed officer would be allocated the Missing Person inquiry and go through the procedure, beginning with the statutory form filling, then an entry on the PNC and then pass the inquiry to someone else when he went on days off, hoping by the time he resumed duty that either the MP had returned home or been dragged from some river or traced to his mistresses home.

"Look, Missus Kilbride. There's more detail I'd like to obtain from you. Are you in a position to visit my office," I glanced about me at the dingy room and quickly thought better of it, "or perhaps it might be more suitable to call upon you at home, say later this morning?"

Again I could hear her hesitate and instinctively knew what was coming next.

"How much… I mean, what are your rates Mister Logan?"

"Don't be worrying about that at a time like this," I smoothly replied and decided to play the guilt card. "Let's just worry about finding your husband and getting him home, safe and sound, eh?"

It seemed to work because she mumbled some sort of a reply that I didn't quite catch.

"Look," I said, "let me have your address and what time would be convenient?" Without waiting for her to reply, I suggested eleven o'clock and she agreed.

Quickly I scrawled her address on the pad and wished her a good morning, trying to sound more confident than I felt.

Almost slamming the phone down, I got one hand over my mouth and, grabbing my stick as the bile rose, staggered as fast as I could to the door that led to the small WC.

Once I'd been sick in the toilet and my body had stopped shaking, I stripped out of the stained tie and shirt and sniffed at my armpits. The dark blue suit jacket was creased and there was nothing I could do about that, but at least I'd the good sense to keep a spare clean shirt and, if memory served me correctly, another tie in the bottom of my desk drawer. The clock was now showing ten past nine, so given the morning city traffic I knew that I'd no time to visit my flat in the south side of the city before my appointment with the distraught Missus Kilbride.

By now the painkillers had done their job and boiling the ageing kettle, I filled the sink with hot water. Balancing on my good right leg and forcing my hand to be steady, I gingerly scraped at my face with a dull razor blade then used a sliver of soap to wash under my arms. The hand towel was about a month overdue a machine wash, but right now it was all I had and used it to dry myself.

As a practising drunk, I always keep a toothbrush and paste, as well as a strong antiseptic mouthwash and a liberal supply of mints, handy in my top drawer. Slipping into the clean light blue shirt and knotting the plain navy blue tie, I stood back and critically examined myself in the cabinet mirror. Lightly dipping the palms of both hands into the frothy water, I stroked them across my head and used a comb to manoeuvre the hair into some semblance of order. I wasn't going to win any beauty contest, that was for sure, but at least now I looked vaguely human. I bared my teeth and checked them for staining. So far they were all my own and not many forty-two year olds can boast that these days, I grinned at my reflection. Leaning on my stick I staggered towards my desk and sat down, reaching for the Glasgow A to Z roadmap. The address Missus Kilbride had provided was, dependent on the traffic and a good run through the lights, less than twenty minutes away. Time enough to make a phone call.

"Good morning, Kirkintilloch police office," said the elderly male voice.

I guessed it was a civilian bar officer who had answered my call.

"Good morning sir," I replied. Start off as you mean to go. A little courtesy wouldn't go wrong. "My name is John Logan. I'm a friend of the Kilbride family. Martin and Phyllis Kilbride that is, of 49 Alexandra Street. Phyllis has asked me to phone to inquire if there has been any word yet about poor Martin? You might recall he was reported to yourselves as missing. Eh, four days ago as of this morning," I read from my pad.

I held my breath. With luck the man wouldn't be too suspicious.

"Can you hold the line please, Mister Logan," he replied.

I waited, one finger on the disconnect button in case the guy got too nosey.

"Aye, here we are," said the voice. I could hear rustling of paper in the background.

"No sorry, nothing since the initial report I'm sorry to say. The missing person's details have been circulated and I can see that there have been two repeat visits to visit Missus Kilbride, but I'm afraid that's all I have. Do you have any information for us sir?"

God forgive me, but I smiled. The news that Martin Kilbride was still missing might be heartache for his wife and any family he might have, but it was a lifeline to me. An earner.

"Eh no. Thanks. Thank you for your time," I replied. "I'll let his wife know that I called you," I glibly lied to the helpful man and then hung up before he could ask anything else.

I was still smiling at the thought of a job. The only thing that could make this morning any better would be a wee dram, but that, I sighed, would need to wait till later.

Locking the office door behind me, I turned to negotiate the dark and dingy flight of stairs to the ground floor when I heard a polite cough.

The small, wizened Oriental man wearing the oversized quilted anorak and standing in the shadow startled me.

"Good morning Mister Logan sir," he said with a slight half bow, "and how is your fine self today sir?"

"Morning Mister Zao," I replied, cursing my luck at having him catch me so early in the morning. "Sorry, you caught me at a bad time. Just on my way to see a client."

I half turned towards the stairs, but he sneaked in front of me. God, for an old guy, he moved like a wraith.

"If I might have a little word sir," he smiled, all teeth, slicked back oily grey hair and eyes like diamonds. By diamonds I mean hard and cold as ice.

"If it's about the rent Mister Zao," I began, giving him my Best smile, "I know I'm two months overdue, but you did say that you would decorate and the smell coming from that sink," I shook my head as if in despair.

I didn't think it necessary to mention it was likely me throwing up into it that was the cause.

"Ah yes," he nodded his head, extending his hands out in front of him with the palms upturned, "the rent. Alas, it is overdue but that is not why I wish to speak with you sir."

I stared quizzically at him, recognising the hesitation in his behaviour. Another client? Surely not! My luck couldn't be that good.

He licked at his lips and I realised he was nervous.

"It is a matter of…some delicacy," he began. "It concerns my daughter, my youngest child. I know that as a policeman…."

"Retired policeman," I interrupted him.

"Ah yes, retired policeman. But still, you know the law sir. And it grieves me to trouble you with such a matter, but perhaps you might be of assistance to me?"

I was conscious of the time and my pending appointment with Missus Kilbride, yet didn't want this golden prospect of another job to slip by.

"Then perhaps, Mister Zao," I nodded politely to him, "if this is a matter of some delicacy then maybe we should make an official appointment? Would my office at two o'clock this afternoon be suitable?"

I held my breath. The last thing I wanted to do was piss off my landlord by running out on him, particularly as I was in arrears with my rent. To my relief he smiled and again made that little half bow of his.

"Till this afternoon sir," he replied then turned and, it seemed to me, almost glided up the dingy stairs out of sight, probably to harangue or appear like a ghost and scares the shit out of some other tenant.

By the time I'd managed to stumble down the worn stairs to the pavement outside, I could feel a trickle of sweat running down my spine. To be honest though, I don't think it was as much perspiration from negotiating the old Victorian built stairs as the whisky oozing from my pores. The exit from the dark close onto Osborne Street and the bright summer morning made my already aching head thump again and I was tempted to down the two remaining painkillers in my pocket. The only thing that prevented me doing so was the little sticky label on the bottle that, when taking the medication, warned against driving and operating machinery, but after downing a bottle of Bells the night before and four tablets this morning, I was in no position to worry about a little thing like that. However, I figured that downing another two tablets just might be bordering on the completely insane. Besides, I'd no emergency stock left which reminded me to call in later to see my pharmacist.

My old Ford Focus estate, an automatic because of my gammy left leg, was parked a few short steps away. Heaving myself into the driving seat, I threw the stick into the passenger footwell and removed the blue disabled badge from the dashboard. There are not a lot of benefits from being disabled, but in a city like Glasgow with its parking restrictions, the blue badge is worth a lot to a private investigator like me. When I'm working, that is, which isn't every day of the week. The fuel gauge was bordering on the red triangle, but I knew from experience I'd about thirty miles or so left in the tank.

I glanced in the rear-view mirror and realised I was probably over the limit, so popped a handful of mints into my mouth from the several packets I kept in the drivers side pocket.

Like I once heard said, drunk driving is only an offence when you get caught and so far, rightly or wrongly, I've been lucky.

It took just twenty-five minutes to reach Kirkintilloch and another few minutes to find Alexandria Street.

I was impressed. The houses, all detached and individually built, were in the main hidden behind large hedgerows and would easily fetch at least half a million each, I reckoned. Mentally I decided to hitch up my daily rates and, depending how that was received, maybe throw in a line for expenses.

Number 49 was a five or six bedroom sandstone villa, partially hidden behind a six-foot hedgerow with a columned entrance that swept to the large double front doors. The grass lawn, or what was left of it, was neatly trimmed though mostly replaced by new monoblock paving that swept round the lawn and, through the gateway, I could see was parked a new, silver coloured top of the range Mercedes Coupe.

The daily rate was hitched up another notch.

Don't ask me to explain it, but I was too embarrassed to drive my ageing Focus into the driveway and park it alongside the Merc, so decided to leave it in the street. An elderly and prim lady walking by with her wee terrier dog viewed me with some hostility till she saw my antics as I tried to exit the driver's door. Believe me, there are better vehicles for a driver with a bum left leg to exit with grace, than a Ford Focus.

The woman's expression changed from Neighbourhood Watch Right Wing Vigilante to a doe eyed Florence Nightingale concern for the poor man. Not so the dog though, that decided I presented a real threat and snarled as it almost pulled the wee woman off her feet in an effort to taste my flesh.

I've never been particularly fond of dogs, not since the time when as a member of a divisional CID arrest team I was first through the door of a council house in Easterhouse to secure the apprehension of a murder suspect and he loosed his large and hairy Alsatian upon me. The dog took me by the left arm and hung on for almost five minutes while I beat it unconscious with the baton in my right hand. It didn't help that the rest of squad, those not engaged in wrestling the suspect to the floor, stood around laughing hysterically at my impromptu waltz in the living room.

That little encounter cost me eighteen stitches and a fortnight off work. A whole two weeks without overtime and at home with a nagging and pregnant wife; not something I'd recommend, at least not with Sally and her mood swings.

So no, I've no real fondness for dogs.

My slow meander up the wide sweeping driveway allowed me time to inspect the property. It seemed to be in good repair and the movement, albeit slight, at the downstairs curtain confirmed there was definitely someone home. The door opened before I had the opportunity to ring the bell.

Maybe from the phone call I'd prejudged Missus Kilbride. What I expected was a distraught, red-eyed woman; say late fifties with perfectly coiffure hair and the obligatory blouse and beads and tweed skirt that were synonymous with the affluent Kirkintilloch folk.

What I got was a woman, yes, maybe in her late forties, but dressed and looking like someone who had just stepped off a Vogue magazine photo shoot.

About four inches shorter than my five eleven, her blonde hair tied back in a ponytail and subtly applied make-up, Phyllis Kilbride proved to be a real stunner. Dressed in a smart lemon coloured linen skirted suit and cream coloured blouse, she had the face and figure to turn any mans head, though I suspected that given her age, her full and rounded breasts might have had a little surgical assistance to be as firm and rounded as they appeared.

"Mister Logan?" she asked, a half smile playing about her full lips.

Those short few words and her accent confirmed it. This was the woman who had rung my office.

As I nodded in reply, I couldn't help it. I felt shabbily dressed and grubby standing facing her and I blushed. Like some adolescent schoolboy caught by his mother staring at the page three girl, I reddened like an idiot and could only nod my head.

"Ah yes," I finally stammered, awkwardly switching my stick to my left hand and leaning on it while I held out my right hand.

Her grip was firm and strong enough to convey confidence without crushing my fingers.

"Please," she stood back, as if sensing I needed the extra room to shuffle by her, "do come in."

With a confidence that I didn't really feel, I walked past her into a light and airy reception hallway, the parquet flooring polished and gleaming. Somehow, I couldn't see Phyllis Kilbride down on her knees scrubbing it and guessed with the money coming into this house, there must be a maid or daily char. That daily rate keeps getting notched up, I inwardly grinned.

She closed the door and invited me to follow her, walking slowly I assumed in deference to the scruffy cripple that limped behind her.

The room she led me to had large, almost panoramic windows that faced out toward the driveway. Two massive and comfortable looking couches faced close to each other and were set at right angles to a large, ornate fireplace. The real thing, I noted, none of that crap electric or gas with fake coals.

Several paintings hung from the walls and though I'm no expert, though they looked expensive. A baby grand piano sat to one corner and ranged upon it were seven or eight photographs in a variety of frames.

"Are these couches too low," she asked, cutting into my thoughts, "or would you prefer a high chair?"

I stared at her. Thinks I'm a bloody toddler does she?

She seemed embarrassed by her comment and glanced at my leg.

"No, I'm fine," I cockily smiled in reply, then sat back and was almost immediately swallowed up in the soft cushions.

To her credit, she didn't laugh outright or even smirk, but the sight of me disappearing must have been the source of some hilarity to her.

With as much dignity as I could muster, I managed to pull myself upright and grinning sheepishly, shuffled forward to perch on the edge of the couch.

"Some tea?" she asked, her voice almost choking with suppressed laughter.

"Ah, yes," I nodded. "Please."

I watched her glide away, the skirt tightening across her well rounded, but firm buttocks and the old devil raised his head. Well, almost. These days my libido is usually determined by my alcohol intake and besides a dame like her was way, way out of my league.

Don't blow this, you idiot, I angrily shook myself. This could be an earner provided Mister Kilbride decides to remain away for the time being. While she was gone I pushed myself up from the couch and took the opportunity to glance over at the photographs on top of the piano.

As I'd guessed, they seemed to be family. Some showed Phyllis Kilbride with a man whom I presumed was her husband Martin. Maybe a few years older, he looked like a model for a SAGA advert. Taller than her, I guessed he was about my height, with salt and pepper hair. Tanned, trim and fit looking, he featured with Phyllis in a number of the photographs, some in formal highland dress, others casual and in one, his hand on the tiller of a yacht with the name Elizabeth displayed prominently on a plaque and what looked like his blonde wife behind him, half turned toward the camera and curling a rope at the stern. I was guessing I know, but it seemed the scenic background looked like the Clyde estuary.

Two of the photographs featured a young woman. Dark haired, she sat on what seemed to be the same yacht and smiled shyly at the camera while in the other snap, taken perhaps a few years later and on the verge of becoming a real beauty, she stood between the Kilbride's, all three formally dressed, but on that occasion her face was blank, almost sullen.

"That's my step-daughter, Sheila," said the voice behind me. "She's almost twenty-four now. Acts like a precocious teenager at time," she sighed.

I turned and saw Missus Kilbride standing watching me, a tray in her hands on which she carried a pot of tea and cups and saucers. But there was something in the way she'd said *"...step-daughter, Sheila,"* some slight sigh of regret, just enough to raise the hackles in the back of my neck and I suspected that the two women didn't get along.

I smiled, really because there wasn't anything else I could do or say. I'd been caught out being nosey and limped towards the couch, taking care this time to sit gently on the edge. If Phyllis Kilbride hoped to watch me make an arse of myself again, it was not going to happen.

Tea poured and with china cup and saucer sitting delicately in my hand, we got down to business.

"Tell me, Mister Logan," she began, "and mindful that you were the first name I picked from the book, what credentials do you offer to…" her eyes betrayed her loss for words, "to take on this case? To search for my husband, I mean?"

I leaned forward to gently place the cup and saucer on the glass topped coffee table, my mind racing as I sought the appropriate reference. Bugger it, I decided. What's a wee lie among the truth, here and there?

"Well," I slowly drawled, "I'm a retired police officer, prematurely retired," casting a smiling glance at my left leg. "During my twenty years with the Force I spent fifteen years in the CID and that included various squads. Since my enforced retirement, I've worked for several distinguished clients," and why I didn't snigger at this point, I'll never know, "as well as a number of large firms."

I didn't really feel the need to explain that 'large firms' was the local council, chasing up Council Tax dodgers, and a debt collection agent, who when she herself did a runner, not only stiffened me for my paltry four hundred quid bill, but Her Majesty's Inland Revenue for several thousand pounds in unpaid VAT, rotten cow that she is.

"And does your…incapacity," said she, politely referring to my bum leg, "cause you any problems in your line of work?"

"Put it like this Missus Kilbride. I never take on anything that might result in physical confrontation. That's why I'm ideally suited for tracing work. Unless," a gnawing suspicion began to eat at me, "you believe that your husband was abducted or his disappearance might be the result of something nefarious?"

I like the word nefarious. Made me sound like I knew what I was talking about.

"Good gracious no," she replied quickly, her hands held up as if in denial. "Martin would never, ever," she stressed, now wringing her hands together, "become involved in anything that might lead to his... his abduction."

The way she said the word '*abduction*' came out like it left a bad taste in her mouth. But somehow, nothing I could put my finger on, I didn't like the manner in which she glanced quickly away and then parted and raised a slim, perfectly manicured hand to brush away a wisp of hair from her forehead. But that's me of course. Mister Cynicism.

"So," I said breezily, reaching to my inside jacket pocket for my notebook and pen, "if you're satisfied that I might be ale to help you, perhaps we might begin with some details?"

"Of course," she replied, edging a few inches closer towards me so that out knees were almost touching.

I swallowed hard and tried to concentrate on taking his full name, date and place of birth and all the little details that I knew I'd need, but her faint scent and her nearness caused a physical reaction that I hoped didn't show through the cheap suit trousers.

"Right," I cleared my throat, "so let's begin. Mister Kilbride....may I call him Martin?"

"Please do," she replied, though didn't suggest I call her Phyllis. Probably something to do with me being hired help, I assumed.

"When did you… or rather, who was the last person to see Martin?"

She reached a slim hand to her throat, the fine gold chain sliding down the well-toned wrist.

"Well, I suppose I was. When he left for his office. Tuesday morning about...let me see? About seven forty-five. And he drove himself. He always does."

"What kind of car does he drive?"

"A Saab. A dark blue coloured Saab coupe. Do you want the registration number?"

I noted it down as she dictated it.

"When did you realise that Martin didn't arrive at his work?"

"Well, usually he phones me during the day. Just a bit of chit-chat, what's for dinner, that sort of thing. If he doesn't phone I think nothing of it, just assume that he's working hard and I'll see him when he arrives home. But that day he didn't phone. At least, I heard nothing, not till I received the call from one of his partners, asking why he hadn't come in to the office that morning. Later that evening, when he didn't come home and I hadn't heard from him all day, I phoned round our friends and some family, but no one had heard from Martin that day. I contacted the local police office, just to voice my concern. The person I spoke with said that the police would need to complete a missing person's form and two young uniformed officers arrived that night."

"Does he carry a mobile phone?"

"Yes, but each time I called it simply transferred to the answer service. On the last occasion I called it," her brow furrowed, "that was about seven-thirty on

Wednesday night, the recorded message said the phone was switched off. I presumed that the battery was perhaps low or out of power."

"The number anyway and the phone company he uses, if you please."

Carefully I had her repeat the number to make sure I'd got it correct.

"I presume that you've contacted all your mutual friends and family?"

"Yes," she sighed, "but of course none of them have any information at all. I've even tried the local hospitals and the police told me they checked their… their..."

"PNC?" I offered. "It's the Police National Computer. It's linked to all the UK forces and if your husband or anyone answering his description had featured anywhere in the UK, whether as an accident victim or even arrested…"

She paled at this.

"Then he'd have been identified and you'd have heard something by now."

"Oh, I see. Anyway, their PNC, there was nothing on it, nothing about Martin."

"What was your husband's occupation?"

"He was a chartered accountant."

She rustled in her handbag and produced a black coloured business card with gold lettering and a four by six photograph.

"Here, I thought this might be of use to you."

The photograph was of a smiling Martin Kilbride, wearing a dinner jacket with a cigar in his hand and sat alone at a white cloth covered table with the remains of a meal in front of him.

"I took that on a winter cruise last year," she said.

I nodded and glanced at the business card. "Boyle and Spencer Accountancy, Waterloo Street," I read aloud.

I smiled reassuringly, though how reassured she was by an unkempt cripple, God alone knew.

"And are you employed Missus Kilbride?"

"Goodness no," she smiled, as though the very idea was preposterous. "Martin insisted when we married five years ago that his wife would be a full time housewife, catering to his every whim."

Somehow the thought of Phyllis Kilbride catering to my whims jumped into my head, but I mentally shook myself and took a deep breath. So, married five years ago. It seems the father and daughter came as a package, then. I glanced down at my notebook.

"I realise the police have been through these questions with you, Missus Kilbride, but are you aware of any reason or threats that might have induced your husband …Martin… to take off without letting you know where he was going?"

She slowly shook her head, her pretty blonde and….Whoa, I told myself. Let's not be getting ahead of yourself here, John my boy.

"No, I can't think of anything. Nothing at all."

She turned her face to stare at me, her soft green eyes boring straight through to the back of my skull.

"I've racked my brain time and time again; checked our mutual accounts and they're perfectly healthy…"

There's my rate notching up one more time.

"....and as far as I'm aware, Martin had no enemies, least none that he ever hinted at."

"I presume that when he went to work on Tuesday morning, he'll have taken his wallet, bank cards that sort of thing, with him?"

"Yes, I suppose so. I've certainly not found them lying about the house, if that's what you mean."

"Can you contact your bank, while I'm here? Find out when the last transaction on his account was?"

She looked puzzled and made to question, but I smiled and continued. "If he is out there and keeping low, he'll need money for a hotel or accommodation, food, petrol, that sort of thing. That means he either carried a lot of cash with him or is using an ATM machine. Follow me?"

Her face widened in understanding. "Of course," she replied, rising from the couch and automatically smoothing the front of her skirt. "I'll just be a moment." This time she hurried from the room as if with purpose, returning a few minutes later, her eyes downcast.

"The last six transactions on our joint account are known to me. They're ones I made since Tuesday. So I'm afraid that he hasn't used his cards."

"Could he have an account you have no knowledge of?"

Her brow furrowed again. "No, I'm sure he hasn't. Martin is a very honest and decent man."

I almost smiled at that one, a bean-counter who is a very honest and decent man. Now there's a contradiction in terms, I thought. I was slowly approaching the million-dollar question. The question that would either be truthfully answered or have me bundled unceremoniously out of the front door.

I licked my lips and pretended to study my notes, then decided just to go for it. "Missus Kilbride," I slowly began. "Is there any marital reason why your husband would leave you without a word?"

She stared at me then broke into a soft smile. "You know, when those young officers came here to the house to take details, they didn't ask about another woman. I mean," she smiled again, "that's what you're implying, isn't it? That perhaps Martin has got himself a….what is it that you call those women? A bit of stuff on the side?"

I smiled back at her and considered that if Martin Kilbride had himself a bit of stuff on the side, then he was a fool. Phyllis Kilbride wasn't just a good-looking woman, but smart as well. No, not smart, unsure where the thought had come from, but definitely intelligent, with perhaps even a touch of deviousness.

I watched as she carefully smoothed down the fold of her skirt, and raised her head to stare at me.

"Believe me when I tell you this, Mister Logan. My husband wanted nothing from any other woman. And I mean nothing at all. I provided for his…." she paused, as if seeking the right words, narrowed her eyes then slowly cocked her head slightly to one side and smiled softly, a sure and confident smile.

"...his every need," she said at last.

I felt my throat tighten and instinctively knew then that wherever Martin Kilbride was, whatever had befell him, his chasing some wee bit of skirt elsewhere was bottom of my list.

'"Right then," I replied, "is there anything that you would like to ask me?"

She opened her eyes wide and tapped her left forefinger gently against her open lips, a silly little habit and I wondered if she realised how provocative it was? Probably, I decided and it also occurred to me that maybe there was a bit of the tease about Missus Kilbride.

"Should I tell the local police that I've engaged you?"

I worked hard at not smiling and cheering out loud. I'd not only got myself a client, but one that seemed capable of paying my soon to be inflated bill.

"I see no reason why not. In fact, telling them might just smooth over any resistance if I should contact them for any reason. I'll leave you to continue to liaise with them as well as your family and friends. Just keep in touch and let them know that any word from your husband, you're the first to be told, okay? You might also contact his associates at work; let them know to expect a call or a visit from me."

"And your fee Mister Logan. How do I pay you? Now, on a retainer or at the conclusion…?"

To my surprise, she stopped, placed a hand against her mouth and blinked rapidly, her eyes brimmed with unshed tears.

"Oh my," she whispered, so softly I almost couldn't hear her. "Martin hasn't been found yet and already I'm assuming the worst."

My instinct was to get close and comfort her, but two things stopped me. One was that going anywhere near her might cause me to forget she was a client and more practically, try being romantic with a gammy left leg. It isn't easy. I know because I've tried, though more usually with a glass in my hand.

And another thing, though I felt bad for thinking it, but Phyllis Kilbride didn't strike me as the sort of woman who run easily to tears.

So I did what these days I do best, sat facing her and looked suitably sombre.

"Please, you must think me foolish," she said at last, sniffing into a white lacy handkerchief as she rose from the couch.

I took my cue and with the aid of my stick, pushed my way to my feet.

Still sniffing into her handkerchief I followed her through the entrance hall to the front door and shuffled past as she held it open.

"You will let me know how your inquiry proceeds."

"Of course," I replied, hitting her with my most encouraging smile.

"Oh, one more thing," I said. "Do you have a mobile phone number?"

She nodded and scribbled down the number on a pad by the phone in the hallway, tore off the sheet and handed it to me.

"Either the house or this number," she said as she softly closed the door behind me.

I was halfway down the driveway when it occurred to me.

"Bugger!" I spat out.

No terms for my fee had been agreed. What I couldn't decide though, was it simply an oversight or had she deliberately manoeuvred me from the house before money was discussed?

Broke as I was, it occurred to me to go back, but my idiotic pride got in the way and I didn't want to appear at her door as if cap in hand and tugging the old forelock. The sudden squeal of tyres on the driveway interrupted my thoughts.

A red coloured Mini had turned into the gateway and sped towards me.

I didn't have time to think, let alone react as it shot past me and came to a shuddering halt beside the parked Mercedes, spraying stone chips from its tyres. Unconsciously, I breathed easier and watched as the drivers door opened and a dark haired young woman, her tied back in a tight ponytail, dressed in a loose fitting yellow tracksuit and carrying a tennis racquet, got out and stared sullenly at me for a few seconds. Then without a backward glance, she strode through the front door, banging it behind her.

Seems the Kilbride's daughter Sheila is home then I thought, as I limped towards my rust bucket.

The trip to visit Missus Kilbride had edged the petrol gauge needle dangerously close to the middle of the red zone and I mentally balanced the few miles I had left to the cost of petrol. I knew exactly how much money I had in my old, well-used leather wallet. One ten-pound note with an additional two, one-pound coins and some loose change, rattling in my trouser pocket. Big spender that I am I reckoned that a fiver's worth would do me at least till I got to the office and then home and the rest could be invested in a half bottle of the cheaper vintage, just to see me through the night.

Filling up with my fivers worth at a Shell garage on the Maryhill Road, I didn't see the grey coloured Renault pulls in to the pump behind me.

"Hello Limpy," snarled a deep gruff voice behind me.

I turned to see an old, familiar face, but don't think I was happy about it.

"Well, well, well. Detective Sergeant Coleman. Maryhill CID letting you out to harass the public these days are they?"

Eddie Coleman, a good four inches shorter than me but a lot broader, though mostly running to fat, stood and stared malevolently at me from the driver's side of the CID car. His face pitted with teenage acne scars and thinning hair brushed forward in an attempt to stave off his baldness, Coleman would never win any modelling contracts, but tried to make up for his ugliness by wearing expensive suits. It didn't really work though, because he still looked like a bag of shite tied in the middle.

"Still the joker, eh Logan? Heard you were a hopeless down and out these days, a drink sodden alcoholic," he sneered. "But still cracking the funnies, eh?"

A cold fury swept over me. Time was that the prick would never have dared spoken to me like that, but since I'd been lamed and retired, well, he obviously thought he could do or say anything he liked.

But the bitterest pill to swallow was that he was probably right.

"How about you then, Eddie," I replied, fighting to keep my voice calm. "Still the cowardly bullying sergeant, beating up handcuffed prisoners?"

His face turned bright red and I knew I'd hit the right spot. He clenched his fists and took a step forward. I grasped my walking stick that little bit tighter and vowed that if he came just close enough, he was getting it right across his ugly mug.

"Sarge," said a low voice, then "Sarge!" but this time with more insistence.

That's when I noticed his partner, a dark haired lassie standing by the passenger door, her face vaguely familiar and looking puzzled as she stared at us both in turn.

"I heard you the first time!" snapped Coleman in reply, his bloodshot eyes drilling a hole through me. "You," he poked a mean finger at me. "You Logan, you'll get yours, I promise you."

"For what?" I replied, my face a picture of innocence.

The short exchange had caused a few other drivers to stare at us both.

"The guys a nutter," I twisted my finger round and round while pointing at my head.

Coleman looked fit to burst a blood vessel and I could see he was straining at the leash to have a go at me. But by now his partner had moved round to the car and was whispering something to him, something I couldn't hear.

"Aye, you're right," he spat through clenched teeth at me. "He's not worth it."

He grabbed the nozzle from its pump and turned towards the cars petrol tank, dragging the thick, protesting rubber hose behind him.

I'd already had my five quid's worth and turned to pay at the small window.

I say the small window because this was Maryhill and nobody except the staff got into the well-provisioned shop. The number of times the place had been robbed had forced the management to secure the door and anything that you wanted from the shop, anything from a pint of milk to shaving foam, the staff fetched it for you and shoved it through the small bandit window, but only after you'd handed over the cash. Not daft, these kids, for that's what the majority of the staff were, youthful students from the nearby Glasgow and Strathclyde Uni's, working part time for peanuts just to supplement their grants.

The downside was that no matter the weather, there was always a queue waiting at the window, whether to pay for petrol or the twenty fags the mammy had sent the kids to purchase. Luckily, today was fine and the one guy in front was leaving as I limped to the pay point.

"Okay big man," said the teenager in greeting from behind the bandit screen. "That CID wanker giving you hassle, is he?"

"Know him do you?" I asked as I waited on the change from my tenner.

"Aye, he's well known round here is that bugger, so he is. Cannae keep his hands to himself. If he's not belting the weans round the ear, he's slipping the hands up the lassies jersey's for a wee feel, so he is, pretending to search them for weapons, so he is. Bloody pervert, so he is."

My ears pricked up at that one. During a spell at Maryhill CID, I'd heard vague mutterings and one particular story, about the dark side of Eddie Coleman, but being the obnoxious man that he is, I simply assumed it was another one of these gossip stories that get richer with the telling.

However, that didn't mean I wasn't going to add to it.

"I'll let you into a wee secret," I drew myself closer to the window, seeing the youngsters eyes widen in anticipation. "He's only annoyed because he thinks I hid the repair kit for his blow-up girlfriend."

The youngster guffawed with laughter as he handed me my five-pound note change and winked.

"Aye, that's a good one," he replied. "I'll be passing that one round my mates, so I will."

I smiled and limped back to the Focus, keeping a weather eye on Coleman who steadfastly ignored me.

But not his partner, who continued to stare at me with a curious expression.

It annoyed me that I couldn't place her. I'm good with faces, but bloody terrible trying to remember names.

Thank God everybody in Glasgow is called Jimmy.

The dashboard clock showed a little after midday, so I decided that I'd call in at the chemists in King Street for a supply of my painkillers. Parking the car, I propped the blue badge on the dashboard and adjusted my face to impress old Mister Cornes with my suffering. Pushing open the door of the dingy little shop, the bell on its spring heralded my arrival and it amazed me again how the old devil managed to keep the place running.

The whole back counter was covered in a fine film of dust as was the enormous bottles that sat on the top shelves with their coloured water contents of red, blue and a sickly green. Dust mites danced in the gloom and everything in and on top of the counters seemed to be a throwback to the Fifties. Even the cardboard DUREX sign, discreetly placed in a dark corner, featured a male and female model whose once fashionable clothes were a throwback to turn-up trousers and elbow length white gloves for the ladies.

The beaded curtain that led to the rear of the shop parted and out he came.

I swear, the wee man can't be any taller than five feet, wearing shoes, and then mysteriously rises to almost six feet. The secret is a running board that he had built behind the serving counter, but if you didn't know it was there, you'd think he'd sprung up from his knees.

As always, Mister Cornes wore a white starched dustcoat, his pens neatly arrayed on the beast pocket and a sharply knotted tie over an equally crisp white shirt.

Thick bifocals sat on the end of a hawk like nose and an outrageous black wig perched on his head. As to his age, it was anyone's guess. He was one of these indeterminate characters who might be anything from forty to eighty years old. "Ah, Mithter Logan, how nith to thee you," he lisped through brilliantly white false teeth. "I trutht you are well?"

I felt like replying that if I were well, I wouldn't be visiting a bloody chemist, but couldn't afford to piss him off, so instead I smiled and replied that I'd come for my regular prescription.

"Ah," he replied, cocking his head to one side and raising his eyebrows as if in regret.

"Is there a problem Mister Cornes?" I wondered, suspecting already there was and feeling a sudden emptiness in the pit of my stomach.

"I've had a phone call from Doctor Goodman, you know, your doctor," he added unnecessarily.

Of course I know who Doctor bloody Goodman is, I felt like shouting, but instead bared my teeth and replied, "Yes?"

"Ah, it theems that Doctor Goodman ith thomewhat contherned about the amount of prethcribed medithines you have obtained in the rethent month and hath athked me to convey a methage, requethting that you call upon her for an appointment at your earlietht convenienthe."

I could feel my legs weakening, the perspiration already forming at the nape of my neck. No painkillers? Bloody hell, this isn't a setback; it's a damned catastrophe!

"Look Mister Cornes," I began, trying to keep the pleading tone from my voice, "I don't think that you appreciate the tremendous pain that I'm currently experiencing. Right now, as we speak, I'm feeling such pain…."

I got no further. The little sod held up his hand to silence me.

"Mithter Logan, you are correct. I cannot imagine the pain that you are going through, but I have my inthtruction. I cannot and will not ithue you with further medication until thuch timeth ath I am authorithed by your GP. I'm thorry, but there it ith. The matter for now ith clothed."

I stared at him open mouthed. It occurred to me to pull him over the counter, stamp on his head and bludgeon him to death.

But of course I didn't. I knew when I was beaten. A four-eyed, five-foot midget with a bad hairpiece had just sentenced me to a day of pain. Bastard!

I stumbled from the shop, banging the door noisily behind me in frustrated anger and made towards my car.

A traffic warden was bent across the bonnet, examining the blue badge.

"What you looking at you, fascist bastard!" I screamed at him.

The man, who in fairness is only doing his job, turned in surprise to discover a raging lunatic waving a stick at him and stared wide-eyed as I stumbled towards him. "Get out of it!" I shouted.

Some workers high on scaffolding nearby must've heard me and began to berate the warden with cries of, "Gerrr-out-of-it!" and "Leave the poor crippled guy alone!" then followed it up with threats that suggested if he didn't hop it, he'd find himself kissing his arse goodbye.

The poor man decided that eighteen grand a year wasn't worth the abuse and literally ran from the street.

With a grateful wave of my stick to my new overhead friends, I climbed into the Focus and drove the short distance to my office.

I still had just under an hour till my meeting with Mister Zao and used the time to boil the kettle for a strong black coffee, pop the last two painkillers and persuade a huffy receptionist to grant me an early evening appointment with Doctor Goodman. Sometimes grovelling does pay off.

I then signed on and used my PC Internet link to obtain the customer service number for the company that served Martin Kilbride's mobile phone. After what seemed an interminable long time going through telephone menus, I eventually got to speak to a human being and just my bloody luck, it was a Scouser.

"Can you slow down please Miss," I politely requested. "I'm afraid your accent is too strong and I'm having difficulty understanding you."

"Sorry love," she drawled with exaggerated slowness, "Now, what is it again that you want?"

In my best, cultured Glasgow accent, I introduced myself as Martin Anderson Kilbride and explained that I'd lost my mobile phone some days ago, that if she could assist me in tracing it I would be very grateful.

Over the past year, I'd recalled reading that a number of the English police forces, during some of their high profile inquiries, had requested the mobile phone companies to bounce tracing signals off mobile phones belonging to lost or abducted children and, though I wasn't a whiz kid when it came to technology, I guessed that Kilbride's mobile phone company must be able to do the same.

"Can you provide me with your password please?"

"Eh, sorry," I replied, "It's just that I've got so many passwords, you know, for the office, my PC, that some of thing," I ended lamely.

"Look," I quickly continued, "can I give you some other personal security information?"

"Yes we can do that. Date of birth?"

I flipped over the page of my notebook. "Seventh of March nineteen forty-six."
"Place of birth?"

"Edinburgh."

"Name of your yacht?"

That threw me for a few seconds, and then I remembered the photograph on the piano. "Elizabeth," I sighed.

There was a slight pause during which paranoia set in and I suspected the woman was tracing the call, but then she thanked me and asked for my, or rather Kilbride's, mobile number. Again, I consulted my notebook and rattled off the digits.

"Right, let me see," she said quietly, almost to herself. "The last time your phone activated was to receive a number of incoming calls, five to be exact, none of which seem to have been answered. The five calls were all received," there was a pause as she seemed to read the information on her screen, "Tuesday and Wednesday and then nothing more. Probably the battery has died," she suggested. "And can you tell me where the calls were received and sort of give me a clue as to where the bloody thing might be," I jokingly urged, feeling my skin crawling as my body craved either an immediate dose of painkillers or a shot of Bells.

"According to the mapping system on my screen," she slowly began, "the phone is somewhere within a two hundred yard radius to the west of a phone mast located in a place called," she gave a short laugh, and then said, "I won't even try to pronounce this, so I think I'll just spell it for you."

She'd only got the first six letters out when I realised what she was telling me. "Polkemmet?"

"Yes, that's it… I think," she guffawed down the line. "Anything else I can do for you love?"

I thanked the woman and hung up.

"Polkemmet?"

Once more I blessed my decision to invest in a good quality computer and ran the Internet programme that geographically mapped the UK. Polkemmet didn't have much going for it, according to the blurb that accompanied the map, other than encompassing a large country park that once formed the grounds of a nearby mansion. It was one of these places that the countryside brigade like to stomp around in their waterproofs and wellies and offered such attractions as horse riding, midges, caravan site, more midges, fishing and yes, yet more midges. Even the talk of midges caused an involuntary itch, though again that might have been attributed to my need for whisky.

I checked there was paper in the printer and made myself a copy of the area, pleased to discover that among other attractions, the mobile phone mast was also marked on the map. Studying the sheet, I wondered what's in Polkemmet that might take Martin Kilbride there? According to his wife, Kilbride's outdoors pursuits were more in the line of yachting than the rural attractions Polkemmet offered. Either way, I didn't intend travelling out there this afternoon, I'd other things planned. Besides, I wasn't too keen on tracing Kilbride right away. There was still the matter of my earner.

Still, I gave a resigned shudder, if that's where the mobile was last heard, then I'd no option but to travel there tomorrow and make some kind of inquiry, while mentally wondering what kind of expenses I'd mark up for the trip?

The door was knocked with a soft tap.

"Come in," I shouted, almost as it opened and in walked, or rather glided, the ghostly Mister Zao.

His hands held in front of him as if in supplication, he bowed formally towards me.

"Is this a suitable time, Mister Logan sir?"

I glanced at the wall clock. It showed two pm exactly.

I half rose from my chair and invited him to sit in one of the two chairs in front of the desk.

"You're always welcome at any time, Mister Zao," I replied in my most sycophantic voice. I make no excuse for grovelling. I owe this guy two months rent so as far as I'm concerned, a little humbleness is called for.

"Now," I begun, my hands clasped in front of me on the desk and once he was seated, "you said this is a matter of some delicacy. How can I help you?"

Zao seemed to take a deep breath, as though he was about to bare his soul in the confessional.

"Look," I told him, "you must appreciate that anything you tell me will not be revealed to anyone. Nobody. I take my clients confidentiality most seriously. Do you understand that Mister Zao?"

Without looking directly at me, he nodded his head and when he raised it, I could see his eyes were bright and his Adams apple in his thin neck working overtime. To my surprise, I realised he was fighting back tears.

"Can I get you a glass of water?" I asked, regretting my earlier decision to save what little cash I had left and forego purchasing a half bottle of the golden relief. He didn't speak, simply waved a hand to tell me not to bother and then, taking a deep breath, composed himself before he began.

"My youngest child, my daughter Tei Pai, she is eighteen years old. She call herself Tracy, give herself a gweilo name…."

He must have seen the curiosity in my face, for he smiled.

"Gweilo. It is you," he pointed a bony finger at me. "White man. European. Understand?"

I nodded, a self-conscious grin on my face as I recalled the names that Mister Zao's race had endured from us gweilo's throughout the years, mostly flung at them by drunks impatiently scrambling for a late night carryout meal.

"Ah, so," he said, shaking his head and sitting there in his badly fitting black suit. It occurred to me that all he needed was a waxed moustache and bowler hat to complete the image of Charlie Chan.

"My Tei Pai, she has got herself a boyfriend. A gweilo. A bad man, I can tell," he nodded sagely. "He have fast car and good clothes and wear expensive watch. I no trust this man."

"But surely having a nice car and good clothes doesn't make him a bad man Mister Zao?" I smiled.

The old Chinese looked at me as though I was stupid.

"He no work," he scoffed, "this Billy. Has a flat in city centre that cost plenty," he leaned forward, rubbing his forefinger and thumb together. "Calls himself a student! Bahh!"

He sat back and folded his scrawny arms across his chest; clearly angry and annoyed that I didn't agree with him about this boyfriend, Billy.

I let him stew for a minute then picked up a pencil and prepared as if I was about to take notes.

"What that smell?" he asked, sniffing the air.

"It's the sink," I pointed the pencil towards the corner. "The smell is coming from the sink."

"Bahh," he dismissively replied. No promise of a plumber or a sanitation man, just simply "Bahh."

I'd need to discuss that before he left, I thought.

"So, what is it that you want me to do, Mister Zao?"

"Stay sober and find out what you can about this Billy," he replied.

I half laughed. Stay sober? What the fuck was that supposed to mean?

He cupped his hand to his mouth as if in a drinking motion.

"You are a good man Mister Logan, but you drink too much. You have bad health too; I can see it in your face. Your face all red lines. Alcohol is not healthy for the body and destroy the mind. Stay sober and get better. I tell you this as your friend, not as your landlord. Understand?"

I didn't know whether to laugh at the ridiculously frank little man or grab him by the scruff of the neck and toss him through the door, but the reason I didn't was simply because he was telling the truth.

So I sat there, staring at him and wishing this was over so that I could get home to my miserable flat and murder the remains of the bottle that I knew was sitting in my kitchen cupboard, shouting out my name for me to come and get it.

"Do you have an address and a second name for this Billy?" I asked at last.

He handed me a scrap of paper with spidery writing that said Billy Crawford flat 21, 18 Lancefield Quay.

"Here, this him."

Zao leaned over the desk and passed me a colour photograph that had been folded in half and showed a pretty girl, Zao's daughter I presumed, standing with a guy who, mouth open, sneered at the camera and was obviously Crawford. Long brown hair to his shirt collar, he looked at least ten years older than her. Crawford had his left arm thrown protectively about the girls shoulder - or maybe I should say proprietarily on her shoulder - and was holding a whisky glass in the other hand. The picture seemed to have been taken in a bar or a club.

"Your daughter is very pretty," I said, more to make conversation than anything.

"Yes," his voice softened, "and I no want her hurt by him. Help me please Mister Logan. Find out what you can about this gweilo, this no gooder."

I think he meant good for nothing, but what the hell, he spoke better English than I did Cantonese.

"Do this for me and we forget two months rent and next months rent also. Okay? If it cost extra, then I pay your going rate."

He stood to indicate the appointment was over.

"How long before you have something to tell me?" he asked.

"I'll get right on it Mister Zao. You have my word that this will take top priority," I cheerfully lied.

I walked or rather stumbled after him to the door, where he turned and nodded towards the sink.

"Next time, throw up in waste bucket, save me cost of plumber," he dryly remarked as he closed the door softly behind him.

The appointment with Doctor Goodman wasn't till five pm, so that gave me time to both get home and shower and also drive past the address on the scrap of paper Zao had given me for a quick look-see. The mid afternoon traffic wasn't bad, but I supposed being Friday, most city office workers had probably skipped off early or perhaps used their flexi-time to get out and take advantage of the good weather. The sun beat down and reflected from the recently constructed shimmering glass buildings that fronted the north side of the River Clyde. Where once cargo and pleasure ships had docked and off-loaded their goods to warehouses, the area was now a large regenerated complex of expensive waterside high-rise flats. Driving along the newly built access roads, slowly and carefully to avoid ripping the already vulnerable arse out of my rusting Focus on the road-humps, it seemed to me that the prosperity of the residents was displayed by the value the few vehicles parked in the allocated bays. I presumed the empty bays belonged to the young professionals who were most likely working and the only buggers that could afford the affluent housing.

When I reached Lancefield Quay, it wasn't too difficult to spot the surveillance vehicle sitting fifty yards from the ornate glass entrance to number 18. A rusting dark blue colour with mud adhering to the wheel arches, the Ford Transit van stuck out like a red-haired Catholic priest at an Orange Walk.

I'd seen plenty of this type of vehicle during my spell with the surveillance unit. I deliberately slowed the Focus and cast furtive glances at the parked cars nearby, but couldn't spot any telltale motors that were two-up, with bored cops inside.

That didn't mean they weren't there, though. I knew that somewhere nearby, there would be a back-up car to support the officers inside the van, just in case of a compromise.

The van faced toward the flats entrance and again I knew from experience that all visitors to the flats would likely be photographed and logged until such times as the van's occupants formed a picture of comings and goings and could identify the strangers from the genuine residents.

Of course, the presence of the van outside the flats might just be coincidence, but old Zao had told me that Crawford was supposedly a mature student with no viable source of income. If that was true then he either had to have private funds, perhaps from his family or more likely, he was dirty. The prohibitive cost of purchasing or even renting one of these places, as far as I was concerned, put Crawford beyond the student loan bracket. No, my gut instinct, when it wasn't threatening to overload on alcohol, told me that Billy Crawford had an income that didn't pass through the office of HM Inland Revenue.

I passed the van without a second look and kept on going. I didn't want my number plate to attract attention and feature in their daily log. Turning at the end of the road I'd a decision to make. Chance one more drive past or, as Big John

Wayne used to say, get the hell out of Dodge.

I couldn't see what was to be gained by risking another look at a front entrance, so chucked it in and headed for my flat over in Shawlands. If nothing else, I'd learned that either the Drug Squad or some other specialist police unit were watching Billy Crawford's building. My guess was the DS and I knew that the DS don't waste their time on junkies these days, but go after the big boys, the dealers.

The one bed roomed ground floor flat in Minard Road was one of my better investments. I'd bought it outright with some of the pay-off money when the police had retired me two years previously, with the intention of renting it out as a possible source of monthly income. I didn't suspect then that Sally, my soon to be ex-wife, was planning to move her boyfriend into our home. Cutting a long boring story short, she got the house and our only child and I got the flat and two days every fourth weekend with my son Paul. To my shame, I've missed the last three weekend visits and the brusque letter I received from her solicitor warned me that she was taking action to prevent any future visits.

Parking in Minard Road is murder at any time of the day, but as luck would have it, a space opened up outside number 29, just as I arrived.

The flat wasn't in bad shape when I first saw it, but I'd let things go and now the two rooms and bathroom needed a makeover. But what the hell, it's not as if I did any entertaining. It was simply somewhere to get my head down, a sanctuary from the world.

Owning a ground floor flat had two advantages. Being on the level, I'd no need to climb stairs with my bum leg and made it far easier to stumble through the front door when I was drunk. The usual pile of junk mail was lying behind the front door and joined the rest that sat on the telephone table. Time was when I'd take the offers of cheap health insurance, cheap car insurance, cheap this and cheap that, stick them all back into their enclosed envelope and return them blank to the originating companies, without paying the postage. That usually took me off their mailing list when they got fed up paying for their own literature, but like I said, I even got bored with that so now I simply bin them.

The telephone answer machine had no new messages. Stripping off my suit jacket I went into the kitchen…. Sorry, did I say kitchen? Scullery more like, then fetched the half bottle of Bells from the cupboard and poured myself a wee curer. When I bought the flat, the seller had described the room as a cabin kitchen, but if this was the type of kitchens they had on boats, they must all be crewed by claustrophobic dwarves. Of course, I'd great plans for making it a kitchen cum dining area cum lounge, back then when I'd first bought the place, but of course I didn't know then that my Missus was screwing my next-door neighbour. Funny how what seems important is nothing really, when your life gets turned upside down.

Everything, all my plans, went to hell when her sexual peccadilloes came to light. All those days and nights, working every hour God sent to improve our life style and all the time that slimy bastard was with her, in my bed. I sipped at the whisky, remembering how Sally had encouraged me to chase the overtime. What a naive idiot I must have seemed to her.

It was almost four o'clock.

I stripped off my sweat soaked shirt and sat down on a wooden chair to strip off my trousers. These days, with my bad leg and poor sense of balance, I don't take chances. It's not the first time I've fell over and banged my head or ended up with a sore face, but usually because I've had a little more than the hair of the dog. Naked, I braced myself against the white tiled wall and, leaning forward into the old steel bath I turned on the electric shower. The force of the water was one luxury that I can't deny. I'd the foresight to screw a stainless steel grab rail onto the opposite tiled wall and, holding tightly to the grab rail, used this to help me step over the lip of the bath. The water cascaded over my body and I remembered I'd left the tumbler of whisky sitting on the kitchen worktop. Bugger it. I'm too wet now to parade through the house, soaking the carpet.

I run a hand across my jaw. The stubble wasn't too bad and I decided another shave wasn't worth it.

I wasn't looking forward to my appointment with Julia Goodman. Not that I didn't need the appointment or that I didn't like or trust her, but because Goodman was too bloody shrewd for my liking. Getting blood from a stone was easier than getting a prescription for medication from her.

I rinsed off and gingerly stepped out of the bath.

Drying myself, I saw from the overcrowded wash basket that another visit to the local launderette was overdue. I'd been promising to get myself a washing machine, but with money being so tight and Sally squeezing me dry, that was on hold for a while. She'd not only gotten half the pay-off money, but almost two thirds of my monthly pension as well. I didn't begrudge anything to Paul and I know that raising a growing eight year old was a struggle, but with her own salary and my contribution, believe me; Sally wasn't doing too badly.

And when our marriage ended, I didn't just lose my wife and son and my home, but most of our friends believed her lies too.

Anyway, what's the use of complaining?

I checked the drawers for clean clothes and saw I was down to just three clean pair of underwear, four pair and one odd sock and one shirt, non-ironed of course. Yep, I'll need to be moseying on down to that laundry real soon partner, I thought to myself.

While getting dressed, I finished the tumbler of whisky and was about to pour another when I checked myself. Doctor Goodman could smell alcohol on a patient's breath at fifty paces, so if I was going to charm her, I'd better be sober. Back in the bathroom, I gargled with the strong minty stuff and gagged when I swallowed some of it.

Almost quarter to five. Time I was gone.

The surgery was a short ten-minute walk. Ten minutes if you've got two good legs that is.

Climbing into the Focus, I reluctantly eased it out of the parking space in the knowledge the space would be gone when I got back. Maybe I should petition the council to paint me one of those disabled bays on the road, I thought?

It took me less than five minutes to drive through light traffic to the surgery, a modern custom built practice just off Dixon Avenue and over five minutes to get a parking space.

I shouldn't have bothered buying a flat. I should have bought some waste ground and turned it into a car park. I'd have made a fortune in a year.

The receptionist glared at me over her glasses. You know the sort; grey-haired, middle-aged spinsters, frosty faced and wearing a tweed skirt and cardigan and whose whole purpose in life is to protect her doctors from their grubby little patients.

Actually, I'm lying. This one was in her late twenties, blonde haired and very, very pretty with breasts that poked out through her thin black, almost sheer blouse and halfway across her reception counter. But that didn't prevent her from glaring at me as though I'd asked her to loan me twenty quid.

"Take a seat please," she crisply instructed me.

So I joined the sick, lame and lazy, seated in neat rows among the plastic potted plants as they coughed and spluttered into their handkerchiefs or onto their sleeves when they thought nobody was looking. The walls were decorated with all sorts of NHS posters that included warnings that threatened AIDS if you engaged in unprotected sex. These days, I'd take my chance for any kind of sex, protected or otherwise. In fact, I almost burst out laughing; I'm so broke I couldn't even pay for it.

At last, I heard my name called and collected my file from the surly receptionist before making my way to Goodman's room.

"Ah, John, come in and shut the door," said the deep, raspy voice. "To what do I owe the pleasure?"

Doctor Julia Goodman, wearing a bright, purple crewneck sweater beneath her white housecoat, sat grinning like a beached whale behind her old, chipped and scarred oak desk. Tight grey hair atop a scrubbed, florid face, her stubby fingers clenched together and an old, worn stethoscope casually slung round her neck, she stared at me with a mischievous grin.

I knew then that I wasn't going to win this one.

"You've had my regular prescription stopped," I blurted out like a wee petulant schoolboy, my carefully prepared script thrown out without a second thought as I sat down and stared accusingly back at her.

"Indeed I have John. Do you think I want to be responsible for you ending up dead with kidney and liver failure? I think not, my young friend. You're much too good looking for that," she teased with a humourless smile.

Maybe at this point I should explain a little of our relationship.

Following the incident that crippled me and my eventual discharge from hospital, during the time when Sally and I were still living together pretending to be man and wife, Julia Goodman, who had been my GP but whom I'd never really had any call to visit, took over my home care and saw to it that any medical assistance or physiotherapy I needed was attended to. For that I am and always will be grateful to her.

But that was then. This is now.

"You know I need those pills Julia," I replied. My God, I can almost hear the pleading in my own voice. How the hell had I come to this?

She didn't answer, but stared at me before using her hands to push her huge bulk up from the desk and waddle over to a small floor cabinet in the corner. I watched her backside wobble as she walked and wondered what I could say to persuade her to scribble me just one more prescription, what promise I could make that she'd believe?

"Ah, here we are," she said, reaching down and grabbing at something. With an effort, she straightened up and I could see that even that short exertion had reddened her face. I didn't need a medical degree to know that if she wasn't careful, if she didn't do something about her grossly overweight body, Julia Goodman was looking at imminent heart failure.

Seated again behind her desk, she tossed a leaflet towards me.

"What's this?" I mumbled at her, reaching for it.

"Its details of an alcohol and drug outreach group, here in Shawlands," she replied.

I stared malevolently at her, or as malevolently as I dared I mean, and tossed the leaflet back at her.

"I don't need this," I scoffed. "I just need some more painkillers. You've no idea what I'm going through."

"Oh but I do," she quickly retorted. "Lack of sleep, stomach cramps, the inability to hold down food, thirst and dryness of the throat, constant headache, the need to dull the pain with alcohol. Am I right?"

I stared at her, my mouth hanging open. I must have looked like some kind of slack-jawed moron. And of course, she was right.

"You've no idea," I spluttered again, my mind working overtime as I tried to think of something that would change her mind. Pushing back my chair, I stood up, but as usual not without the help of my stick.

I tried to appear angry, but it didn't work with her. Julia Goodman had practised medicine for thirty years in the Gorbals, among the junkies and the work shy; been bullied and threatened and on one occasion, had her car torched right outside her surgery window. So what were the chances of a crippled drunk like me intimidating her?

"Like I said John," she calmly replied, "whether right now you appreciate it or not, I'm doing this in your best interest. As far as further medication is concerned, you are barred *sine die*, so get used to it. There's no easy way for you to bear this, but I want you to consider seeking the help of this group," standing now, she waved the leaflet under my nose.

I raged and I shouted and I screamed at her, but all to no avail.

During the ranting the blonde receptionist, alarm on her face, hurriedly pushed through the door, but Goodman, blank faced, waved her away. I didn't see the patients or the reception staff watching me as I stumbled from the surgery. I didn't see the curious stares of the pedestrians as, tears of anger burning my eyes I slowly made my way along Dixon Avenue to my car. I didn't see the sympathetic looks of passers-by when they saw me weeping in the driver's seat.

I sat there sobbing quietly and feeling sorry for myself for what seemed like ages, but was in reality no more than ten minutes. I found a used handkerchief in the pocket of my jacket and wiped my runny nose. Taking a deep breath, I started the car and drove home, or rather, back to the flat. I've never really considered it home, if you get what I mean.

Home is where my son is and where I used to be - should be.

With uncommon luck, the space I'd vacated almost an hour earlier was still empty and, at my second attempt, I parked the car.

I sat there for another five minutes, my thoughts dulled by the knowledge that, other than the remains of less than a half bottle of whisky, I'd nothing to see me through the night.

Then I remembered the seven quid or so that I had remaining and looked over to the small licensed grocery shop on the corner.

I stumbled through the front door, almost falling in my eagerness to get to the kitchen and polish off the half bottle of Bells before I started on the new one. Holding the bottle like some precious relic, I carried it through to the room I laughingly called the lounge; white painted walls to create the illusion of space, two old and fading green cloth covered couches and a coloured brick fireplace that was fashionable in the seventies. The television sat in the corner on top of a light coloured wooden unit that housed my CD player and collection of Tambla Motown music. On top of the television sat a framed photograph of a shyly smiling Paul in school uniform, taken on his first day at primary school.

The day before his mother tore him from my life.

Dressed in the ridiculously baggy shorts over bony knees and school blazer a size too large, it is his eyes that are the most startling feature, eyes that are mine, deep and blue. Except these days my eyes are more inclined to resemble an AA road map, all red lines I mean. I uncorked the bottle and raised it to my lips and was about to take a pull at it when I saw the flashing red light on the telephone answer machine.

Curious, I thought, I didn't usually receive calls at home these days, not since Sally had spread the word about me being a rotten, violent bastard.

I pressed the rewind button and listened as the tape whirled round in its casing. The call started with the time received, just over an half an hour previously, then the harsh voice of Detective Inspector Michael Farrell crackled through the small speaker.

"Hello Logan, you drunken old fart, how's it hanging? Hate these bloody things so if you're there, pick up, eh? No? Okay then, play hard to get. Your old mate

Mickey here, but of course you'll have guessed that. Word is that you were seen snooping round the River Clyde area this afternoon, cruising past a certain building that my lot have a wee interest in. Give me a call when you get this, you know the number."

There was a slight pause, as if he was remembering something, then:

"Oh, and don't call the office. Get me on my mobile, okay?"

The line went dead and the tape whirled back to the beginning.

I sat there, thinking about what Mickey had said. If nothing else, it confirmed my suspicions that the Drug Squad had an interest in 18 Lancefield Quay and Mickey, forewarning me not to contact him at his office, was tipping me the wink that I'd been spotted. Must have been the back-up team that saw me, I guessed, some former colleague recognising me as I drove past because I'd never bothered registering the Focus with DVLA, in my own name.

The tape machine settled into receive mode again and I nestled the half bottle against my cheek, aching for a sip of the magic potion but curious as to what Mickey had to say. With reluctance, I placed the bottle on the low coffee table and hobbled into the small hallway to where I'd hung my jacket and retrieved my small diary from the inside pocket. Back in the lounge, I quickly scanned my contact list and dialled Mickey's mobile phone number.

It was answered almost as the line connected.

"Can you speak?" I asked him.

"Not at the minute, dad," he replied. He's no fool, Mickey Farrell. I realised he must be standing close enough to someone to be overheard. "'Just having a chinwag with the team. Be with you in about thirty or forty minutes. Fish suppers alright?"

I'd have preferred a bottle of Bells, but grinned at the handset and blew him a kiss.

"That'll be fine, son," I replied, getting into character, "I'll have the table set."

I replaced the handset and reached for the half bottle, stroking it tenderly as one would a lover.

But I didn't want to be sozzled by the time Farrell arrived, so twisted the cap back on and stowed the bottle on the ledge under the table to await the arrival of my old friend.

I must have dozed off while I sat on the couch. The close doesn't have a security entrance and I jerked awake as Farrell noisily banged on my front door. Hobbling to open it, he pushed his bulky, six foot frame past me reeking of the cheap French cigarettes he favours and carrying a plastic bag of beer cans in one hand and a steaming brown package that could only be the fish suppers, in the other.

"Thought you were setting the table, you grubby little man?" he shouted an admonishment from the kitchen cum scullery.

"And hello to you too, Michael," I grinned to no one in particular as I steadied myself on my stick.

I followed him into the back room and he already had two places set out on the scarred wooden table and two wooden chairs drawn up facing each other. As I watched, he rubbed a dinner plate against the trousers of his ample backside and placed it down at my side, then repeated the motion with a second place for himself.

"Hope these are clean," he growled at me before dumping a portion of fish and chips on each plate.

How do you reply to a guy that's just wiped your plate on his arse? I lowered myself into the chair as he dumped a can of Tennents lager in front of me.

"Get that down you, you'll feel better," he ordered me.

He sat down and began to wolf down the food. It was obvious Mickey came from a large family, the protective way he hunched over his plate.

"I'm starving," he said between mouthfuls. "Been out all day and not a bloody thing to show for it."

Then he stared meaningfully at me.

"Except you, of course."

He tipped his head back and swallowed deeply from his can of lager.

"So, first things first then. You look like shit. Still hitting the bevy and those bloody pills then?"

I could literally feel the hot food plummeting to my empty stomach and reminding me how hungry I was.

"Don't you start," I mumbled in resentful reply. "I've had enough problems with my GP this afternoon. Bloody old cow refused me any more medication."

He chewed thoughtfully and nodded his head.

"Must have realised how close to becoming a junkie you are then, eh?"

That stopped me. I stared at him, at his salt and pepper bearded face, his thinning, collar length hair gelled back into an untidy ponytail. The anger welled up within me. The sanctimonious shit! Who the hell is he to call me a bloody junkie?

He must have seen the rage in my face, because he put both hands up as if in surrender and stared back at me.

"Look, John, I'm one of the very few friends you've got left. Don't go falling out with me because I happen to tell you the truth. We both know that you've had a drink problem since it happened and that you've become reliant on the painkillers. Jesus! After what you went through, all those injury and domestic problems hitting you at the same time, it's not beyond belief that you'd seek to dull the pain with the booze and the pills. But you're killing yourself, as surely as if you were opening a vein and letting your lifeblood drip away."

The greasy food suddenly seemed indigestible and I threw my cutlery down onto the plate, I almost reached for the can of lager then, but something stopped me. I knew that he'd win, that he'd see it in my face, that I needed the drink.

He poked with his fork at a piece of fish, the silence between us as physical as a brick wall then decided enough was enough and drew a packet of fags from his jacket pocket. Lighting one drew a grimace of distaste from me. Of all my bad habits, smoking hasn't been one.

"You got any plans to tell me why you're warning me off Lancefield Quay?" I said at last.

He chewed noisily at a mouthful of chips, masticating the food like some bearded ogre crunching bones.

"We've had an interest in a guy that lives in that block. We think he's the middle man for some wealthy dealers in the north side of the city."

"Middle man? Middle between whom exactly?"

"Strictly need to know John. Sorry."

My body ached for a pull at the can of lager or, even better, three fingers from the half bottle nestling beneath my coffee table. But I knew from long experience that if I waited, didn't press him, Mickey would open up. Couldn't hold his breath, Mickey Farrell, let alone keep a secret from an old and trusted mate. He placed his knife and fork neatly together on his empty plate and, with a loud and fragrant burp sat back, the can of lager tight in his big, right fist.

"So, any chance you can tell me why you were cruising round that area?"

"Client confidentiality," I replied.

"Don't give me any of that old bullshit, John Logan," he snarled as he leaned towards me, his hot breath drifting across the gap between us. "Remember, I'm the one that warned you and wrote your mysterious appearance on our surveillance plot out of today's log, otherwise you'd have some of my boys knocking on your door and demanding to know what you were snooping around for. So let's cut the crap. Why were you there?"

"Who saw me?" I asked, trying to divert his anger.

He smiled at that.

"Same old Detective Sergeant Logan," he shook his head, his anger abating as quickly as it rose. "Confuse the suspect by going off at a tangent. You haven't changed have you? But the only problem here, old son, is that I'm not a suspect and I know you too well."

He smiled at that and I had to assume, like me, he'd had a sudden flash of memories, of good times working together. Realising that I wasn't going to be blustered into telling him anything, he sighed and grinned at me.

"One of the back-up team recognised you. You won't know him," he said, forestalling my question, "he arrived as a rookie in the surveillance unit just about that time you copped it. But he'd heard the stories," he grimaced, "about the wife beating."

"Who hasn't?" I replied, taking a slug of lager. A few drops dribbled down my chin and I used my shirtsleeve to wipe my mouth.

He grinned again. Mickey is one of the few who knows the real Sally, the Sally who isn't the victim she likes to portray.

"The guy were looking at is a real lowlife called William Crawford. Stays in a two bed roomed flat at 18 Lancefield Quay. Calls himself a mature student and does a bit of minor dealing in the clubs and pubs round the Charing Cross end of Sauchiehall Street. Bit of a player with the ladies too, by all account. Doesn't care what age or type, as long as they've got a pulse, if you get my drift."

As if accepting that he'd started so he might as well finish, he continued. "Heard a whisper that our young Mister Crawford had holidayed recently in Palma and stayed in the same hotel as a Columbian that the Civil Guard were watching. Seems the two were more than friendly and that provoked a wee interest from the Spanish, who contacted our Customs, who in turn came to us looking for more information on Crawford. To cut a long story short, the Spanish have revealed the Columbian, his name doesn't matter, is the European end of an operation that's bringing a shipload of cocaine, not sure how much, but a lot anyway, into one of the Spanish ports aboard a Venezuelan freighter. Our Mister Crawford hotfooted it back to Glasgow about a week ago and approached our very own Jackie Dewar with a proposition."

Now that was a name I hadn't given much thought to in the recent past and I involuntarily shivered, the thought of Jackie Dewar immediately dragging up a faded but terrible memory.

"Dewar?" I slowly replied, "I thought he was doing real heavy time?"

"Overturned on appeal. Do you not read the bloody papers, you tosspot? Claimed the evidence was tainted by Drug Squad officer's intent on convicting him at any cost. There's an internal inquiry going on as we speak. One of the bags of cocaine discovered in his car is from a batch with the same purity and origin as a bag that had already been seized and was lost…."

"Lost?"

Mickey grimaced.

"Yeah, lost from the production room at headquarters. A kilo bag," he added.

"Don't ask," he mournfully held his hands up.

"Suffice to say, it was enough to suggest the stuff had been planted. Seems the real unpublicised story is that Dewar had just bought it from one of our own, but of course he isn't saying who. Needless to say if that information had become open knowledge and hit the papers, public confidence in the police drug squads would have evaporated overnight and every convicted druggie for the last ten years would have claimed he or she had been fitted up. The court appeal system would have been overwhelmed and we would likely have had dozens if not more, released pending those appeals. Anyway, Crown Office and Dewar's solicitor worked a deal and the result is he's free and right back into it. Living in one of those renovated apartments that used to be part of the old GPO building in George Square."

I knew the flats. When they were being sold off a couple of years previously, the starting price was almost half a million each. Seems Jackie was doing not too badly for an almost illiterate scummy thug from a council housing estate.

Do I sound resentful?

"So," I asked, "this guy Crawford is trying to source part of the shipment for Dewar?"

"That's the story. Mind you, we've watched him for almost a month now and apart from dealing a wee bit of personal now and again, the bugger hasn't put a foot wrong."

He stared at me, a half smile on his whiskered chops as he drew deeply on his smelly French weed.

"So give, ya gimpy wee shite. What's your interest in that building? Is it Crawford? Have you turned something up? Give."

I wouldn't have tolerated that kind of abuse from anyone else, but Mickey Farrell was different. Apart from being one of my oldest and few remaining friends, the ugly sod had helped me out of more than one scrape. Besides that, even with two good legs, it's unlikely that I could have wrestled the big, rugby mad brute to the ground; anyway, not before he'd have pummelled me to death.

So I gave.

"A client, a Chinese man, has asked me to find out what I can about Crawford. His daughter is keeping company with him and he's not a happy chappie."

"Young Oriental bird, with long black hair? Aye I've seen her. Looks like a wee schoolgirl she does. Stays over sometimes at Crawford's flat. Haven't got a name for her. Is she on the dope?"

"That I don't know, but if she is, the father won't be pleased and he certainly hasn't told me."

"You know that you can't repeat what I told you John? You can't tell the father anything. I can't afford to have this operation compromised, not at this stage. We're getting close to the witching hour. Customs have recently heard from the Yanks DEA, their satellite monitoring of the Venezuelan ship puts her on our side of the pond and the Spanish reckon she'll dock sometime with the next few days."

"Why not just let them, the Spanish I mean, hit her and take out all the coke?"

He shook his head sadly.

"Politics, my old friend," he wryly smiled, "you're well out of it. The management on our side are being pressurised by the Customs who want a large seizure on our turf, followed by heavy sentencing, to deter other drug importers. Well, that's the official version. What's really got up their noses is Dewar walking out of what seemed to be a watertight case and giving the Scottish Judicial system the finger. That and they're trying to identify the viper in the nest, the one that stole the kilo of coke from our supposedly secure production room."

He pushed the dirty plate to one side and using his middle fingernail, began picking at a lump of food debris trapped between his upper front teeth. Mickey was in his element now, a natural storyteller.

"So," he finished off the lager, reached into a trouser pocket and produced a packet of spearmint gum, "what it boils down to is the Spanish intend letting the shipment be taken from the freighter, probably in one of these seagoing containers, we think, and then allow the coke to be divided up. They've agreed that they'll permit the foreign consignments to be dispatched across their borders and then hit by the police of whatever country receives a consignment. The Spanish Civil Guard will then deal with their own importation. That way it'll take away from the source that provided the original information about the shipment."

He smiled.

"Don't ask me who the source is, I've no idea. But I'm betting its some American DEA informant in Columbia. All we have to do here is concentrate on the arrival of our batch that we assess is to be received by our very own Jackie Dewar. Or at least by his network."'

"Any idea how large a delivery Dewar is expecting?"

"Can't say old pal, but what I have heard is that Dewar is borrowing heavily from all over the place to fund the coke. He's into some of the heavy mobs in London and Manchester and apparently at least one Manchester based dealer is trying to muscle in with backing too. If you want my considered opinion," he cocked his head to one side and raised an eyebrow.

I nodded, my interest like a worm on a hook that he was about to reel in.

"I figure from what I've heard we're talking at least eight, maybe as much as ten million."

I pursed my lips and blew.

"If that's the purchase price, what's the profit margin in that I wonder?"

"Sadly, coke's not too difficult to obtain these days, but if Dewar floods the market the price will drop and he'll lose a lot of money. No, I see him hanging on to this batch for a while, storing it and organising its sale piecemeal. But he won't want to hold it too long either. That amount of coke will attract buyers from all over Scotland and the North of England".

"Any idea where the deal will take place?"

Mickey shook his head. "Not a clue John, but if I know Jackie Dewar, he'll want testers before he purchases and then it will be a cash delivery, a truckload of money upfront for a truckload of charlie. Straight swap, done and dusted."

He gave me a wry smile. "Just think of the money the Treasury would make if they ever legalise the stuff."

He shook his empty can.

"Another?" I asked.

"Naw, time I was away home. I've Crawford to baby-sit again early tomorrow morning".

He scraped back his chair and grinned at me.

"Mind what I said now Johnny boy, not a word to your Chinky man now. And do me a personal favour will you? Try and lay off the booze and the pills. Too many of my old pals are turning up their toe these days."

He hesitated at the door. It was obvious something was on his mind.

"Sally," he said, biting at his bottom lip, the confession bursting from him. "Never could believe her, anything she said. You never knew, I couldn't tell you John, but she tried it on once. With me," he said, then lamely adding, "but I didn't. Honest mate," as if the revelation would shock me.

But it didn't surprise me. I already knew. She'd boasted about it one night, after she'd had her nightly tipple, as she liked to call it. Sneering as she tried to persuade me that it was Mickey, my old Squad pal, who had suggested the relationship. I hadn't believed her, knew that for all his faults, Mickey Farrell just wasn't the type. He'd been happily married for fifteen years or so to a really nice and attractive woman and knew what It was to have a faithful and loving wife. I guessed he'd spurned her advances and in her embarrassed and shamed anger, she'd turned spitefully and insisted he had propositioned her, finally convincing herself that it was she who had rejected Mickey.

I didn't see him out, merely nodded. Then he left and I heard the front door bang behind him. Like me, Mickey Farrell was going home to a cold and empty flat, because a couple of years previously, Mickey's wife had succumbed to cancer, whereas mine had merely stabbed me in the back.

Funny, but as I hobbled back into the front room and sat down, it never occurred to me then, not till later I should say, but right then, my mind preoccupied with what Mickey had told me, I never gave another thought to the half bottle nestling under the coffee table.

CHAPTER 2

The next morning found me lying uncomfortably on my couch. Sore and aching, but sober. That didn't stop the pounding in my head, but for the first time in as long as I could remember, I attributed that to the awkward position I'd been lying in and not the whisky. Carefully, I eased myself into a sitting position. The sunlight shone through the unclosed curtains, filling the room with more light than my eyes could cope with at that time of the morning. It was almost six-thirty, according to the clock sitting above the fireplace.

While I made my toilet, I ran the shower then stood under the heat till my skin felt as though it was blistering. It didn't help my head, but did take away some of the ache in my body.

I boiled the kettle for coffee and because the milk was going off, settled myself to take it black. The worrying thing was I'd no painkilling tablets left to wash down and contented myself with four Paracetamol, hoping that they'd be enough to get me through the morning.

I planned to travel through to Polkemmet and try to locate Martin Kilbride's phone. I'd already convinced myself I was going to find a love nest, some cottage tucked away in the Country Park and Kilbride living it up with a girlfriend.

I figured the journey would be no more than fifty or sixty minutes, depending on traffic conditions on the motorway, but I already knew the petrol in my car wouldn't get me there near there without a top up. I grinned self-consciously. My monthly retirement money wasn't due for another week and I was already at the limit on my bankcard. Problem is that most of the local garages know me and wouldn't give me a second chance, with my practised stammered excuse there must be a problem with the bank, so I'd need to chance on filling up out of the city.

But first, there was something far more important to organise.

I pulled up outside the laundrette and mentally crossed my fingers as I swung my black bin bag in front of me and pushed through the doors.

I was in luck.

Wee Annie was on duty. Eyebrows raised and chubby hands on ample hips, she cocked her head to one side and scowled at me.

"Mister Logan, my favourite private dick," she slowly drawled in a deep voice. I say drawled because Annie, just over five feet tall and almost as broad, wore a cowgirl skirt so tight it threatened to split at the seams, plaid shirt decorated with pearls, fancy stitched high heeled boots and her long black hair braided in a ponytail. The only things missing from her outfit were a ten-gallon Stetson and holster on her hip. A slash of scarlet lipstick and heavy pancake make-up on her chin and cheeks failed to hide the slight dark moustache that trailed under her once broken nose. A devotee of the American cowboy era, Annie was a regular at the Grand Ole Oprey club in Paisley Road West, where every weekend, lawyers and dustmen, nurses, cleaners, some cops even and every trade and profession you can think of, gather together at the Western theme club where they shed their every day lives and become the heroes and villains of the old Wild West.

Annie, if memory serves me correctly, goes by the name Six-gun Sally.

"Hello," I sheepishly replied. I say sheepishly, because I can't recall if I settled my previous laundry bill.

"Long time no see pardner," she drawled in her pseudo American accent, reaching for my bag. "So, where have you been hiding then?"

"Here and there," I replied with a smile. "Sorry, I'm not sure Annie. Am I up to date or do I owe you…."

"No, you paid the last time," she hastily replied, glancing at me from beneath her unplucked eyebrows.

I suspected I hadn't in fact paid and she was being kind and did my best to ignore how really hairy she was. Hadn't really noticed it before, but probably because every time I called in I was either getting drunk or recovering with a hangover. I narrowed my eyes. In fact, I'm almost certain that was a faint shadow round her chin. She couldn't be….? No, I quickly dismissed the thought.

"So," she interrupted my daydream, "will you be wanting this lot back this afternoon? If you are, remember its early closing today. Half-past four. I've the club to get ready for tonight," she grinned, making a pretend gun with her forefinger and thumb that she pointed at me.

Just as I was about to reply that yes, I'd be back in time to collect my laundry, she stared meaningfully at me.

"You know, if you're not doing anything tonight. Maybe you'd like to come along? I mean, as my guest," she blushed and bit her lower lip as she gazed at me with wide, open eyes.

"Eh, I'd love to," I replied, the guilt of my lie betrayed on my face, "but I've a job on this evening. A surveillance," I almost blurted out.

Funny that. When the occasion demands it, I can lie and fib with the best of them, but when it comes right down to it, I find it difficult being deceitful to an honest soul like Annie.

She nodded and smiled, her disappointment evident on her face.

Awkwardly I shuffled to the door, ignoring the disapproving look of the old busybody who was sitting in front of the dryer and pretending to read her book while she ear wigged everything I'd said. Seems she didn't believe me either, then.

The day dawned bright and sunny and the drive east on the M8 through the city centre was the usual chaotic avoidance of the Saturday morning early shoppers, but once I'd passed Cowcaddens, the traffic thinned and I'd a relatively trouble free journey to the fuelling station at Harthill, where I slapped a packet of ham sandwiches and bottle of water onto the petrol bill that I paid by cheque, one of the few petrol stations that, thank God, still accepted cheques. Sometimes I get lucky.

Fortunately, the teenage girl was too preoccupied talking to her fellow assistant and didn't give it a second glance. Back on the road, I continued on to junction four, where I came off the motorway and made my way back to the Country Park. I stopped at the Park entrance and consulted the printout I'd got from my computer. Slowly I made my way in on the dual tarmac roadway then turned left onto a single-track that took me into a densely wooded area. I'd travelled no more than a few hundred yards along the rutted track before realising I was hopelessly lost, that there was nothing on the printout that indicated any kind of reference point, at least, not from where I sat with a curtain of greenery over my head.

I parked the Focus in a widened part of the track that allowed vehicles to pass and climbed out.

I'd figured I'd have some walking to do and prepared myself with a pair of stout Doc Marten shoes and was wearing a tee shirt beneath a black roll neck sweater and an old pair of brown corduroy trousers. I didn't need a jacket and left the car locked, but decided to take the sandwiches and bottled water with me in a plastic carrier bag. Been a long time since I was on a picnic, I grinned self-consciously. Before I set out, I again studied the printout like I knew what I was doing and reckoned the area from where the mobile phone emanated the signal must be somewhere to my left, westwards. What I needed to find was some kind of track, some sort of way through the dense foliage through which Martin Kilbride had apparently made his way. The recent spell of good weather had hardened the track. Sure, there was plenty of tyre-track evidence that vehicles had used the baked track, but unless I was completely wrong, I'd say most of the tyre-tracks belonged to off road vehicles. This wasn't the type of route that was likely to be used by a top of the range Saab coupe.

I made my mind up. I'd leave the Focus and trudge along the track, try and find a way into the woods that could be used by a vehicle or at least, by someone on foot.

Now, I'm no Indian tracker and a smiled faintly. It occurred to me that maybe I should have brought laundrette Annie or one of her cowboy friends on this little jaunt with me. Stumbling along the uneven ground, I was grateful for the cool shade the overhanging trees afforded me.

After twenty minutes of fruitless searching, I realised that I was hungry and, propping myself against a tree, sat down with my legs splayed out in front of me. I tore the cellophane from the sandwiches and slowly munched my way through half of them, enjoying the relative peace and calm for the woods.

In the near distance, I could hear the sound of something large pushing through the shrubbery. According to the blurb I'd read about the park, deer roamed freely so I guessed I wasn't so alone after all. I washed the sandwich down with a mouthful of water and then struggled to my feet.

That's when I saw it, the whiteness of a broken branch, a whiteness that stood out from the dark brown and green surrounding it.

Now, don't get me wrong. I'm no bushman, but even a city slicker like me can recognise that a broken branch signifies someone or something has passed this way. Sure, I'd completed a two-week rural surveillance course in my prime, living rough and freezing my balls off in the forest around Loch Ard, playing at hiding in bushes and ditches for a fortnight and maybe just then some of the training came back to me. Maybe just a little, anyway.

I moved closer and saw that the broken branch wasn't alone. A number had been broken and placed back into the ground, as though still growing, creating a curtain of green. A curious excitement gripped me and I began pulling and pushing at the thick foliage. It gave way under my frenzied assault and I saw that it hid a disused track that led further into the woods. It didn't take a genius to work out someone was trying to hide this narrow passageway and I determined to find out why.

Clumsily, using my stick to clear a path, I shoved through the bushes and into the clear track then followed my nose, for now I could smell an old, familiar stench, that of burned plastic and leather.

Another fifty, maybe sixty yards later, I found the car. Or what remained of it. I must've been holding my breath and to be honest, half expected to find a fried corpse shrivelled in the driver's seat but thankfully, the car was empty and I breathed a silent prayer of relief. There weren't any keys in the ignition, but in the driver's footwell was what seemed to be the casing of a mobile phone, burned beyond any hope of obtaining information from it.

Whoever had torched the car hadn't waited to see the end result that was obvious, because though the interior was completely destroyed, the bodywork still remained to clearly identify it as a Saab coupe, dark blue in colour and with the registration plate that indicated it belonged to the missing Martin Kilbride.

Reaching into the driver's side, I tugged at the lever that remotely operated the boot and, heart in my mouth, stumbled to the rear of the car.

Taking a deep breath, I raised the boot lid and peered in.

Empty.

I can't say exactly how long I sat there, my bag in one hand and staring at the burnt out vehicle. I'd seen a lot of torched cars in my time. Some torched for fun by so-called joy riders, some torched by their owners for the insurance money, while others as a result of collisions and occasionally with some unfortunate soul screaming for help from inside.

But this, I shook my head. My gut instinct was telling me that this stunk to high heaven and I'm not referring to the smell of plastic.

The longer I sat there and stared at the burned wreck, the more I considered the reasons why the Saab had been torched.

My first thought was that whoever had set the fire, had botched the job. The blown out windows seemed to indicate the doors had been closed when the fire was started inside and even though I guessed it had happened some days previous, the smell of petrol was still pungently strong.

I could see the petrol cap was in place and it was fortunate that the tank hadn't ignited.

"So," I wondered aloud, "why destroy just the interior and let the rest survive the flames?"

The car is registered to Martin Kilbride, so there was no need for him to deny any connection with the vehicle, no need for him to eliminate his trace from the interior of the vehicle. I glanced at the back of the car, at the registration plates. Even had they been removed, the engine block and chassis numbers would still have identified it as being registered to Martin Kilbride.

It seemed then that it probably wasn't Kilbride who had set fire to the Saab. Why would he need to destroy his connection with the vehicle? No, I concluded, someone trying to both hide the vehicle and deny any forensic connection with it, did this.

There could only be one logical answer. Whoever had caused the fire wasn't bothered about the outside of the vehicle. It was simply the interior that was the target of the fire, where a scene of crime examination might turn up a trace of the last occupant or whoever had dumped the car in this out of the way place. The culprit simply wanted to erase any trace of his or her connection with the Saab. Which led me to another realisation.

If it wasn't Kilbride who had torched his car, who did, why, and where the hell is Kilbride now?

CHAPTER 3

I drove back towards Glasgow, my mind racing.

I considered Id two options open to me. I could drive to Kirkintilloch and inform the foxy Missus Kilbride that I'd discovered her husband's car, but she in turn would be bound to let the local coppers know. Problem with that option was that the uniform would then hand Kilbride's file to the CID, who'd be a little more circumspect and with the finding of the burnt out car in such suspicious circumstances, likely treat the disappearance with a lot more misgiving. Kilbride's disappearance would then become a criminal investigation rather than a simple missing person. That would result in me being out on my ear, becoming no more than a witness to the finding of the Saab and so, I realised, bang goes my earner. Or I could hold back on the find of the Saab for a few days more, maybe tell her I was conducting searches in the Polkemmet district and try to establish if he knew anyone in that area.

I suppose that I didn't really need any persuading. I'd replaced the broken foliage at the start of the track and left the entrance to the track the way I'd found it. I had known then when I was sticking the twigs back in place, even though I wasn't admitting it even to myself, that I'd choose the second option; try and spin this inquiry out for a few more days.

After all, I needed the money I consoled myself. And if I'd read Phyllis Kilbride correctly, another two or three days at most without news of her husband wasn't going to crack this lady up.

You might ask did I feel any guilt at keeping this to myself. Truthfully?

I glanced at the petrol gauge as it crept towards the red line.

Not a bit.

Having made my decision to keep the finding of the Saab to myself, I decided I'd keep the news for up for two, maybe three days at most. I knew that once I revealed the discovery and the CID taking over the inquiry that at least would give me some time to put a decent bill together. Until then, I'd go through the motions, interview Kilbride's associates at work and maybe some friends, put some typed witness statements together in a fancy folder to at least demonstrate I was trying to find the wayward husband.

Frankly, I couldn't care less if Kilbride turned up, even less if he was alive or dead

My concerns were more pressing, such as where my next half bottle was coming from and scraping enough dough together to recover my laundry from the doe-eyed Six Gun Sally.

Arriving at Glasgow city centre, I drove to Waterloo Street and managed to secure a disabled parking bay right outside number 1192. Switching off the grumbling engine, I could see in the wing mirror a uniformed parking warden sauntering towards the Focus, his blue hat pulled low over his forehead, his ticket machine slung on a leather strap round his neck and shoulder and his hands quivering with anticipation as he watched me through narrowed eyes open the drivers door. I waited till he drew abreast then casually slung my blue disabled badge onto the dashboard. His face frowned with disappointment and he ambled away as though indifferent to me, but I knew better.

Call it my little quirk, but I do love to stick it to these officious bastards.

The double entrance doors to 1192 were highly polished mahogany and led into a spacious hallway where a female concierge presided behind a wide desk. The large brass plate attached to the wall and beside the elevator listed the location of all the offices in the ornate Georgian building. There were no call buttons beside the lift doors so I assumed it was security controlled and the concierge operated its opening at ground level.

The young blonde woman behind the desk smiled a friendly greeting at me.

"Can I help you sir?"

I limped over to her desk.

"Mister Logan," I introduced myself. "I'm visiting Spencer and Boyle. I'm here to speak with someone from the firm about Mister Kilbride."

She didn't acknowledge if she was aware of Kilbride's disappearance, but merely nodded and pressed a preset button on her phone.

I listened as she informed whoever was on the line that I was downstairs and nodded at the handset, evidently receiving some instruction. Replacing the phone in its cradle she smiled at me again.

"Ms Carlisle will meet you on the fourth floor," she told me, and then I saw the grimace.

"I'm afraid the lifts out of order again Mister Logan. Do you think you'll..."

She glanced at a locked door on the opposite side of the hallway and then more subtly at my stick. I knew what was coming next. Would I manage the stairs with my bum leg?

I grinned more heroically than I felt. The thought of climbing all those stairs sickened me to the pit of my stomach. Ordinarily I wouldn't mind four flights, provided I took my time, but the way I was feeling right now, with my stomach churning and perspiration oozing from every pore in my skin, it occurred to me to maybe I should just cancel and phone in my interview. Stupidly, male pride got the better of me because I didn't want to seem like a wimp in front of the good-looking concierge.

"No, I'll manage thanks," I assured her with more confidence than was good for me.

She must have pressed a remote button beneath her desk for I heard the door click open.

With a brave backward wave I limped over and pulled open the heavy fire door, steeping inside to the unexpected chill of the small foyer. A closed emergency exit door with a push bar was to one side with the stairs facing me. The polished wooden handrail atop the fancy wrought iron supports that adorned the stone steps seemed to curl up the building like a giant snake, to the sixth floor. I heard a door bang closed from above me then a muffled discussion from what seemed to be two people descending the stairs.

With my stick in my right hand, I supported myself with my left on the banister and began the sickening climb to the fourth floor. I hadn't reached the first flight, when head lowered and concentrating all my efforts on my movements, the two men were almost upon me.

"...don't care! Just get him found! Put the word out…...."

The speaker stopped talking as the two figures rounded the half landing and saw me.

"You all right there Jimmy?" asked a gruff voice, though more out of curiosity I realised than concern about my plight.

"Aye, fine," I gasped with a half nod, my head still lowered.

The two men stepped silently past me, but I felt rather than saw the younger one in the snazzy Italian suit giving me a curious glance.

I didn't turn my head, but heard them open then close the ground floor door.

The breath rattled in my chest and my hands were shaking.

I hadn't recognised the older man, but I'd known and dealt with his type all my working life. He was obviously a minder, cropped greying hair and a bullish face, wearing an ill-fitting suit that must have been made by a drunken tailor and sporting his scarred face and knuckles like visible trophies.

But the other guy, the younger of the two, him I'd never forget.

The last time I'd seen Jackie Dewar was in the box of the High Court in Glasgow, when he stood trial. The time before that was when giving me a panic-stricken backward glance as he ran southwards on Helen Street from the car I'd just rammed. But not his accomplice. No, his junkie passenger stood his ground and put two bullets into me in the seconds before our armed back-up dropped him stone dead.

I took a few seconds to compose myself, drew a deep breath and began to climb again. After what seemed an interminably long time, but was likely no more than five or six minutes, I reached the half landing below the fourth floor. My heart was hammering in my chest and truth be told, I don't think my infirmity was as much to blame as my lack of fitness.

A thin trickle of sweat was sliding down the crease of my back and I had to resist the urge to tear my shirt open and rip the tie from round my neck.

"Mister Logan?" asked a concerned voice above me.

I raised my head and stared at the woman who stood holding open the door to the fourth floor suite of offices.

Talk about a vision of loveliness. The woman standing at the top of the stairs looked like she was in her mid to late twenties, but her truer age was likely early thirties.

"Good morning, I'm Alison Carlisle."

The old macho thing again unconsciously kicked in and I tried a smile, but it must've looked like I was about to puke for the woman's face creased in further concern and she almost stepped forward as though coming down the stairs to assist me. Maybe it was the expression on my face or maybe she just didn't want to seem patronising, but she stopped and simply smiled at me, waiting on me making that final effort.

I'd like to say I hurdled up the dozen or so stairs, but get real. I'd already climbed far more stairs today than I was used to in the recent past, so limped, staggered, crawled, call it what you must, but I made it - and at least under my own steam. She held the door to permit me to squeeze past her.

I smelled her scented fragrance, but God alone knows what she sniffed from me. At her invite, I slowly followed her through a large, brightly lit, airy room with glass doors leading off it and where three women sat at computer consoles, and into a smaller office. Perhaps it was their interest in their work or possibly I'm just not that attractive to women any more, but none of them gave me even the slightest glance.

The office wasn't overly large, but big enough to accommodate a working desk in one corner and a small coffee table with two soft chairs in the other corner beneath the panoramic window that faced onto Waterloo Street. Ms Carlisle invited me to sit at the coffee table then her face again creased with......maybe concern isn't the right word.

"Is the seat too low?"

I decided some honesty was in order and that I'd already overstretched myself today. I nodded to the wooden chair facing her desk.

"Perhaps I might...?" leaving the sentence unfinished.

She smiled, a very professional smile, and pulled the chair aside, inviting me to sit.

I lowered myself wearily into it and watched, as she walked no, rather glided round to her own chair.

Faced with the good looking Ms Carlisle, her blonde hair piled on top of her head and wearing a navy pinstriped-skirted business suit, I must have looked like a refugee from an Oxfam clearing shop. I could see faint white crease lines at the corners of her eyes that must have escaped the sun, for the rest of her face sported what looked to be a recent, but fading tan and genuine too, none of your sunlamp stuff there, I thought. Seated facing me across the desk with her hands neatly folded in front of her she smiled again, that smile that seemed to convey her full attention, but really meant "Here's your hat, what's your hurry?"

I'm no expert on jewellery, but I saw that on the middle finger of her right hand she wore what looked to be an expensive looking diamond encrusted dress ring. The third finger of her left hand was bare. So, nobody special yet, I thought?

"I'm the office manager here, Mister Logan," she broke into my thoughts "and I've been instructed by the partners Mister Spencer and Mister Boyle to answer any questions you might have in relation to Mister Kilbride. So, how can I help you Mister Logan?"

"I take it Missus Kilbride will have been in touch and informed you that I have been tasked by her to inquire into her husbands disappearance?"

"The senior partner, Mister Spencer, had a word with me yesterday afternoon." Her eyes narrowed and she almost gushed. "Of course we're keen to assist in any way we can, but I don't think that there is much more I can tell you that hasn't already been disclosed to the police. Mister Kilbride...Martin," she corrected herself, inferring in the deliberate slip of the tongue that she was much more than an office manager, but on a par with management, "was at work on Monday and left for home about six that evening. I'd already left for the day, but our charwoman Missus McGowan recalls Martin saying goodnight just as she was about to begin cleaning his office. Other than that," she shrugged, "I'm afraid we've had no word from him since then."

"Is there any reason, any business reason I mean, why Mister Kilbride might have disappeared?"

She tilted her head slightly to one side and smiled at that; a broad, but very cold smile.

"I'm sure that you'll appreciate Mister Logan that I'm not at liberty to discuss any business matters with you, but I can assure you that no, there is absolutely nothing connected with this office that might cause Martin to…" she hesitated, as though the very word was repugnant to her, "…to disappear."

Now maybe I was a CID detective too long and maybe sometime I've grasped at straws, adding two and two together, but coming up with five. Admittedly, there were another couple of businesses above this office suite and according to the brass plate in the entrance foyer, at least one below this floor. Sure, Jackie Dewar might have come from any of these other offices. But that persistent wee bell that I'd trusted before was ringing in the back of my head. That little tinkle that told me that prior to my arrival he and his ugly minder had just visited the offices of Spencer and Boyle.

Right now, though, I guessed that getting anything useful from the frosty Ms Carlisle wasn't on the cards. But no harm in trying, I decided.

"Is it possible then to perhaps have a look at Mister Kilbride's office? I'd like to try and see if there's anything in there that might relate to his disappearance."

There was that smile again. Yeah, it was definitely mocking, that's what it was.

"Oh, I'm afraid that's quite out of the question. Mister Kilbride's office hasn't been disturbed since he left and there are client's confidential files on his desk. We really do expect him to turn up anytime," she cooed, "and I'm certain this little…." she fought for the words, "…this little jink of his is probably just a domestic issue that he's resolving."

"So you believe that he was unhappy at home then?"

"No!" she snapped as she sat straight back in her seat, her eyes widening, nostrils flaring, and face reddening. "Not at all. I wouldn't suggest such a thing. Not at all."

I was warming to this. It had been a long time since I'd had the opportunity to really question someone.

"But you seem to think this is some sort of domestic..."

Ms Carlisle held her hands up, cutting me off.

"A poor choice of words Mister Logan. I certainly didn't mean domestic with his wife. I meant domestic as in his private life and not connected with his business life."

By now there was a full-face blush and I was revelling in her discomfort. She isn't such a smart-arse now is she? I almost smirked. I decided to change tactics.

"So how did you get along with Mister Kilbride, Ms Carlisle?"

"Oh, very well, very well indeed. Martin and I have worked together for over five years. He and the other partners, Mister Spencer and Mister Boyle are excellent employers. We're all very happy working here."

Well, that's definitely a first, I dryly thought. I've never really known any group of people who all get along together. Usually there's some sort of envy, jealously or backbiting. Instinctively, I marked her comment down as a lie. It was then I made my mind up to have a little fun.

"Is there anyone that Mister Kilbride was particularly close to? How about you, Ms Carlisle? I've seen photographs of Mister Kilbride. He's a handsome man and if I may say, you're a very attractive lady."

Not often you witness someone's face turn three or four colour shades within a few seconds, but that's exactly what happened here.

Alison Carlisle turned from deep red to a cold pale and several tones in between. "As a matter of fact, I do mind you saying, Mister Logan," she replied through gritted teeth. "I find that suggestion most impertinent and just short of offensive. I consider that this interview is now over."

She stood up sharply, both hands slapped flat on the desk to reinforce her point. I thought it was time to placate her.

Opening my hands as if in surrender, I remained in my seat and smiled at her, giving her my most reassuring beam.

"It wasn't my intention to offend you, Ms Carlisle, but I've been hired to ask the questions the police probably won't. I'm sorry if you feel that way, but if Mister Kilbride has left his wife for another woman and if I trace him and he doesn't want to return home, that's not really my business. There's nothing in my brief from Missus Kilbride to discover her husbands….secrets. She simply wants to establish that he's safe, that he hasn't come to any harm. The question I asked was posed not at you personally, but to anyone who might be sheltering him from his wife, to give him the opportunity to contact me if indeed he is going through some personal domestic strife, that's all. As I say, I simply want to establish his safety, nothing more. If I can satisfy his wife to that end, then my jobs done."

Like hell, I thought. Evidence of Kilbride's infidelity might be worth a few bob to the anguished Missus Kilbride and something I could offer as a bonus. After all, chasing council miscreants, missing persons or divorce work, it's all the same to me. Anything to make me an earner, I inwardly grinned.

She stared down at me and finally slowly sunk back down into her chair.

Now don't get me wrong, I knew I hadn't convinced her or anything. No, I wasn't that good. I could almost hear her brain ticking over and she must have made her mind up that sleazy though I looked, I wasn't stupid.

"Mister Logan," she began and did my ears fail me or was that a hint of respect in her voice, "I can assure you that in all the time that I have known, I mean, worked with Martin Kilbride, I have never known him to conduct himself with any hint of impropriety. Yes, I agree, Martin is indeed a handsome man, but I assume you've met his wife Phyllis. Can you see him cheating on her?"

She had me there. Phyllis Kilbride was a real eyeful, I grant her that. But nothing is as greedy or as stupid as a man with a hard-on and let me tell you; I've seen some stunningly beautiful wives pass through the divorce courts as the plaintiffs, so don't give me any bull about completely faithful husbands.

"So, in short terms Ms Carlisle, you're telling me that you know of no business or personal reason that Martin Kilbride would take off without any word?"

She hesitated. Nothing that was immediately evident, but I saw it in her eyes; a definite and clear hesitation. She fixed me with an unwavering stare.

"No, no reason at all," she lied.

For that's what it was, a barefaced lie.

I knew it, she knew it, but she didn't know that I knew it.

If you see what I mean.

With that, she stood again and without preamble, offered me her right hand.

I'd one last gesture. Reaching into the side pocket of my jacket, I produced a business card, admittedly crumpled and a little worse for wear that had the office address and phone number on it and handed it to her. Her mouth creased with distaste as she took it between her forefinger and thumb of her left hand.

"I'm sure that you have enough to do Mister Logan, so I won't keep you any longer."

Actually, I thought that was my line, but I didn't argue, simply shook her hand and headed out the door. Alison Carlisle didn't accompany me this time. I figured she'd want to update her bosses that the scruffy guy was on his way. And maybe, just maybe, they'd have a wee smirk that I'd wasted my time.

But I knew different.

It was much easier descending the stairs than climbing them, I can tell you and within two minutes I was back in the entrance foyer. The good-looking blonde concierge was still behind her desk, head bowed and writing laboriously in some kind of ledger. And who says computers have completely taken over, then?

"Hi," I breezed towards her, flashing her a big, cheesy smile. "That's me been fixed up."

I pretended to turn towards the door and then, as if remembering something, turned back towards her, just like the TV detective, Colombo.

"By the way, I was on my way up the stairs when two guys passed me by. One of them said hello and I thought I knew his face, but for the life of me I can't recall his name. You know how it is, you meet so many people. Young guy smartly dressed. Does he work here?"

She screwed her mouth and her pencilled eyebrows knitted together as she tried to recall whom I was talking about.

"Was one the men…." she bit her lip in embarrassment.

I forced a laugh. "Like a boxer, you mean? A right ugly bugger? Aye, he was with him."

She giggled and blushed. "I didn't mean ugly, but he did look a bit like a boxer." She shook her head. "No, they don't work here. But they're here quite regularly," her brow creased as though recalling previous visits. "They were just visiting an office upstairs again."

She leaned forward and quietly whispered, "That's three times in as many days," like I was her new best friend.

I raised my eyebrows questioningly and she took the cue.

"Same as you, Spencer and Boyle."

"Oh, pity," I tapped at my head with my free hand, "Maybe his name will come back to me. It's an age thing. I think it's the start of Dementia, but I keep forgetting I've got it."

That got me another giggle and I waved cheerio as I limped towards the exit. I waited for a few seconds in the shadowed doorway till my eyes adjusted to the bright sunlight and that's when I saw him, the minder. He was standing across the road at the corner of Wellington Street and Bothwell Street, holding a newspaper up and pretending to read it as he lounged against the corner of the building. But he wasn't reading the paper; he was watching the doorway, waiting for me to exit. A large, well-built and quite ugly man, wearing a badly fitting suit, with scars on his hands and face. A bit of a stick-out, if you get my point.

Okay, I accept that my old Focus is a rusting heap and not worth the cost of having it removed to a scrap yard, but thankfully one of the things that still worked on the old wreck was the remote control that unlocked the door. From the safety of the darkened doorway I pressed the small button and saw the indicator lights flash in response. Quickly I limped the few yards to my car and hastily pulled the door open then scrambled untidily inside. Slamming the door shut behind me, I activated the locking mechanism. The thug hadn't expected me to be parked right outside, which was obvious. I say obvious, because the noisy car horns and his red, angry face that appeared at my passenger window indicated he'd run across the road when he'd seen me get into the Focus. He tried to wrest the passenger door open and slapped at the glass with his free hand, but I just smiled at him and started the engine.

Don't get me wrong. At another time when I'd use of both my legs and wasn't feeling like crap as I was today, I might have been capable of getting out and having a right good square go with the bastard, right there and then in the street. But those days were long past and I wasn't the hot-blooded man I once was. The sad thing is because of my gammy left leg, I'm so much more aware of my own vulnerability.

Now he was like a man demented, kicking at the side panels in his frustration and shouting all sorts of obscenities, so much so that a mystified crowd was gathering to watch his antics. Easing the car from the parking bay, I drove off into the traffic, watching in my mirror as he took another spiteful kick at my rear bumper and waved a fist at my departure. My hands were welded to the steering wheel to stop them shaking. Frightened though I'd been at the unexpected attempted assault, I couldn't help but grin, more to hide my relief at my escape than humour at his failure to catch me.

I drove through the midday traffic towards my office.

So, Jackie Dewar had recognised me after all, I mused.

But why did he leave his minder to have a go at me? Just what did Dewar want with me, a broken down detective from his criminal past? Revenge? For what? He'd been caught the day after I'd been shot, but I had been the only eyewitness to see him flee the scene and there was no forensic evidence to tie him into the car I'd rammed. At the trial the jury had decided that my word wasn't enough to convict him and with a Maryhill pub full of paid witnesses providing an alibi, he'd walked from the drug bust charge.

A grim faced traffic woman was hovering in Osborne Street, so there were plenty of spaces for me to get into and with a cheery can't touch me smile I abandoned the blue-badged Focus right outside the close entrance.

I swear Mister Zao must have been watching for me because there he was, just as I arrived at my office door, the perpetual smile creasing his already wrinkled face even more.

"Ah, Mister Logan sir," he began, giving me his respectful little bow, "you have news for Zao?"

There was no way that the little guy was going to allow himself to be fobbed off. That was evident because he was standing too close to permit me to turn and close the door on him.

"Come in," I invited him, which was a bit pointless because he was through the door before I'd got the key out of the Yale lock.

Zao stood patiently waiting while I shrugged out of my jacket and slid into the chair at my desk.

"Take a seat," I said, but he merely shook his head and stood watching me.

"News?" he asked again.

I hadn't written anything down, but not because of Mickey Farrell's warning. No, it was more because I really hadn't bothered and decided to wing it.

"Mister Zao, I've made inquiries like you asked and in the matter of…..."

I half coughed to hide my embarrassment. God, what was his daughters name again?

"Tei Pai?" he prompted me.

"Yes, of course, Tei Pai. I've spoken with a former colleague…."

"Policeman?"

"Eh, yes, a police officer. And I've learned that the man that Tei Pai has been seeing, this William Crawford…."

"He drug dealing shit like I tell you, that what you find out, yes?"

Jesus, there was no need for me to even fob him off with a lie. Old Zao had already made his mind up, it seemed.

"Well, what I have to tell you," I replied, trying to make it sound official, "is that Crawford is known to the police and it might be prudent for…."

His eyes narrowed. Clearly I'd confused him.

"Prudent. I should say better for your daughter, if she didn't see this guy Crawford again. You understand?"

Zao simply nodded in understanding. All I'd done was simply confirmed his suspicions, that Billy Crawford was the wrong sort of guy to be hanging about with his wee girl. But then again, he's a father. Is there such a thing as the right guy for a man's daughter?

"The police, they arrest this gweilo?"

I shook my head. "The police won't arrest a man without evidence, Mister Zao. You've been in this country long enough to know that. They won't touch him unless they catch him dealing drugs."

His eyes narrowed and an uncomfortable chill run through me as I guessed what might be going through his mind. I figured a wee warning might not be amiss at this point.

"Look," I sat forward to emphasis the point, "If the police arrest Crawford while he's going out with your daughter, that just might implicate her too and I'm sure that's the last thing you want. Better just to get her away from him and let the police deal with him in their own good time, eh? After all, once she's away from him, what happens to Crawford no longer affects you or your family, does it?"

He didn't answer, but stared directly at me. An uncomfortable stare that made me realise no amount of warnings would get through to this little man. Suddenly, Mister Zao no longer appeared to me to be a worried father, but more a loose cannon that just might interfere with Mickey Farrell's operation. And that, I dreaded the thought, would lead right back to me.

"Mister Zao? You are listening to what I'm saying, aren't you? You do realise that if you are thinking of involving yourself with this man Crawford it could do more harm than good where your daughter is concerned? Mister Zao?"

It was as if he suddenly came back from wherever his devious mind had taken him. His smile flashed on like a sixty-watt bulb and he grinned at me.

"You no worry Mister Logan sir. Zao will see to daughter's...."

He struggled for the word.

"Welfare?" I suggested.

"Ah yes. Tei Pai's welfare," he slowly agreed. But I knew in my heart of hearts the little man wasn't finished with Billy Crawford. No, my gut instinct told me the wee sod was up to something.

He turned abruptly to leave, wrinkling his nose at the overpowering smell.

"I leave bottle of strong bleach outside your door for that," he pointed to the sink. "Forget owing rent. That finished for work you do for Zao."

"And next months?" I asked, chancing my luck.

"For that, you kill Crawford," he solemnly replied, then burst into cackling laughter as he shut the door behind him.

Well, the arrangement had been two months back rent owed and next months that was due, but as the rock god Meatloaf says, two out of three ain't bad. And besides, I'd hardly done enough investigation to merit a days pay let alone two months back rent. My head ached and the pain in my leg began to assert itself once more. Only now, I had no medication to ease the discomfort.

I'd nothing pressing to attend to, unless you consider picking my washing up from Six Gun Sally, so figured another visit to Missus Kilbride might be in order.

I didn't bother phoning this time, but decided to chance my luck and call uninvited.

Maybe, I hoped, the visit will take my mind off the dull ache at the back of my head and the gnawing cramps in my stomach.

Back in my car I groaned when I saw the petrol gauge resting just at the tip of the red. I knew I'd just enough to travel to Kirkintilloch and back to my flat, but after

that it was gas fumes or the bus. The Saturday afternoon traffic thinned once I was clear of the city centre and I'd a trouble free drive to the Kilbride house. This time I decided to drive straight on up to the front door and to hell with image. The red coloured Mini was parked...sorry, did I say parked? Abandoned more like, just by the front entrance, but there was no sign of Phyllis Kilbride's silver Merc coupe. I pressed the bell and the door was opened almost immediately and made me suspect the Kilbride's daughter had been watching me arrive. With her dark hair tied back in a ponytail and dressed in a white polo shirt and short, white tennis skirt that showed off her long, tanned legs to perfection, she was stunning; there was no question of it. As lovely a young woman for her age, as was her stepmother for hers. She glanced briefly at me with what seemed like a slight sneer, and then looked beyond me to my car. Her gaze returned to me.
"Yes?"
The tone in which she used that one word summed up Sheila Kilbride. A snobby, spoiled brat, used to getting her own way and derisive of anyone who hasn't had the good fortune to experience the same affluent upbringing.
I suppose that some people might have been slightly intimated by this kind of reception, but after my long years in the CID, I'd encountered all sorts of greetings when I called. And Sheila Kilbride, when it came right down to it, was just another cheeky wee lassie.
"Miss Kilbride?" I beamed at her, "John Logan. I'm in the employ of your stepmother, Missus Kilbride. Is she at home?"
I'd already guessed the answer to that one, but I banked on the daughter's curiosity in getting me through the door.
"She's not at home. My stepmother, I mean. What do you want with her anyway? Is it about my father?"
A look of genuine concern drifted across her face.
"Has something happencd to him?"
For that brief second, and I mean a second, Sheila Kilbride's vulnerability peeked from behind her mask of scorn.
"No, nothing like that," I replied, oozing charm like I was squeezing it from a tube, "but there is some more information that I need…..to help me find him," I added.
She sighed and I saw her shoulders slump. I suppose that looking at me, she didn't see me as any physical threat and her initial reluctance to allow me into the house was swayed by the sight of me leaning heavily on my stick.
"You'd better come in," and turned away, leaving me to step up and close the door.
I wondered at the east coast twang in her voice and followed her into the front lounge. She indicated I should sit while she remained standing, her back to the large ornate fireplace and I assumed she felt by looking down at me, it gave her some sort of superiority. This time, I carefully lowered myself onto the edge of the massive settee. I couldn't see Sheila Kilbride offering me a cup of tea, let alone a high chair.

Now, let me tell you, it can be quite disconcerting being in the company of an extraordinarily good looking and shapely young woman, particularly when she's standing in front of you wearing a micro tennis skirt and tight top, her arms crossed in what I knew to be an aggressive pose that also accentuated the swell of her breasts. But that, as they say, comes with the territory. Some things I just have to suffer.

"I know that Phyllis has hired you to find my father," she carefully began, "but what I don't understand is why?"

She must've thought the question puzzled me and began to explain.

"I thought that if he has taken off for whatever reason, then surely the police would be handling this. I mean I know she contacted them and everything, but surely they can do the job, with all the resources at their disposal. Why does Phyllis need you?"

I decided that honesty might just win her over.

"I agree, the police do have the equipment, but what they don't really have is the manpower, Miss Kilbride. They can include your father's details in their computers and even, in the fullness of time, broadcast an appeal with a photograph, but what they don't have is a dedicated officer or officers to physically search for him, if you see what I mean. Mister Kilbride is one of hundreds of persons who go missing through the course of a year. Some for personal, family reasons; others because of medical conditions such as stress and even more who simply wish to disappear from a life that they can either no longer bear or believe offers them no future. And if there is no suggestion that your father has been the victim of a crime, then he will simply be treated by the police as a missing person, presumed to have taken off for his own personal reason.'

"But my father wouldn't just go off like that," she burst out, her left arm cradling the right as she gnawed at the nails on her right hand.

For the first time I saw her eyes moisten and I realised she was close to tears. Seemingly now, the hero at this point usually springs to his feet with a clean handkerchief and hands it to the good-looking woman. But not me, I'm afraid. My bum leg means I don't go springing anywhere anymore. And though I always carry a spare, clean hankie in my pocket, some inner gut feeling made me hesitate. Something about Sheila Kilbride's demeanour, her distress just didn't ring true.

So I watched as she dabbed at her eyes with the heel of her hand and slowly moved to sit on the sofa opposite me.

The short skirt rode up around her thighs and try as I might, I couldn't help but notice the strong, tanned legs, knees demurely pressed together and hands clasped upon her lap and I'm guessing I must be approaching that certain age.

"So," I began, clearing my throat and forcing myself to stare at her face, "do you have any idea as to why your father might have disappeared without giving you any notice of his intention?"

She shook her head.

"What about his business affairs? Did he have or have you any knowledge of a problem at work?"

"No, nothing like that. As far as I know, Dad is very successful at what he does. Accountancy I mean."

She glanced at me, her eyes boring through me. "But I suppose you already know that?"

Now, here I go again, about to add two and two to make five and took the shot in the dark.

"What about his business associates or his personal friends, Miss Kilbride? I mean, have you ever heard your father mention a man called Jackie Dewar?"

I watched her frown as she seemingly tried to recall the name, and then shook her head, but something about her expression puzzled me and no, I couldn't explain it.

"Dad never discusses business with me and usually not at all at home. He makes it a point that business is for the office and home time is for leisure."

"You say usually not at all at home. So he has had business dealings here, in this house I mean?"

"The odd telephone call, as far as I'm aware," she sighed, "but nothing more than that. I don't really know for certain."

Her eyebrows knitted together.

"In fact, Mister eh…?

"Logan," I smiled lamely at her, "John Logan."

"Mister Logan," she almost smiled, her face softening as she recalled her father. "Dad's work was almost totally confined to the office. Apart from bringing his briefcase home, I can't ever recall him receiving clients here… or where we used to live. Before he married Phyllis, I mean."

I desperately wanted to ask her about her relationship with her stepmother, but realised that I couldn't justify such a question, particularly if it wasn't relevant to my search for her father. But Nosey is my middle name. If I phrased it correctly…...

"So, you and your father resided elsewhere and I presume you moved here when he married his present wife?"

I couldn't fail to notice the tightening of her lips and the narrowing of her eyes.

"Phyllis decided that their….relationship," she almost spat the word out, "must begin afresh and all their past baggage left behind, hence moving from Edinburgh to this place," she cast her eyes about her.

Ah, I realised. That explained the slight east coast accent.

"And did you resent the move?"

I knew I was pushing into personal territory here, but in for a penny, in for a pound.

"Of course I resented the move," she barked at me. "I was eighteen. I left my friends, my school, everything I'd known."

I pushed the boat that little bit further.

"So you don't have a comfortable relationship with your stepmother?"

Her eyes flashed and she scowled at me, but curiosity was written all over her face.

"You don't think….I mean, why are you asking me these questions? You don't suspect…?

"No," I gushed in reply, assuming my very best 'don't be silly', yet reassuring face.

"I don't think your stepmother has anything to do with your father's disappearance. On the contrary, I believe she's truly concerned and extremely anxious to try and discover his whereabouts."

Well, convincing her though I might be, I had to admit its one line I hadn't thought of. But something else had occurred to me.

"Your father I believe is a keen sailor. Does he still sail and is the yacht," I half turned towards the photographs on the piano as I nodded toward them, "that features in the picture over there. Does he still own the Elizabeth?"

She visibly brightened at the mention of the yacht.

"Yes, daddy keeps her docked at the Inverkip Marina these days, but he doesn't sail as much. Not like when mum was alive. That's whom he named her after," her voice quietened, "my mum. Elizabeth. That was her name," she added unnecessarily.

"Phyllis doesn't like sailing and prefers cruise liners with ballrooms and the Captain's table rather than chunky sweaters and deck shoes," she replied with a definite sneer.

She sat back on the sofa and run her hands across her head, sweeping her hair back from her face and sighing loudly, the very act causing her skirt to ride further up and expose yet more of her thighs.

Now, you might at this point think I'm nothing but a dirty lecherous old bastard, or at least a nearly middle aged lecherous bastard, but I'm not stupid and realised it was an act. She was deliberately tempting me with the glimpse of flesh. Not that it wasn't a rare treat for someone whose recent sexual exploits were confined more to memory that actual experience, but curiously, and stop me if you think I'm fibbing, I'm far too long in the tooth to be seduced by a flash of leg from a barely out of her teens temptress.

"Do you know if the police have checked the Elizabeth for your father," I asked her, "or even if she's still moored at Inverkip?"

She stopped still and stared at me.

"I have no idea. Could he be there, do you think?" she burst out with an excitement in her voice. Funny, but I still believed she might be acting, don't ask me to explain it because I'm just a mere male and what man among us can really tell when a woman is acting?

"Let's not get ahead of ourselves Miss Kilbride. It's only a suggestion and your stepmother told me she has provided the police with as much information as she could and I would suggest that will likely include the possession of and location of your father's yacht. However," I struggled to my feet, "it won't do any harm to double check. I'll contact the police and see if they have called down and checked the yacht. Either way, I'll be in touch," I promised her, turning towards the door.

She scrambled to her feet, demurely pulling at the short skirt and followed me to the front door.

Look, she began, biting at her lower lip, wringing her hands as though in anguish, "I'm sorry if I was a bit off-hand with you to begin with, it's just that…."

She choked off then and the mask slipped, just for a brief instance and I saw her for what she really was, a young and vulnerable girl, constantly competing with an experienced and worldly-wise stepmother for the attention and affection of her father.

Now don't misjudge me. That didn't excuse her well-bred contempt for the common man, on this particular occasion, me. But what it did was remind me that for all her social breeding, evident wealth and obvious attractiveness, Sheila Kilbride was one unhappy young woman. The cynicism I'd adopted long ago as a copper, reinforced when I'd learned to endure the lies my ex-wife bandied about, crumpled slightly and I sought some words of comfort.

But then she straightened and, the mask now firmly in place, stared me straight in the eye and said "I'll inform my stepmother you called," before firmly shutting the door in my face.

As I slowly walked to the Focus, it occurred to me that next time I called at this house, I should use the servants entrance at the rear.

CHAPTER 4

The petrol gauge wasn't looking any healthier and I decided to coax the Focus back to my flat via the laundrette, to collect my washing.

The evening traffic had by now eased slightly and by the time I'd arrived at the north end of Maryhill Road, I was doing a comfortable thirty behind a Tesco lorry. The driver of the lorry clearly wasn't used to this part of the city, for while I concentrated on his red brake lights that flashed at every turn and bend, I failed to notice the marked police Traffic Department car that sat on my tail and only became aware of it when the driver sounded his two-tone horn and I saw him in my rear view mirror indicating for me to pull over.

Shit! I thought, but at least I'd not had a swallow since early morning and had half a pack of peppermints since then, so it was unlikely he'd smell any alcohol. Still, the peppermint smell might make him suspicious.

I remained seated and, turning the engine off, watched in the rear view and nearside door mirror as the passenger slid from the his seat and approached my door.

As subtly as I dared, I fetched the blue disabled badge from the driver's door pocket and slid it onto my dashboard. Well, it might not get me off any charges but anything is worth a try with the Beasties, I reckoned. I could see the Traffic driver was using his microphone and I guessed he was checking the registration number of the vehicle. I slid the window down as the cop approached and his shadow blanked out the sun as he leaned a grey beard in my window, or at least as far as his bulk would permit.

"Well, well, John Logan. How's it hanging you perverted wife beater?"

Now, had anyone else greeted me like that I might have been inclined to lose it a bit and drag his head through the window while I pummelled him senseless, but to my surprise, the cop turned out to be none other than PC Walter Bartholomew, known throughout Maryhill as Wally-One-Nut on account of him losing a testicle to cancer.

He'd lost weight since I last seen him and was looking pale, his eyes watery and his face drawn

"Don't be shaking hands or anything stupid, John," he hissed quietly at me. "Not while that prat of a sergeant of mine is watching us."

"Look," he quickly continued, "pretend you're checking your jacket for your licence or something while I talk, okay?"

I nodded and theatrically patted at my pockets as he instructed.

"The word has been put out on you to the beat cops and the Traffic that you've to be given a pull and turned over. Don't ask me why, though. And that idiot I'm with is dead keen to impress so…oh, oh, here he comes. Now remember, just follow my lead."

I glanced in the rear view mirror and saw the Traffic sergeant getting out of his car and swagger towards my driver's door.

"So, sir," Wally barked at me, "if you don't have your documents with you I'll need to be issuing you with a HORT1 form. You'll recall what that is of course?"

I silently nodded, remembering it as the form that obliged me to produce my driving documents at a named police station within a given time; seven days as I recalled.

I watched as Wally produced a small, buff coloured book from his belt-pouch.

"What we got here then, Constable Bartholomew?"

I glanced back over Wally's shoulder to where his sergeant stood scowling.

Almost straight off, I recognised the type. Career minded and to hell with anyone that stood in the road of his advancement.

"Just issuing the driver with an HORT1 form sergeant," replied Wally, who continued to write in his book without glancing up.

"So, where are you off to then Mister Logan?" the sergeant didn't so much ask as sneer at me.

Your first mistake pal, I inwardly smiled and knew then that if I didn't seize the initiative, this guy was about to try and make my evening very miserable.

"Is this a genuine road stop," I innocently began, "or are the police conducting a campaign of harassment against me?"

The sergeant blinked rapidly and stared at me with surprise.

Wally coughed, more to hide his amusement that anything, I guessed.

"Well, sergeant, I asked you a question?"

"I have no idea what you're talking about," he scoffed.

"Then how did you know my name unless you were ordered to stop me?"

"I….I don't know what you mean."

"Your officer here," I nodded towards Wally, "addressed me as sir. He didn't use my name. But you did and that indicates to me you've been told to stop me. Isn't that the case?"

"I got you name from our PNC check on your vehicle registration," he replied, but his reddening face told a different story.

"Strange that," I smiled at him, "seeing as how at this time I've just purchased the car and not yet forwarded the change of ownership documents to Swansea."

The sergeant's Adams apple was by now doing cartwheels in his scrawny neck and it was clear he hadn't been expecting anything other than a straight stop that would permit him yet another opportunity to intimidate a helpless driver.

Caught out in the most basic of lies, he almost barked at Wally, "Constable, finish up here. We've an urgent call to attend."

I was tempted to continue my verbal assault on the skinny bastard, but a raised eyebrow from Wally put paid to that. As the sergeant stormed back to their car, Wally handed me the tear off form and staring at me, loudly said "Make sure you read the instructions, sir."

Without a backward glance, he made his way back to the Traffic car and had hardly got his backside on the seat before it roared off past me.

I swallowed hard. Don't make the mistake of thinking that I'm a bit of a Jack the Lad or anything. That small confrontation with the law on any other day could have seen me facing a driving ban and once more, as I'd done a thousand times before, I vowed to cut down on the booze. I sat for a while, allowing my breathing to ease into a regular pattern and for the slight shaking of my hands to cease. I stared at the crumpled HORT1 form and smoothed it open. None of the boxes had been ticked, but instead saw that Wally had scrawled a mobile phone number across the page. I smiled, thanking God that the old cop was one of the few of my former colleagues who didn't believe me to be a real arse.

Taking a deep breath, I switched on the engine and slid into the traffic towards the city centre.

The scruffy old boy that had the afternoon shift in the launderette was just bringing the metal shutters out of the rear of the shop when I arrived. Wheezing heavily, he took a break as he watched me scramble from the driver's door.

"You're lucky you caught me pal," he coughed heavily and spat a globule of phlegm into the gutter, "I was just about to lock up."

His chest rattled as he led me into the shop and pointed to a black bin bag on the counter.

"Annie left that for you, ironed an all," he grinned. "I think she's got a wee fancy for you, pal. Doesn't iron the clothes just for anybody. Giving her one are you?"

He began to laugh, a cackling laugh that turned into a panting as he fought for breath, the legacy of sixty cancer sticks a day for what was probably a habit spanning fifty years.

I've been to a few post mortems in my time and let me tell you, when you've seen the pathologist removing a pair of lungs dripping with nicotine, I guarantee it will put you off the fags for life, no matter how many a day you've been on.

"How much is that then?" I asked, reaching into my pocket as though I was searching for the money. But I'd already guessed he'd have cashed up and wouldn't want to be opening the till again. Not when he'd a bus to catch.

"See Annie tomorrow about payment," he generously suggested, "unless of course you might be seeing her tonight?" he leered at me, making an obscene gesture with his right forefinger while creating a circle with his left thumb and left forefinger.

I decided it wasn't worth getting into a debate with the depraved old sod; not so much because I wanted to deny any shenanigans with Six Gun Sally but rather that I was keen to get away before the old git decided that maybe he'd better take the payment after all.

Bundling the wash into my rear passenger seat, I grinned inanely at him as he cursed and struggled to lift the steel shutters onto their brackets. With an apologetic smile, I limped to the all night grocery mart next door where I knew they sold strong Paracetamol and packets of ready cook pasta. Tempted though I was to throw down a few tablets in the shop, I decided to wait till I got home and lo and behold, discovered an empty parking space right outside my close.

See, sometimes God does smile on the unfortunate.

I took five minutes to put the washing away, boil a pan of water and check my answer machine - empty of course.

Emptying my pockets of the small change that remained and the useless bloody advice leaflet Doctor Goodman had given me, I was tempted to have a shower before I phoned the number Wally Bartholomew had given me. But first, I'd a more urgent call to make.

"Hello, Strathclyde Police, Kirkintilloch office," the female voice answered.

"Hi, my name's John Logan," I introduced myself, "can I speak with the officer who has the missing person inquiry for Martin Kilbride please?"

"Just putting you through to CID now sir," the woman replied.

CID? Bugger it! My chances of remaining with the case just evaporated, I thought. If the inquiry has been turned over to the CID, there's every likelihood they'll freeze me out.

"Hello CID, can I help you?" inquired a male voice.

"Eh, I'd like to speak with the officer who has the missing person inquiry, Martin Kilbride?"

"Who's calling please?"

It occurred to me then to give a false name, but if Phyllis Kilbride has already said I was employed to assist finding her husband, they might just be expecting a call from me anyway.

"John Logan," I said, unconsciously holding my breath.

"Hold on Mister Logan," said the anonymous voice.

The detective must've pushed a secrecy button, for the line went dead and just for a second I almost believed he'd cut me off.

"Mister Logan? DC Helen Burns, how can I help you?"

"Ah, it's about the missing person inquiry..."

"Martin Kilbride, yes, my colleague told me that. And your interest is?"

"I'm employed by Missus Kilbride to find her husband. In a private capacity," I replied.

There was a definite pause before she answered.

"You'll be John Logan, the former police officer, now working as a private investigator, is that right?"

Seemed little point in denying it.

"Does that create a problem, DC Burns?"

"Not as long as you don't interfere with my inquiry Mister Logan, so why exactly are you calling? What is it you want?"

No hanging about with this bird, I thought.

"As you'll no doubt be aware, Martin Kilbride owned a yacht, the Elizabeth, moored down at Inverkip. I was wondering if you'd searched her yet or even if you can confirm she's still at anchor there?"

"Yes," she dryly replied, "I am aware of his ownership of the yacht and no. According to the harbour master, the Elizabeth slipped her mooring on the night Kilbride disappeared. She didn't log a destination and apparently it....wait a second. Do you have something for me?"

"Eh, regretfully no," I hastily answered, "but I'm instructed by Missus Kilbride to turn over all and any relevant information to yourselves, the police I mean," I smoothly lied.

There was another pause and I figured Burns was wondering if she should go on and tell me more.

"Look," I decided to try my luck at persuasion, "I know that you'll likely be up to your neck in all sorts of Divisional work and probably this inquiry is the last thing you need. My interest is purely financial; after all, I'm getting paid for finding Kilbride. I suspect you'll have some boss breathing down your neck for updates on how you're getting on with tracing Kilbride, so how do you feel about a little cooperation; me doing the leg work and passing anything relevant to you that you can report to your boss as your effort?"

"And what exactly do I have to do in return for this legwork?" she dryly asked.

"Nothing comes to mind other than perhaps letting me know if our inquiry paths cross over. To be frank, I think that travelling to Inverkip would be fruitless if you'd already closed off that avenue of inquiry, so there's a starting point, if you like. You were about to tell me about the harbour master?"

I kind of held my breath, silently praying that she'd take the opportunity to use me while providing me with the information I'd need. It crossed my mind at this point to reveal the presence of his car, but somehow that little gem seemed worth holding onto meantime.

"Right," she finally decided, "we'll call it a mutual cooperation, particularly as you are working for Missus Kilbride. When I interviewed the harbour master," she continued, "he told me that unless the yachts that are moored at his marina intend a foreign sailing, it's unlikely they register a one or two day local trip with him. In most cases, it's a nod and a wink and a reliance on local staff with elephant memories, what boats are coming and going, I mean. Curiously, the harbour master's records indicate that the Elizabeth hadn't been taken out for several months and the only time anyone had seen Kilbride about the yacht in recent weeks was a fortnight ago, when he'd provisioned the yacht with dry stores; cans and packets of food. He'd also left instructions that the water and diesel tanks were to be filled. Naturally, the staff thought the yacht was being provisioned either for a trip by Kilbride or, as happens to many of the boats down there, hired out for a summer trip."

"If it had been provisioned for a hire," I interrupted "wouldn't Kilbride have mentioned this in case the staff got suspicious of strangers hanging about or boarding the yacht?"

"I did ask," she admitted, "but no, Kilbride didn't say why or whom the boat was being stocked for."

"And it was definitely Kilbride who stocked the boat and made the arrangements for the water and fuel?"

"Definitely," she replied. "He's well known down there and seemingly well liked. A good tipper, apparently."

"But nothing to indicate he's the person who took the Elizabeth out on Tuesday night?"

"Nothing. And, before you ask, no trace of his vehicle in the surrounding area."

Okay, okay, I admit I felt a bit guilty about that, but like I said, it might just pay off to keep the Saabs whereabouts to myself right now. But again, that begged the question, if it was Kilbride who sailed the yacht from the marina, how did he arrive in Inverkip? By bus, train or private car? And if he was simply intending escaping from whatever demons followed him, why go to the extraordinary lengths of concealing his car in the forest at Polkemmet?

Too many questions and not enough answers and to be honest, I'd been a detective too long not to realise that what seemed like a straight forward missing person inquiry now stunk worse than a sumo wrestlers three day old jock strap.

"So, apart from your faithful promise," Burns interrupted my thoughts, "do you have any information that you might wish to share?"

"Like I said DC Burns….sorry, is it Miss or Missus?"

"Like it matters?"

"No, it's just…well, if you call me John that makes it much easier, eh?"

"Yes, John, and you can call me DC Burns, okay? So, once again…..John… do you have anything for me?"

That put me firmly in my place, I reckoned.

"No, nothing for the moment," I almost whimpered in reply, "but I'll call in as soon as I have."

"I'll expect your call then," she replied, and then hung up without a cheery bye.

If nothing else, the call confirmed the CID was now treating Kilbride's disappearance with a little more suspicion.

Helen Burns. The name seemed somehow vaguely familiar. During my spell with Maryhill CID prior to being transferred to the Drug Squad, I'd met and worked with most of the divisional officers, but couldn't recall Burns as being in the CID. But time had passed and no doubt I'd be hard pressed to recognise any of the old department. I got up from my desk and more to give me a bit of exercise, thought I'd take walk down to the street and to the dairy across the road to fetch some milk.

Which reminded me of the phone call I'd to make.

Fetching the crumpled HORT1 form from my jacket pocket, I flipped open my mobile and dialled the number.

"Hello?" Wally Bartholomew answered. There were loud voices in his background.

"Wally, its John Logan. You okay to speak?"

"Hang on, love," replied Wally, "I'm in the muster room with the lads."

I could hear him making his way to a quieter area and from the echoing noise, guessed he was in a toilet room.

"I'm sorry about that wee thing today John. That prat nearly wet himself with excitement when he saw your old Focus go by. Fairly took the wee shite down a peg though, you did. Unfortunately I can't put the story out because knowing some of the loudmouths that work here now, he'd know it was me that passed it round and I'd get my one good ball in a sling with every dirty job he could lay on me."

I smiled at Wally's description. Never one to mince his words was Wally.

"I'm just pleased it was you Wally. But you didn't give me your phone number just to apologise. So, what's on your mind?"

"Thought I'd tip you the wink," his voice lowered. "You had a run in recently with that wee bugger from the CID, Eddie Coleman?"

That seemed to confirm my suspicion as to why I'd got the pull from the Traffic sergeant. But of course, I'd already half guessed. It didn't take a detective to work that one out.

"Yeah," I admitted, "met him with a policewoman yesterday in the petrol station in Maryhill Road. Exchanged a few words, but nothing friendly."

"Wee, good looking dark haired bird with a permanent scowl?"

"That description sort of fits her," I replied, though I couldn't be sure about the scowl.

"That'll be Helen Burns, his partner."

Yet another piece of the jigsaw falls into place, I realised.

"Anyway, I don't know what you said to the potted faced wee shite, but he's got it in for you big time. Passed the unofficial word round the Traffic and uniform patrol supervisors that you were a waster and your car was worth turning over. And if you don't mind me saying so, you gimpy wee bugger, you're an easy target for some of these excuses we call cops these days."

No, I didn't mind Wally saying so. Truth be told, he was right. I made myself an easy target, drinking like a fish and throwing down the prescribed medicine then driving the next day.

"So if you can take a friendly warning, John," he continued, "then watch your back, particularly when you're passing through the Maryhill division, eh?"

"Thanks Wally, I appreciate the warning."

"No thanks needed, son. I don't forget favours. No, I don't forget things like that." I heard a door opening in Wally's background, and then he said forcefully, "So I'll let you know when I'll be home for my dinner all right?" and the call terminated. I smiled quietly at Wally's pretence.

You might wonder why Wally went to such lengths to warn an alleged wife beater and all round bad guy? Well, it goes back to a time when Wally, a widower, found himself diagnosed with the big C of the testicular kind and also discovered his eighteen year old daughter Janice was into a local dealer for a few hundred quid, due to her burgeoning reliance on smack. I was still serving with the Maryhill CD back then and learned about it from one of my touts. Suffice to say I reckoned the big guy had enough problems with his health and took it upon myself to visit the dealer who, finding himself hanging from the eighth floor balcony of his high rise flat, agreed to quash the debt and refuse the lassie anymore heroin, no matter how much she pleaded. I also managed to pull in a favour from a health worker and got Wally's daughter into a rehab clinic. The last I heard, she got cleaned up and turned her life about.

But of course, that was back in the day when I was fit enough to handle things like that.

Okay, I know I'm bumming here, but I've had so few successes in my recent past that surely I've the right to boast about one now and again, eh?

Eddie Coleman. What a shit. One of many I'd encountered in the job that'd had a personality by-pass. So, you might also ask, why does Coleman hate me so?

It goes back to when we were both Detective Constables at Maryhill. He'd pulled in a suspect for a robbery; nothing major, a corner shop hold-up where the balaclava-clad culprit used a penknife to threaten the ageing female assistant and stole thirty quid from the till. Coleman decided his suspect, a known junkie, was the robber and while he was beating ten shades of shit out of the junkie up a dark close to extract a confession, I'd arrested the real offender, a spotty faced adolescent who cried from his school all the way to the police station.

Coleman never forgave me for that and blamed me for the subsequent discipline inquiry against him. It still amazes me that he got away with it and the whisper was the poor sod that Coleman beat-up had been threatened again that if he spoke up to the rubber heels mob, it would be the worse for him.

I stretched my left leg to ease the throbbing pain at the hip and tried to recall Helen Burns. Sure, I'd seen her at the Shell garage with Coleman, but that was about as far as my recollection of her went. Still, it was a valuable piece of information and I now realised that anything I told her would likely be passed to her boss, detective sergeant Eddie Coleman.

The pain in my leg was now getting beyond bearable. Easing myself to my feet, I shuffled forward and literally tore open the cheap plastic carrier bag and then wrestled with the boxed Paracetamol packaging. Such was my haste I dropped the box and scrambled down onto the floor to retrieve it, ripping the foil apart and cramming four tablets into my dry mouth.

I had to get something to swallow them down. Whisky would have been nice, but I'd learned early on in my addiction…. whoa, did I use the word addiction? Jesus, I must really have listened to Julia Goodman after all.

I limped over to the sink and poured myself a large glass of water in a dirty mug and swallowed the lot, gasping as the cold water hit my empty stomach.

With the tablets washed down, I knew it would only be a matter of ten or fifteen minutes before they kicked in; not as good as the prescribed medicine, but hey, beggars can't be choosers.

Standing there, I began to chuckle, then laughed out loud.

Slowly, I shook my head. I'd become the very antithesis of everything I'd worked against as a cop.

Reading cheap American detective stories during lengthy surveillance operations, I remembered the heroes had been either high flying Los Angeles gumshoes or down at heel New York private dicks. Me? I was just a down at heel dick, slowly sinking in a pit of whisky and prescribed tablets. How far, I wondered, was I from the very bottom'?

The phone chirruped behind me.

"Yes?"

"Mister Logan, its Phyllis Kilbride. I understand from my stepdaughter that you called by the house this afternoon. Do you have something to report?"

I wasn't certain, but felt there was a slight hesitation in her voice. Was she, I wondered, expecting bad news?

"Regretfully no, Missus Kilbride, I simply wanted to update you that I've been in contact with the local police and to inform you that the CID, a detective officer has been assigned to the inquiry."

I almost slipped up and said the case rather than the inquiry, but that might have had her thinking that her husband's disappearance was now criminal rather than simply a missing person. Nor did I mention that I'd spoken with Burns after I'd called at her house. As far as I was concerned, it was academic and besides, what she didn't know wouldn't hurt her.

"What did this detective Burns tell you?" she asked.

"I discussed your husband's yacht, the Elizabeth and learned the police have discovered the yacht sailed from Inverkip the night your husband went missing. Do you have any knowledge as to were the yacht is now? I mean, did you know your husband had provisioned the yacht for a trip?"

"No… no," she stuttered, sounding bemused. "I didn't now that Martin had even been in Inverkip recently. Was it Martin that took the yacht out?"

"I'm not sure," I replied, "the harbour master has no record of the yacht departing and Tuesday night was established from memory by the marina's staff of last seeing the Elizabeth moored. But then again it isn't apparently unusual for boats that simply take off for a few days local sailing. It seems that the records are more geared towards foreign or lengthy sailings."

Now, I know it was a cheap shot, inferring that Burns locally made inquiry was my own, but hell, I had to show something for my pay. Which reminded me.

'"I hate to sound mercenary, Missus Kilbride," I grovelled, "but in regard the matter of my fee...."

"Yes, yes, of course," she answered, if a little absentmindedly. "I'll forward a cheque to your office. The address as on your business card I presume?"

"That'll be fine," I replied," and if you could cross it made out for cash, that'll save me the hassle of getting to the bank. I'm so useless at my own accounts," I cheerfully lied, rather than admit the bank would likely seize any cash paid in and set it against my extensive overdraft.

Fortunately, she didn't question this arrangement and said "You'll keep me informed of anything that detective Burns tells you, anything that she turns up?"

"You'll be the first to know," I assured her, before she hung up.

It was a little later, as I idly stirred the pot containing my pasta meal, that I realised I hadn't mentioned to the lovely Missus Kilbride that DC Burns had been assigned the inquiry and that Burns was a woman.

Later still, fed and lounging on the couch, my gammy leg propped up on a low padded stool and the television volume turned low on the Channel Four news programme; I idly glanced at the leaflet Doc Goodman had given me. I realised that unless I made some kind of effort and convince Goodman that I was trying to get off the medication, I might lose her support and then, God forbid, where would I be?

The four-page leaflet advertised the South Side Voluntary Help Group and offered a range of support that included counselling in drugs, sexual abuse, financial problems and all sorts of other issues. A contact phone line was apparently manned from early morning to late evening and all calls, the leaflet assured, would be treated in the strictest confidence.

I took a deep breath and reached for my mobile.

"How can I help you?" the male voice answered.

Shit, I hadn't even considered how I was going to approach this and stammered that I'd been given a leaflet by Dr Goodman, that the doctor had figured I might be able to speak with someone regarding my reliance on prescribed medication....

"Look," the guy interrupted, "rather than discuss your condition...."

Condition, I thought? What condition? I didn't say I'd a condition.

"...on the phone," the guy continued, "If you're happy to come in and speak with someone, we've a resident counsellor with whom I can make an appointment for you."

I heard the guy rustling what sounded like paper then he asked, "Would 5pm tomorrow evening be suitable?"

I didn't have time to think and mumbled that "Yeah, that would be fine."
"Okay then, the address is on the leaflet. Just tell the desk you'll be here for the 5pm appointment."
It was only after I'd hung up I realised the guy hadn't asked my name.

CHAPTER 5

The sun streamed through the cheap nylon curtains and awoke me just after seven the next morning. Unusually, I had no hangover and though my leg was cramped from sleeping in the same position through half the night, I'd no ill feeling other than the usual aches and pains.
I took my time shaving then the hot shower beat me into full consciousness and I rubbed myself vigorously dry, curiously eager to eat and get out into the bright sunshine. In the bedroom I smiled at the pile of newly ironed clothes and promised myself I'd buy Six Gun Sally a small bunch of flowers in appreciation. I hadn't felt this invigorated for some time and while I munched through the remains of last nights rubbery pasta and a fried egg....I know, don't ask....I dressed in a newly ironed light blue shirt, navy tie and clean if slightly worn chino's and corduroy jacket and thought about my conversation with Phyllis Kilbride.
It seemed obvious that she knew Helen Burns had been assigned the case, prior to calling me. The logical answer was, of course, that Burns herself had called upon Missus Kilbride and declared herself as the officer in the case. But why then would Kilbride not mention this to me? Why would she refrain from stopping me and informing me that she already knew of Burns inquiry about the Elizabeth? Unless she had learned from someone else that Burns was on the case, but had not herself spoken with Burns.
And if the CID is now on the case, why am I still working it?
I fetched a small used notebook from the kitchen drawer and fumbled about till I found a biro that worked and stowed them both in my inside jacket pocket. One thing I'd learned while serving in the CID was note taking and I figured it was about time I got back into the habit. Besides, producing a notebook in front of a client always looks so much more professional.

The traffic was light and with one wary eye on the fuel gauge, I made it safely to my office. Yes, God is kind even to non-believers and once more I found a parking space right outside the close. Jacket casually slung over my right shoulder, I gingerly made my way up the darkened stairs, grateful for the coolness of the tenement close after the blinding sunlight.
"How you this morning, Mister Logan," said the quiet voice behind me.
"Jesus, Mister Zao, can't you shuffle a little more loudly? You almost gave me a

heart attack," I whined.

The old guy chuckled at my discomfort and followed me into my office.

With more aplomb than I felt, I settled myself into my chair at my desk and asked him what I could do for him.

To my surprise, old Zao dragged the wooden chair out from opposite my desk and sat himself down, a first that I could recall.

He licked his old cracked lips and audibly took a deep breath.

"My daughter Tei Pai," he began slowly, "she a good girl, always study, get good grades. Want to be doctor. Like her uncle back in HK."

He saw my curious glance.

"Hong Kong," he explained. "My brother is doctor. He family eldest and so is," he struggled for the word, "is educated by family, you understand?"

I nodded, not certain where this was going but hey, this is my landlord so the last thing I'm going to do is piss him off.

"I not so fortunate. I second son. No more money for school and I get in with wrong crowd," he half smiled as though disclosing a family secret, "and end up here."

By here I took it he meant Glasgow and I knew he owned half the tenement buildings in Osborne Street and with the average rent for a city centre property being bloody high, I suspected the old bugger wasn't doing too badly.

We sat in silence for a few minutes and I patiently waited. It was easy to see that he was struggling with something, something that he wanted to say or to ask. English not being his first language, he either didn't know how to tell me or more likely was uncertain whether he could trust me.

"You have children?"

Now that took me unaware, his change of subject throwing me for a second.

"Eh, yes. Paul. A son," I explained, "he's eight years old. Lives with his mother. I don't see him very often, well, not as often as I'd like. Because of his mother," I added lamely, though I didn't add she was an unfaithful, torn faced bitch.

"Then you know what children mean? They are your life, your future. They are the currency of your being."

Nine in the morning, I wryly thought, and I'm sitting with Confucius talking philosophy or whatever the hell it's called.

I decide to take the initiative.

I leaned forward and with my elbows on the desk and my fingers joined to make a pyramid, asked him outright.

"What is it that you want me to do for you Mister Zao?"

He sighed heavily, as though about to discharge a great weight, looked briefly down to his feet then said, "I want you to kidnap my daughter."

Well, work me over with a leather cudgel and stomp me to the ground. I couldn't have been more taken aback than if he'd sexually propositioned me.

"What?" I almost got to my feet, but there's my gammy leg again, reminding me not to make any sudden movements.

"Kidnap your daughter?" I hissed at him, suddenly conscious that I was lowering my voice as though I was already complicit in a crime.

He stared at me with sad eyes and I saw what he had become. A father who doted on his child, who worried himself sick about her, but who no longer had any influence over her.

I kind of recognised and sympathised with his position, if you follow me.

"I want her home," he almost whispered, the defeat evident in his eyes, "away from that man Crawford and his evil ways."

I took a deep breath, my mind racing as I tried to find a way to explain that this was Scotland, that abduction meant jail. And I meant jail. Solid time. Years watching your back in some of the worst prisons in the UK. And for a former cop, that was tantamount to exposing yourself to murder or worse. Yes, I mean worse. Some of these head cases in Barlinnie or Peterhead have been locked away without the charms of women for a long time and have developed what I can only imagine are some strange and weird sexual habits. I involuntarily shuddered at the thought and knew that if I ever found myself in one of those places, with my bad leg, I'd be fair game for any nutter that took a fancy to me and believe me, I'm no spring chicken either.

"Look, Mister Zao," I began to reason with him, "even if you did abduct, I mean, kidnap Tei Pai, there's no guarantee that she'd stay with you. And if the police became involved…."

"They already involved," he curtly told me, his eyes flashing with sudden anger, "and they do nothing. Nothing."

I sat back, my mind working overtime.

"What do you mean?"

He shifted uneasily in his seat, almost squirming.

"Come on Mister Zao," I cajoled him, "if you're to trust me and if I'm to help you?"

I left the rest unsaid, conscious that his mind was working overtime.

I knew from experience when I was with the drug squad working on some of the Triad inquiries, when they tried to infiltrate the Scottish drug scene from their base in Manchester, that the Chinese believe the police to be socially inferior, as well as corruptible and that any interviews I participated in with Chinese suspects invariably met with little or no response to questioning.

But this, this was different. I stared hard at Zao. This little man I knew, who to the ordinary punter looks shabbily dressed and apparently insignificant, has a razor sharp mind and doesn't miss a trick. But the same man was in a situation he hadn't before encountered and he was at real low ebb. Well, he must have been to consult last chance Logan.

I sat still and figured that all I had to do was sit and wait; sit and listen.

Three, maybe four long minutes passed and I said nothing, just stared at him. Passing traffic noise and the sun both beat through the unwashed window and dust mites danced in the air. Finally, as though coming to a decision, he raised his head and looked me in the eye.

"The police drugs people. They sit and watch Crawford," he hawked a goblet of spit with vehemence onto the floor. Great, I thought, I'd better mind that I don't slip on that one.

"I have man who tells me things. Man who owe Zao money, great deal of money, you understand now?" He licked his lips and stared at me, uncertain if he should tell me more, but continue he did. "But this gweilo Crawford, he not the one who is top of tree."

My ears pricked up at that. Just how much did Zao know and more importantly, from whom did he get his information? A cop? I knew that if I pressed him, he'd close up and that would be it.

He shook his head, almost in sadness. "My Tei Pai get caught up in this. She go to jail. Worse," his thin frame shuddered, "she get hurt."

He stared me in the eye.

"That happen, I kill Crawford. That why you must help me get Tei Pai out of his hands before I get to kill him."

Now, I'd seen the photograph of Crawford and there was no doubt in my mind the guys a bruiser and looks like he can handle himself in any kind of ruckus. You'll know the type. A poster model for men's underwear; tall, muscled and with a full head of blonde hair, he looked to some women every inch the ideal man. But looking at the little Mister Zao in front of me, just at the moment, just then, I knew that if Zao went after Crawford, then Crawford was a dead man.

My mind raced. Maybe after all I hadn't quite stopped being a drug detective.

I leaned forward, eager to placate this little man and, yes I admit it, maybe somewhere along the way help him out, though please don't tar me with any white knight brush.

I asked him how he knew the police were watching Crawford?

An almost sly expression began on his face then changed, as if with resignation, he knew he'd already started and might as well finish.

"I have," he hesitated, as though searching for the right word, "friend who know Crawford and his boss."

"This friend," I pressed him, "can't they help you with getting Tei Pai out of Crawford's clutches? His hands, I mean?" seeing the confusion in his face.

He seemed to deliberate in this question and slowly shook his head.

"I already owe my friend a debt that I repay. Every month," he sighed. "I cannot ask for more."

I absently nodded my head, as though in understanding.

"Look, I began, thinking that I'd better say this in simple English, "I can understand what kind of pressure you must feel that you are under, but abduct......kidnapping Lei Pai is not the answer. Trust me. You don't wish to hurt your daughter. I know that. What if she resisted? What if she screamed? You can't tie her down, keep her imprisoned in your home. Not forever."

I was thinking on my feet here, if you'll excuse the colloquialism.

I had already realised, much to my honest to goodness surprise, that old Zao actually *liked* me. What a scunner, I thought, particularly as I was about to use the sad old bugger to further my own end.

"It seems to me," I wasn't so much thinking as now dancing on my feet, "that one option to save your Tei Pai would be to get Crawford out of her life. What if he was arrested?"

He glanced sharply at me.

"I mean, I still have some contacts in the drug squad. What if I was able to tell them about Crawford and his boss? Give them something that might provide them with enough evidence to arrest Crawford, get him out of Tei Pai's life for a few years. That way, it'll give you time to maybe talk some sense into her. What about that idea?"

His brow furrowed as he considered my suggestion.

"I would need to give you details, yes?"

"Yes, Mister Zao. Enough to interest the police to take some sort of action against Crawford and maybe his boss," I replied, my mouth suddenly dry with the realisation that there was a lot more to Zao than I'd ever guessed.

Slowly, he nodded his head.

"Crawford, he middle man for very bad man. Scotch man who live here in city. I only know of him by..." he seemed to be confused "by name you know…"

"Reputation?" I suggested.

He nodded his head again.

"Reputation," he repeated. "His name is something like Dewa," he said, pronouncing the name as though gasping like a floundered fish.

I must have visibly startled, because Zao asked if I wanted water.

Jackie Dewar. The lowlife bastard. It had to be him.

"But I cannot tell you all," he continued. "There is a police…."

He stopped dead at that, knew he'd said too much.

I stared at him again.

"What you trying to tell me, Mister Zao?"

Then it hit me what he'd already told me, that the police are already involved and his inference that he has a friend who knows Crawford and Crawford's boss. A shiver run up the back of my spine.

"It's a police officer, isn't it? Your friend is a cop."

He didn't answer, just stared hard at me, his lined, pale face growing even paler as I watched.

Abruptly, he pushed back the wooden chair, the legs squealing on the cheap linoleum floor.

"I say too much already. You tell your police friends that they better arrest Crawford before something happen to him. Something really bad," then turned and without another word, left the office.

I sat staring after him and again, a cold shiver run through me.

Whoever Zao's friend was, there seemed little doubt he was either a cop or worked for the police and knew enough to tell Zao that Crawford was under surveillance by the drug squad, as well as knowing that Jackie Dewar was Crawford's boss.

I dug out my A4 pad and resorted to my old habit of putting pen to paper, listing the questions that were going through my mind.

Why were Dewar visiting Boyle and Spencer's offices and presumably, what was Dewar's connection to Martin Kilbride.

What was the real reason for Kilbride's disappearance and where the hell was the yacht Elizabeth?

Who's the cop feeding Zao his information and what's the debt old Zao owes the cop?

But more importantly, how could I use this information and who would I tell?

I was mulling over my conversation with Zao when the phone rang and made me jump.

"Hello, Logan Investigations" I answered, "John Logan speaking. How may I help you?"

"DC Burns. You said you'd get back to me with anything you found about the MP, Martin Kilbride," the voice said, almost like an accusation.

I took a deep breath.

"Mister Kilbride is one of several inquires I have ongoing at the minute, DC Burns and I'm kind of tied up with a client. Can I call you back?"

The office door opened and there she stood, mobile in one hand pressed against her right ear and a brown paper bag in the other hand.

"Is it the invisible man you're tied up with then," she asked, still talking into her mobile.

Caught red handed as it were, I could only look sheepish and returned the phone to the cradle.

"Come in, take a seat," I invited, because really, what else could I say?

Burns glanced round the room, her eyes taking in everything.

"This place have a kettle?"

"I can offer you coffee, but only if you take it with powdered milk and no sugar."

"That'll do then," she replied and placed the brown bag on the desk.

I limped over to the table and switched on the kettle at the wall, knowing it was already half full. An old habit of mine, refilling it after I use it.

"What's that bloody smell?" she asked, wrinkling her nose.

"Drain problem, but the landlord's fixing it," I lied with ease.

She sat down on the chair recently vacated by Zao and opened the paper bag, offering me a sugary doughnut while helping herself to one.

"So, what you got to tell me, detective sergeant Logan?"

I spooned some milk into two mugs, smiled and hobbled back to the desk, placing her coffee in front of her and taking the offered doughnut.

"Long time since anyone's called me by that rank," I replied, settling myself back into my chair.

She half smiled.

A pretty young woman, late twenties I guessed. Her coal black hair was tied back in a ponytail that reached just beneath her jacket collar, clasped with a broad, grey coloured hairclip. Not a bad figure beneath the charcoal grey skirted business suit either and no ring on the fingers of her left hand. In fact, none on her right hand fingers either. A bulky dark grey shoulder bag hung to her slim waist from her left shoulder and I guessed contained her notebook and probably handcuffs, as well as other female odds and sods that most women can't be without.

"Well, I've nothing that you likely don't already know. You've met with Kilbride's wife?"

"No, not yet," she shook her head, "but according to the uniforms that attended the initial and follow up calls, she's a bit of a looker. I've arranged to call upon her at her house at 3pm this afternoon."

"She's a looker all right," I agreed. "In fact, from my perspective, if she was my Missus, I'd be reluctant to go chasing another bit of skirt with her waiting at home for me."

Burns smiled at that.

"Ladies man are you? I heard you were more into a bit of battering, rather than loving."

I smiled back, a tight smile. She was, after all, Eddie Coleman's partner.

"That's an old story now and like a fine wine, it gets better as time passes. Course, it depends on who's telling the story, doesn't it? And if it's Eddie Coleman, then I'm already tried and convicted, aren't I?"

She looked down at the desk and sharply back at me.

"Coleman's an arse and don't dare to presume to judge me because I work with him. That's a resource issue, not by choice."

I smiled at that. Resource issue. Time was that you would work with your partner of choice, or neighbour in police parlance, because you made the best team. Nowadays it seems the diversity brigade have even determined what makes a good working relationship. Better to be seen to be politically correct, regardless of results achieved. Anyway, I inwardly shrugged; it had nothing to do with me anymore.

"So," she pressed, "have you got anything new on Kilbride's disappearance?"

I placed my hand on top of the A4 pad that lay in front of me, conscious that the names I'd written might attract her attention.

"Coleman investigating this with you?" I asked, hoping to gauge how she really felt about him.

"No," she shook her head. "Obviously, he's my supervising officer, but there's nothing in this inquiry that will get him ahead," she almost spat out "so he's got no interest in the case. You'll know Wally Bartholomew then?"

Now that took me by surprise.

"I know Wally," I cautiously replied.

"Wally was my tutor cop when I started. Keeps me updated, what's happening in the uniform side and the likes. He says you're a good man. Not to believe all the shite that Coleman tells me about you."

I tried to avoid swallowing, the comment of unexpected support again taking me by surprise.

"That's nice of him. Now, in answer to your question, DC Burns...."

"Helen. My name's Helen."

"Well Helen, in answer to your question, no, I haven't got anything new re Kilbride's disappearance."

Now, don't ask me why, but sometimes I do the most brainless things and curse myself stupid after I've done it. Sometimes, to be brutally honest, I can be a right plonker and let my mouth run away with me. Maybe it was the comment about Coleman, or maybe it was the inferred compliment from Wally. Maybe I just wanted to show off to this pretty young woman, that even though I was a crippled former detective sergeant, I still had it. Maybe even that I'd just sold my soul for a doughnut. Whatever it was, I went ahead and asked her, fully aware of what I was about to tell her.

"Have you visited Kilbride's offices, Boyle and Spencer, in Waterloo Street?"

"No, not yet," she shook her head, the questioning look in her eyes betraying her interest. "Is there something there I should know about?"

"I was there yesterday. Spoke to the office manager, an Alison Carlisle. Definitely knows a wee bit more than she was prepared to tell me. But the curious thing is that when I was going up the stairs," I almost gave an involuntary shudder when I recalled the pain, "I bumped into an old acquaintance. Jackie Dewar, Do you recognise the name?"

"Jackie Dewar," she slowly repeated. I could almost hear her brain ticking over. "Is he not the guy that shot you?"

"No, that was his sidekick, his minder. But he was there at the time and charged with possession all the same, but got away on a Not Proven. Seems to have got himself a new minder these days, a big guy, face like a well skelped arse. Looks like an ex-boxer. Maybe an inch or two taller than me, might have been well built at one time, but running to fat these days, I'd say."

She nodded her head in recognition. "That'll be Scorcher Lamond. Alex Lamond. And you're right. He is a former boxer. Does his heavy for Dewar, twisting arms and belting faces. Real hard man with the junkies and the ladies, I hear."

The scorn in her voice made me think that Burns was aching for an opportunity to get to grips with Lamond, but she didn't explain and I didn't ask. Seemed there might be more to Burns than I first thought.

"So," she asked, her pretty brown eyes narrowing, "what's your take on why Dewar and Lamond were visiting this firm then?"

Did I say pretty eyes? I know, I know. I'm just a sucker for good-looking women. "Well," I'd already made my decision, so I decided to go with my gut, "I figure that it's too coincidental that Kilbride is missing and Dewar, one of the top targets for the drug squad should happen to be visiting Kilbride's firm and my source tell me that it's not the first visit Dewar has made to Boyle and Spencer's offices. I didn't think it necessary to explain my source was the young blonde receptionist and it didn't take a genius to work out that Jackie Dewar must be an ongoing target for the squad. Better to let Burns think I was still in the game, as it were.

"One other thing that puzzles me I said," on a roll now. "When I spoke with

Missus Kilbride, she seemed to be aware that you had been given the inquiry to find her husband. I know that she told me just as the uniform handed the inquiry over to CID and it was before you made the appointment to meet her, so how could she know that you'd landed the inquiry?"

Burns shook her head. "No idea, unless the uniform told her."

"No, that can't be right, unless procedure has changed. They'd simply pass it to the CID and it would be allocated either by the detective inspector or whoever is in charge. Somebody told her your name, but I can't imagine why. Do you intend asking her?"

Burns seemed to give it some thought.

"No, that's something I'll keep for the minute. Kilbride's disappearance is still a missing person inquiry, but if his body turns up, it might be a relative question. What do you think?"

"I agree," I told her and smiled. "You're thinking ahead and that can't be bad, keeping your options open."

She stood up and brushed some crumbs from her skirt.

"Keep the rest of the doughnuts and remember Logan, anything at all, you've got my number, okay?"

Now, not many women these days are happy to give me their phone number, but this one came with a veiled warning that I didn't ignore.

"What about Dewar?" I reminded her.

She stopped at the doorway, one hand on the handle and pursed her lips.

"I've a pal in the Fraud Squad. I'll give her a phone and ask her if she knows where Dewar's laundering his ill-gotten gains or if there is anything suspect about Kilbride or his firm. Maybe try to connect the dots. Either way, I'll give you a call but," and she poked her finger at me "don't forget you and me, it's a two way street. Okay?"

I raised my hands in surrender and grinned, but thought if she finds out that I've knowledge of where Kilbride's burnt out car is, my balls will be well and truly kicked.

I gave her a dog-eared calling card that bore my name and both the office and scribbled my mobile number on the back.

She took it and stuffed it into her police notebook cover.

"Happy to help, detective," I called out to her back as she closed the door behind her.

With a sigh of relief, I settled back into my chair and thought, what the hell, another doughnut won't kill me.

I killed the rest of the afternoon resting my leg and practising long forgotten breathing exercises to try and dull the ache.

I kept going over it in my head, trying to connect Dewar to Kilbride's disappearance.

If Kilbride is dirty I thought, conscious that I was using present tense in the belief he yet might still be alive, maybe he's ripped off Dewar and sailed into the sunshine. The only connection I could guess at was Kilbride being an accountant was ideally suited to hide Dewar's dirty money in investments. Clean it through legitimate business deals. Jesus, I thought, my brain ticking over like a rusty old Lada, and with some knowledge of Dewar's past successes in drug dealing, Kilbride might have been laundering six figure sums, maybe even seven figures. Reason enough for him to disappear if he believed that Dewar had discovered Kilbride was ripping him off, good-looking wife or not. And if what my old mate Mickey Farrell has told me is correct, Dewar might not have been unduly suspicious till this new deal arrived last week via Billy Crawford and told Kilbride to start getting his assets into cash.

I sat bolt upright, or as near damn as my leg would allow.

The snatch of conversation I'd heard on the stairs, Dewar telling Lamond to find him. It must have been Kilbride they were discussing.

The time was about right. Kilbride was now missing six days, as of this morning. That just fits in perfect. I leaned back in my chair, my hands clasped behind my head and smiled to myself.

CHAPTER 6

I didn't realise until I startled awake, that I'd dozed in the chair. Rubbing my neck, I hobbled over to the mirror above the washbasin and splashed some cold water on my face, rubbing it dry with the dirty towel that daily I forgot to take home and have washed.

Crap. I'd forgotten the appointment with the counsellor at five.

Shaking the sleep from my eyes, I closed and locked the office door and made my way to the Focus.

Stupid making an appointment at that time, I realised, for the traffic out of the city across the Albert Bridge and through the south side of the city was nose to tail. By the time I turned into Coplaw Street, it had turned ten past five. Fortunately I found a parking space near to the old, Victorian mid terraced house at number 155 and once again, the trusty old blue badge came into play. Stick in hand I limped up the stairs and pressed the buzzer next to the unpolished brass plate that said South Side Voluntary Help Group. The old wooden door sported a broken panel at the bottom, with fading boot prints on it where it seemed an irate visitor had decided to vent some frustration.

A smiling, middle-aged man opened the door. Lanky and balding, wearing thick lensed, John Lennon type specs, a bright green shirt and yellow tank top and flared trousers, I couldn't help but notice he wore Scooby-Doo slippers on his feet. God, I thought, please tell me this isn't who I'm here to meet.

"Hello," I slowly began, preparing myself to turn and get the hell out of Dodge, "I'm here for a 5pm appointment, but got a bit stuck in the traffic. Sorry."

The guy smiled and beckoned me in.

"I'm Jimmy. Yeah, I checked the log," he replied, "you've a meeting with Alex."

I inwardly sighed with relief and from his voice, recognised him as the guy I'd spoke with on the phone to make the appointment.

"Please, follow me," he said and turned to lead me along a hallway to a door that led into what I guessed must have once been a reception room, when the house was in its full glory. He pushed open the door and led me inside.

The room's decor obviously hadn't changed much since it had been a family home. Pastel green wallpaper on all four walls with a variety of cheap prints, mostly of farming scenes and probably bought as a job lot. A fluorescent light hung from the ornate ceiling rose. A faded green leather Chesterfield couch sat to one side while angled in the far corner stood an old and scarred oak desk, behind which sat a wooden swivel chair of the type more commonly seen in Western movies. A grey coloured, office type plastic chair, much favoured by doctor's waiting rooms, was at the other side of the desk. On the floor behind the door sat a grey metal filing cabinet with a variety of files stacked neatly on the shelves. Next to the cabinet was a four-drawer box shaped filing cabinet of the type that locked. All the drawers were closed. No carpet, but floorboards that were varnished and shining bright.

The large, panoramic window was closed with dark, heavy brown curtains pulled back and tied with thick, brown cord. Through the window, clean I noticed, I could see through the fading light the rear of tenement buildings across the back courtyard.

"Alex won't be long, if you'd care to take a seat," he pointed to the couch and quietly pulled the door shut behind him as he left.

I stiffly made my way to the plastic chair.

Curiously he still hadn't asked my name and I guessed that was the policy here. I hadn't realised there was an old-fashioned wall clock on the opposite wall, not till the silence of the room echoed its loud ticking.

I shifted nervously on the unforgiving chair. Bloody thing certainly wasn't designed for comfort, I thought, shifting my weight to ease the ache in my leg.

Yes, I'll admit it. I was nervous. I didn't relish the thought of admitting to some guy, some stranger, that I was reliant on prescribed medicine.

Addicted. No other word for it.

I sighed and the noise sounded unduly loud in the room. According to the wall clock, four minutes passed and I was getting a bit pissed off waiting, then the door opened to admit a woman.

Age, and I have to say here that even though I'm former CID, I'm crap at telling women's ages, probably late thirties to forty, maybe five four in her stocking feet and, I couldn't help but notice, a shapely figure. Her face bore no make-up and was framed by dark hair curling to her collar. She wore a white blouse open at the neck with a string of small pearls at her throat, trim waist with a plain black pencil skirt to her knees and black high-heeled shoes.

I watched as she closed the door behind her and smiling at me, walked to the seat behind the desk.

I saw she carried a cardboard file and a notepad under her left arm and a biro pen in her hand, all that she placed on the desk in front of her as she sat down.

"Sorry," I began, slightly confused "I think I've an appointment with Alex?"

She smiled again, revealing a set of perfect white, even teeth.

"Yes, that's right. I'm Alex, or more correctly," she bobbed her head slightly and made a slight almost comical grimace, "Alexandria. Alexandria Haldane."

She rose from her seat to reach across the desk to shake my hand.

Awkwardly, I pushed up from the plastic chair and took her hand, a firm grip with nails neatly trimmed short, but without polish. On her wrist she wore what looked like a man's watch, stressed brown leather strap and white face and though I'm no expert, it looked to me to be expensive. It seemed at odds with the neatly attired, feminine Ms Haldane.

She saw me looking at the watch and explained, "It was my fathers watch. My mother gave it to me when he died, nearly three years ago now. I'd always admired it."

I kind of shrugged as though in understanding and didn't really know how to respond to that.

"Now then," she turned and glanced down at the file that lay before her, running her tongue over her upper lip. That's when I realised it was just an empty cardboard file and she probably expected that today's session would likely be the first entry.

"I know we haven't been introduced and if you'd rather remain anonymous, I'm happy to respect that. However, it would probably be a lot easier if I had a forename so that at least we can begin to find out why you're here and how I can help you?"

At that she sat back and I took it that was my cue to speak.

"John. My name's John Logan. My doctor referred me to your group. Doctor Julia Goodman. Her practise is down at..."

I saw her nodding.

"Ah yes. I know Doctor Goodman," she interrupted. "She did say you might call by. She expressed some concern for you, but didn't tell me the full story. Said I'd be better hearing it direct from you."

"You were that sure I'd attend here then?" I replied, trying not to sound cool and yet cynical, but failing miserably.

She folded her hands in front of her on the desk.

"No, not certain, but Doctor Goodman did hint that if you were hoping to continue visiting her at her practise as her patient, she didn't leave you much choice."

Inwardly I cursed the old bugger. My anger must have showed in my face.

"I've known Julia Goodman for a long time," she quietly continued "and while over the last few years she has previously referred some of her patients to the group, for various reasons, she seems to have a particular interest in you, Mister Logan. Julia isn't the sort of doctor that simply patches and prescribes; I can tell you that my experience of her is that she takes a real interest in her patients, the ones worth saving I mean," she almost sighed.

An awkward silence again fell between us.

"Look," she sat back in her chair, unclasping her hands and laying them flat on the desk "why don't we treat this as an introductory session. I can sense you're not overly comfortable being here. Or perhaps it's the fact I'm a woman? Would you prefer to speak with a male counsellor?"

"It's nothing to do with your….gender," I paused, searching for the right words, conscious my leg ached and of the tightness in my chest.

"I've just not had the will to speak about what happened to me. I went through a lot at the time. I was injured when I was working as a police officer and pensioned off. I went through a messy divorce that left me bereft of friends and I've no family to speak of. My name and reputation was tarnished, my ex-wife is trying to deny me visitation rights with my son and to top it all, I'm struggling with pain on a daily basis and doctor fucking Goodman won't give me the fucking pills I need till I come here and spill my fucking guts to you!"

Her eyes were wide opened and it was then I realised I was shouting.

The door behind me opened and the lanky Jimmy came spilling into the room.

"Everything all right Alex?" he asked nervously, one hand holding the door as if ready to bolt and slam it shut in my face if I went for him.

She had both hands held up, as if placating both Jimmy and I together.

"Fine, Jimmy, fine," she said in a calm and unflustered voice and then turned towards me. "We are fine, aren't we Mister Logan?"

I could feel the fine beads of sweat on my forehead and my hands were shaking. God, how I needed a handful of painkillers washed down with a neat glass of golden liquid.

But I nodded my head anyway.

"Yes, sorry," I lamely replied. It was an indication of how uptight I was. I seldom if ever raise my voice, but that's just me. I didn't turn, but heard Jimmy shut the door behind me.

"I can't imagine what kind of physical pain you must be experiencing and I won't make light of your personal situation. I'm here to listen, talk with you if you wish and if I can, help you resolve your reliance on prescribed medication. I don't expect this will happen overnight, but I'm willing to work with you and to try and find a solution to your problem."

So it was a problem now, I noted, not an addiction.

"Can you get me some painkillers?" I asked. "I mean, right here, right now? Can you sort this gammy leg for me? Can you get me access to my son?"'

I pushed up from the desk to my feet.

"I'm sorry Ms Haldane, I think I'm wasting your time," and turned to leave.

And it was then, right as I was reaching for the door handle, that she stonewalled me.

"I was, am," she corrected herself, "an addict."

That stopped me dead. I turned towards her.

She stared at me, through me almost as she spoke in that same, calm voice.
"My addiction was drink," she continued, now that she had my attention.
"Alcohol. Vodka, whisky, lager, wine. You name it. If it was alcohol I swallowed
it. Daily. Hourly. Every chance that I got to drink, I took it. I didn't care how I got
it or what I was doing. I was your typical, happy drunk. I was always the life and
soul of all the parties, the good time girl. Oh yes, that was me. One for the road
and to hell with convention."
She didn't raise her voice, didn't stand, just continued sitting at her desk, hands
clasped in front of her, staring at me with those lovely, dark, solemn eyes.
"Then I killed my daughter."
I stood motionless, almost scared to breath. I could not believe what she was
telling me, but somehow, I also knew it to be the truth.
I wasn't conscious of groping my way back to the plastic chair, of sitting down.
Her eyes continued to bore into mine.
"Hayley had just turned nine. My husband and I, he was an IT consultant and ran
his own business. We had it all. The nice house in Newton Means. The top of the
range cars and the annual holiday to Florida. I worked part time as a nurse in the
Victoria Infirmary. Did compressed hours and usually took at least a half bottle of
vodka in with me, just to get me through the shift in the general ward I worked in.
Course, I knew all the tricks, the mouthwashes, peppermints and suchlike. I could
handle the booze, couldn't I?"
The pain was etched on her face and I saw that she was lost in some dark
memory. I could hear myself breathing, but sat stock still, afraid to break the
solemnity of the moment, the recounting of this woman's own agony.
"And how did I get to work? By car of course, driving a fancy, sports BMW
coupe that my affluent lifestyle rewarded me with. The same car," she stopped
speaking, as though to compose herself, "the same car in which I took my
daughter to school each morning. But of course, I'd go to bed each night if not
fully drunk, then certainly nearly there and each morning? Always a pick-me-up
to get me started, ready for the day. A splash of lipstick, hair brushed and a vodka
and tonic and hey, ho, off we go."
"I thought that nobody knew, that nobody guessed. But Hayley knew. Just nine
years old and she knew. She tried to tell me that she didn't like me drinking when
I drove, but she was just a wee girl, I told myself. What could she know?"
She slowly shook her head.
"My husband knew as well. But he chose to believe there was nothing wrong, that
as long as I acted the dutiful wife, so long as it didn't interfere with his own life,
his golf outings and social life, then it was okay."
I saw that her interlocked fingers were white at the knuckles as she fought to
maintain her composure, but her voice didn't falter as she continued to torture
herself.
"It was a Thursday morning and the roads were wet after a heavy rainfall, but
that's no excuse. I just didn't react fast enough when the lights changed to red and
tried to get through the junction. I was late for the school, you understand."

She sighed and took a deep breath.

"The van coming through the green light hit me side on at the passenger door. I had minor, superficial cuts and bruising but Hayley was critically injured. She took three days to die. Three days in which I comforted myself by getting drunk, but only after the court released me on bail from the drink driving charge." Curiously, she half smiled at me, but I knew that there was no humour behind the smile.

"I was convicted of causing my daughter's death by drunk driving and only escaped prison because, frankly, my life was destroyed. I'd lost my daughter, my husband blamed me and threw me out of the house and in time, divorced me. The Nursing Council, because of my conviction, struck me off the register and so I lost my profession and my only source of income. I moved back home to my parent's house where I watched my father slowly die of shame, though the official diagnosis was cancer, but I'll always believe that the cancer was exacerbated as a result of my drunken actions. My mother still blames me, but she's my mum and so, she's stuck by me. She's a far better mother than I was. Or should have been. In time, my only remaining friend Tricia, who is herself a counsellor and has dealt with her own demons, finally introduced me to Bill."

She must have seen the quizzical look in my eyes and smiled a sad, slow smile.

"You might know Bill better as Alcoholics Anonymous?"

Still too surprised to comment, I merely nodded my head in understanding.

"It wasn't easy to begin with. My first problem was admitting that I had a problem. Then when I realised that I was an alcoholic and finally admitted the fact, then eventually came the understanding and the grief. The knowledge of what I had done, who I had hurt, not least myself. Each day is a struggle, but I couldn't have managed, would not have got this far if I hadn't been helped, not least by Tricia, who became my sponsor."

She sighed deeply.

"So you see, Mister Logan, I do understand what you might be going through, if not the physical pain, then certainly the mental anguish. I can't solve your problems, only you can do that. But if you're willing to try then please believe me, I'm willing to help.

It's not every client I bare my soul to," she continued, with that half smile again, "but you needed to know I'm not some wee hairy with an HNC in sociology from the city college that is determined to sort your life out for you. I've lived the pain and still do. Julia Goodman tells me that you're a good and decent man, that I should do what I can to help you. So, are you willing to give me a chance?"

You know, it's been my experience that sometimes in life there are decent people in the world; maybe not a lot, but there is some.

"Right," I softly replied, "before we start, is there any likelihood of a decent cup of coffee?" I asked, sitting down and laying my stick on the floor.

CHAPTER 7

Now, don't go thinking that was it, I'd turned a corner and that because of some sob story from a counsellor, albeit a very pretty counsellor, I was on my way back to the straight and narrow.

So a couple of hours later, I'm driving the old Focus automatic and, I should have explained, it's an automatic on account of my leg you understand? Anyway, I'm heading back to the flat and thinking of nothing but the aching pain in my leg and how the hell am I going to get through the night without medication. Admittedly, I was surprised just how much I'd opened up to Alex Haldane, probably more than I intended, but something about her demanded the truth. She was, I believed, a woman who had been to hell, visited for a while and clawed her way back. I wished I had her guts.

The pain in my leg doesn't go away. That's it in a nutshell. It's there to stay and so in some sort of perverse way, I'm living with it in a reluctant partnership.

Driving now on automatic pilot, I'm starting to recall the time I'd spent in front of the desk, telling Alex… yeah, I know what you're thinking, but she insisted…; telling her the story of my life. Well, the recent bad part I mean. Discovering my unfaithful wife was shagging my neighbour, then three weeks later the shooting incident when I took two nine-millimetre rounds in the leg. I'm lying in hospital, sick with worry and wondering if the elderly, toffee-nosed bastard of a surgeon, who hardly gave me the courtesy of speaking to me would save my leg or amputate it, as he favoured. I didn't know then about the stories that were circulating among our friends and my colleagues at work, courtesy of my dear wife Sally, who cried that when I was drinking, I'd abuse and beat her. It didn't help that being in hospital, I wasn't around to defend myself and that some of her cronies began to remember bruises that they'd seen on her arms, her legs and body. It didn't take much persuading by Sally's lawyer to get them to speak up in court

Just a shame that none of them seemed to recall that before we'd married, Sally worked for a theatrical make-up company and part of her job was demonstrating the products.

Boy, was I the number one patsy.

I pulled up outside the tenement just as a van was pulling out from the kerb and blessed the God of parking places for his kindness and consideration.

Locking the car, I glanced at the night sky, absent-mindedly noting the gathering clouds as I limped towards the tenement building and pushed open the door that led into the common close. The stair head light bulb must have popped, I thought as I tentatively stepped into the darkened close and crunched broken glass beneath my feet, one hand feeling along the wall while I used my stick to ensure I didn't stumble.

The powerful flashlight snapped on and blinded me, seconds before a fist caught me in the stomach and drove the breath from my lungs.

I staggered back and would have fallen but for the hands behind me that caught me under the arms.

Two of them, I thought briefly. I say briefly because almost immediately I was stood upright by the one behind me. The guy in front with the torch belted me again, this time on the side of the head, with what seemed like a sledgehammer, but likely again was a fist.

"Tut, tut, DS Logan," said the voice behind me, "Cannae hold your drink, eh?"

Right then, I swear, a drink was the last thing on my mind. Then his words hit me, only literally, I mean.

DS Logan? Who was this bastard?

I tried to twist round, but the voice at the back still held me tight while the bear in front grabbed a handful of my hair and held my head up.

"Not his face, Scorcher," came the sharp command.

Scorcher Lamond, I realised. So the guy at the back must be Jackie Dewar.

The blow, when it came, again landed in my midriff and again I doubled up in pain and gasped for air.

"Dewar, you bastard," I managed to wheeze, trying to suck air into my lungs, sounding like a sixty a day coalminer with asbestoses.

My back was slammed against the wall and I was pinned there by the shoulders with Lamond's powerful hands, while Dewar played the torch onto my face to completely dazzle me.

"Long time no speak, DS Logan," said the shapeless form that was Dewar, from the darkness behind the light. "Hear that you might be doing a bit of business with Martin Kilbride's wife, eh?"

No beating about the bush then.

"What's it to you, Jackie?" I replied, trying to sound full of bravado, but to be honest I was prepared to give him any information he wanted rather than suffer the indignity of having his minder work me over. The world's full of heroes, but tonight, ladies and gentleman, it's not my turn.

"Let's just say you and I can do bit of business, Logan, eh," he sneered.

I almost laughed at that one. Do business with Dewar?

But I didn't laugh. My mind was racing and I realised that if I was going to get out of this without serious injury, the wisest course of action would be to listen, then comply.

That's when I took another one to the gut, not as hard this time so reckoned as Scorcher was holding me up, it must've been Dewar having some fun at my expense.

I slowly nodded, really because I was still trying to breathe and unable to speak. I pushed back at the shapeless lump that was Lamond.

Dewar must have tapped Lamond or something, because the bear relaxed his hold on my shoulders and then caught me as my knees buckled and, with surprising gentleness considering he'd just walloped me a few times, lowered me to a sitting position on the ground.

My back against the wall, I looked up at the light and said "First things first. Get that fucking light out of my eyes."

Dewar laughed and switched the torch off.

"So, what is it you want, Jackie?"

"You're working for Martin Kilbride's Missus," he repeated, "trying to find her man, eh. Have you traced him yet, eh?"

Now, in the movies, the hero always comes out with some wisecrack that usually earns him a slap or maybe he fights his way out of situations like this.

But in real life, I'm looking at best a kicking and at worst, I don't even want to think about that one, so I decided this wasn't the time for lies. Maybe I'd get away with a wee bit of economy with the truth, but definitely not lies.

"Not yet," I replied, inferring that in time I'd get my man.

"Are the polis close to finding him, eh?"

"No closer than I am."

"So, DS Logan," he leaned down and sneered at me "how close are you, eh?"

"If you tell me your interest, I might be able to answer that one," I replied.

That cheeky response earned me a stinging smack across the side of my head.

"Let's just say that Kilbride and I had a falling out and I'd like a word with him, so here's the deal, Logan. You find Kilbride and I'm first to be told, understand, eh?"

"Seems fair, if you're hiring me too," I slowly replied "so how do I contact you?"

"Hiring you? Are you a halfwit or something? I thought it was your leg that got damaged, not your head, eh."

"Well," I reminded him, "you did say we we're going into business together, Jackie, so fair's fair. You want me running around for you, it's going to cost petrol money and my time. And like I said, I need a contact number."

"You've got balls Logan, I'll say that for you," he guffawed, "so here's my deal. You find Kilbride and you get to keep your good leg in one piece. A double barrel at close range can make an awful mess of bone and tissue and as for contacting me, no sweat. I'll stay in touch with you. Remember, I know where you live, eh."

I heard Dewar shuffle in his pocket and then he threw some notes at me.

"Here's your petrol money" and laughed all the way out of the close with Lamond strolling behind him, the width of his silhouette almost filling the door frame.

I sat for a couple of minutes, then groped around to find the notes Dewar had thrown down, found my stick nearby and managed to get to my feet.

You might be wondering why I lifted the notes and didn't I have any pride? My reasoning is that money doesn't hold grudges and after all, I did need to pay for the petrol. Sometimes the old proverb that beggars can't be choosers comes in handy.

I felt nauseous and the bile rose in my throat as I staggered to my door.

My hand shook as I tried to insert the key into my lock.

I groped for the hallway light switch and got to the toilet just in time to discharge my guts into the bowl. I retched a few more times, wiped my face and sat shaking on the edge of the bath to compose myself.

Now, one thing I've learned in life is that life itself is a learning experience.

So what did I learn from my encounter with Jackie Dewar?

For one, I'd made the definite connection between him and Martin Kilbride and

I'm guessing that it was less of a partnership and more of an employer and employee relationship. That could only mean that as I suspected, Kilbride was laundering Dewar's money.

Recalling what Mickey Farrell had told me a couple of days ago, was it coincidental then, that Kilbride took off just as Dewar was drawing in all his assets for this Columbian coke deal? Is it likely that Kilbride was siphoning off money from Dewar's ill-gotten funds and feared Dewar had or would find him out and decided to leg it, possibly with the cash?

I reasoned that Dewar wouldn't normally care if Kilbride took off, but would care very much if he took off with Dewar's money. So much so that Dewar was even prepared to use me, a former cop and one of the manky mob, to help him track Kilbride down. That smelled to me as a hint of desperation. From that I deduced, I always did like that word, that Dewar was pressed for time, that maybe the coke deal was a lot closer than Mickey Farrell's squad thought.

If I'm right, I thought, how much are we talking about and more importantly, where the hell was Martin Kilbride?

Idly I glanced at the notes Dewar had tossed down to me. Four twenties.

As they say, money has no conscience, so at least the night wasn't an entire waste of time I smirked.

The following morning I rose bright and early. The ache in my guts from the pounding Scorcher Lamond gave me had overtaken my aching leg and so I skipped breakfast. Showered and shaved, wearing a clean, light blue shirt with dark blue knitted tie, pressed khaki chinos, all courtesy of Six-gun Sally, buffed black shoes on my feet and my light tan sports jacket, I inspected myself in the wardrobe mirror and was reasonably pleased that I'd scrubbed up neat and tidy. I might have looked the part, but God, I'd have killed for some painkillers. I did consider now that I'd some cash in my pocket, hitting an off-licence for a half bottle, but right now the last thing I wanted was to smell of booze.

Now don't go thinking that the meeting with Ms Alex Haldane had some sort of magical effect on me, that I was suddenly weaned off the golden nectar. No. Let's just agree that right here, right now, that more than anything, I could have murdered for a drink. Just a nip would have done, something that would have settled my stomach.

But I'd more pressing things to attend to first, so maybe later I promised myself. For once I was pleased to have some money, albeit I didn't want to linger on the source of the windfall and just after 8am, confidently drove into the ESSO garage on the Pollokshaws Road. Standing at the pump, I could see the acne ridden teenage assistant at the window had recognised me and was hesitating, deciding whether or not to take a chance on me having cash. Give a dog a bad name, I thought. I grinned at her and waved one of the twenties and she smiled, almost in relief, and activated the pump.

It took me a good forty minutes to drive through the city to Martin Kilbride's house.

I didn't phone ahead, taking the chance that my early morning visit would catch the elegant Missus Kilbride at home. I drove the Focus into the driveway, seeing both the Mercedes and Mini parked beside the front door and gingerly climbing from the car, limped towards the front door.

Before I got there I could hear the sound of raised voices and the door was snatched open.

Kilbride's daughter Sheila, hair tied back and wearing a short, grey coloured dress with a wide red belt and carrying a tan leather briefcase in her left hand, stood in the doorway, her face expressing apparent surprise at my presence.

I could see she'd been crying.

"Did you find him?" she asked.

My face must have registered my response, because without waiting for a reply, she pushed past me, causing me to stumble.

I'm not the most stable guy at the best of time and listen here, I'm talking about my balance, not my mental well being, and but for my stick would have fallen over.

Sheila stopped and turned toward me, concern on her face and her free hand outstretched. But then seeing I was okay, turned and got into her Mini before racing off at speed down the driveway. I watched her drive off, but didn't see any red brake lights as she exited into the main road and heavy traffic and I winced, then silently exhaled, thinking she'd be lucky to get where she's going without doing herself or some other poor sod a mischief.

I turned towards the still open door just as Phyllis Kilbride arrived.

This wasn't the cool, composed and elegant lady I'd previously visited.

Hair in disarray, eyes blazing and her mouth curled in a snarl, she was barefooted and wore a gold coloured, knee length silk dressing robe that was flapping open and revealing both perfectly round and naked breasts that juggled as she staggered to the door. A flimsy pair of black panties completed the ensemble and it was evident that she was drunk. I didn't need to be a detective to realise that.

Her glazed eyes and the half full bottle of vodka clutched in her left hand was a glaring clue.

If Sheila was surprised to see me, Phyllis was bloody shocked.

She stood stock still, her eyes opened wide and her mouth widened.

"Mister, eh, eh…." she pointed the bottle at me as she tried to recall my name.

Now call me old fashioned, but as much as I was enjoying the sight of her full and voluptuous breasts, I felt obliged to indicate to her that she was openly displaying her charms. She giggled and made a half-hearted attempt to pull the robe together, but again it fell open and she didn't seem too concerned that I was staring at her. I kind of formed the opinion that maybe Phyllis wasn't too averse to showing off her lovely assets.

"Come in, come in," she slurred at me and walked off towards the reception room that I'd previously visited.

So there I am, living every guy's dream. A good looking, almost naked foxy blonde, invites me to follow her and all I can think is that I hope she offers me a drink from that bottle of vodka.

Sad bastard that I am.

I closed the front door and watched her perfectly round bottom in the flimsy robe wiggle her way through the hallway into the lounge.

"Take a seat, Mister, eh..."

We'd already been through this so I told her, "Logan. John Logan. You hired me to find your husband Martin?"

That got through to her. She sat down heavily on the couch and dropped the bottle, then leaned down and snatched it up almost immediately, but not before spilling some of the liquid on the highly polished wood floor. Again, her robe fell wide open, but either by design or accident, I now wasn't sure.

"Come and sit here," she leered at me, patting the seat beside her.

"Sorry, my leg, I lamely explained," pointing to it and exaggerated my limp as I sat down on the opposite couch.

She sniggered as though in disbelief, that offering herself as she was to a gimpy guy, she was getting a knock back.

Don't get me wrong; I'm no saint and another time, another occasion. Well, who knows?

But not now; not here and certainly not in the drunken state Phyllis Kilbride was in.

I watched as very unladylike, she lifted the bottle and took a mouthful, swigging the stuff back like a professional. Some dripped down her chin and she used the back of her hand to wipe her mouth. One thing that life taught me is that alcohol is a great leveller and drunks have a habit of always either telling the truth, the truth as they believe it, or alternatively make poor liars.

I knew I was taking advantage, but this I thought is the ideal time to get some answers from the inebriated Missus Kilbride, assuming she stayed conscious long enough as I watched her take another pull at the vodka bottle.

"Have you heard anything from Martin, Missus Kilbride?" I began.

"Phyllis," she slurred in response, "call me Phyllis, dearie."

I tried not to smile, realising the posh Essex accent had been replaced by a Cockney drawl.

"Phyllis," I started again, "have you…"

"No, I ain't," she cut me short, almost spitting the words out. "The bastards took off and left me high and dry. The banks won't even let me draw any money. Shut the account off until he gets back. Telling me I can't get my money out," she wailed.

"Telling me because it's a joint account and the bloody police have told them he's missing, I can't draw nuffin till he's back, the lousy git."

Bugger, that meant it was also unlikely I'd be getting my retainer any time soon.

Now call me cynical, as likely you already have, but it seemed to me the previously cool Missus Kilbride might not have been telling me the whole truth when she had told me that her marriage to Martin was a bed of roses. I decided to test this idea.

"Thing's not too good between you and Martin then?" I asked, discretion not being one of my finest qualities.

She stared at me, her jaw slack, a slight bubble of spittle at her lower lip, and then grinned.

"He looks the part, doesn't he?" she said, pointing vaguely at the photograph of her husband that sat on the nearby table, the one of him holding the tiller of his boat. "But it's a front," her voice lowered as though fearing we'd be overheard. "He's nothing but a fraud. A good looking fraud, I give you that," she sneered, "but not the man he pretends to be."

She tapped the side of her nose with her forefinger.

"I know the real Martin Kilbride."

Here we go, I thought in anticipation of a few dark secrets.

"Can't get it up," she nodded her head, "not without me doing things for him, know what I mean?"

I didn't, but I could guess and I also guessed I was about to be told.

Now this isn't exactly what I had in mind when I thought she was going to burst to a few home truths, but I figured better to let her ramble and try to steer her to what I needed to know. Like, where the hell her husband might be?

"Dressing up. He likes me to dress up for him. Nurse, policewoman, tart, French maid. I've a whole wardrobe of costumes upstairs. Those and some toys too." She giggled coyly at me.

"Would you like to see them?"

I smiled and declined her offer. Had she been sober, I might have considered it, but then again if she'd been sober, she wouldn't have made the offer. The one thing that her statement told me was that if Martin Kilbride needed sexual encouragement with a good-looking woman like his wife, it was highly unlikely he'd been chasing some skirt. But then again, I'm hardly an expert in matters of the heart or nether regions, given my past record I mean.

A thought occurred to me.

"Did you sail with Martin, when he took the boat out?"

Her head began to droop and I thought she was about to pass out.

"Phyllis!" I barked at her and saw her head snap up, then asked her again.

"No, no way I was going out in that little boat. I prefer the cruises, dear," she simpered, taking another swig at the bottle. "But he'd take his precious daughter out on the boat," she almost spat out, "the little tart."

No love lost there then, which seemed to confirm the spat I'd heard when I'd arrived at the house.

A thought occurred to me.

"Does the name Jackie Dewar mean anything to you, Phyllis?"

"Dewar, Dewar," she repeated in a slurred voice. "Cheeky bastard! Phoned here and demanded to speak with Martin. Told him to fuck off," she replied, then giggled and covered her mouth with her hand and added "Sorry."

"When was this, when he phoned I mean?"

She narrowed her eyes as though in concentration and I hoped she remembered before she passed out.

"Days ago. In the morning. Said he needed to speak with Martin," she repeated. "Swore at me, called me a cow, no," she shook her head, "worse than that, I can't remember. Bastard."

Her head began to droop and as her eyes grew heavy, she leaned back into the couch and I figured she was about to fall asleep.

Another thought struck me and I was annoyed with myself I hadn't considered it sooner.

"Phyllis, Phyllis! Do you and Martin have a cottage anywhere, a holiday home? Somewhere in the country, maybe near Stirling?"

She stared at me and tried to focus.

"I hate the fucking countryside. Too many of those damned midge bugs. Biting me all the time. I hate going there."

I leaned forward, realising I was onto something.

"Where is this place, Phyllis? Where can I find this place?"

Her eyes drooped again and I got to my feet and limped over to sit beside her. She smiled in anticipation and leaned into me.

"You know," she cooed, "you're not a bad looking guy and placed her left hand on my crotch while leaning her head against me."

I put my arm about her shoulder and drew her against me, trying awfully hard not to get excited about her nakedness. This close to her, I realised that vodka wasn't the only alcohol with which she'd imbibed. She was reeking of the stuff and I thought must've been at the booze all night, probably when she discovered her bank account was meantime frozen.

"So tell me again," I lied, "where is your cottage, your holiday home?"

She drew slightly away from me and stared as though as though confused.

"Why do we need to go there, dearie? We can just go upstairs," she said while stroking my crotch and leaning into me, her face upturned and smiling vacantly.

It didn't escape my notice she still held onto the vodka bottle and yes, I admit it, I was really, really tempted to take it from her and help myself to a long, deep and satisfying swig.

"Course we can," I smiled back and pressed her once more, trying hard to ignore the vodka. "So, where's this place again?"

"Gar bloody something," she slurred. "Gunnick or something, I really can't remember. I only went once. Stirling way, where the castle is. Bloody church bells! You'd think they'd let people sleep late on a Sunday, wouldn't you? Why can't I sleep late on a Sunday? I mean, I work hard all week keeping house for him, don't I?" she simpered.

Curiously, the Essex accent had re-emerged and she smiled and continued stroking my crotch and unwilling though I was, felt myself responding to her touch.

Right, I decided, I'd probably got as much as I could from her, if you know what I mean and to her apparent surprise, lifted her hand off me and stood up.

"Where you going?" she slurred again, her eyes suddenly suspicious.

"To find your husband Martin."

"But, what about us?"

I smiled down at her, deciding the best option was to humour her.

"I'm going to do what you asked me to do, Phyllis, remember?" while deftly avoiding her reaching again for my crotch, "and to find your husband, okay?"

She continued to stare at me and sat back, as though in resignation.

"Go, go, do whatever the fuck you like," she hissed, then started crying. "You men, you're all bastards. Always fucking leave me," she wailed.

This, I wisely decided, was when I got out and made my way to the front door with Phyllis now screaming a few nasty expletives at my back.

I was grinning at my narrow escape and opened the door, only to be faced by none other than DS Eddie Coleman and his partner, Helen Burns.

"I can hear you're still winning friends," smirked Coleman "or is that another woman complaining because you've belted her, Logan?"

So there I am, standing in the client's doorway, two cops facing me and with the sound of verbal abuse coming closer from behind me.

I could see Helen Burns eyes open wide and Coleman leering over my shoulder and turned to find Phyllis Kilbride standing behind me, her robe again askew and tears streaming down her face, but this time minus the vodka bottle.

I presumed the crying was the shame of rejection by a crippled guy, or maybe self-pity had caught up with her. However, shocked that she might have been with her unexpected visitors, she also had the good sense this time to hurriedly close her robe.

Burns glared at me and crooking her right forefinger, beckoned towards me then turned and walked towards the nearby CID car, a dark green coloured Renault Megane with the additional telltale second radio antennae on the roof. I limped after her, blessing my good sense that I'd not after all succumbed to the temptation of the vodka bottle. Burns stopped and turned, leaning her back against the car, arms folded and tight lipped, her eyes burning a hole straight through me. I couldn't help but notice that angry though she undoubtedly was, with her coal black hair hanging loose about her shoulders and dressed in a maroon coloured trouser suit, she was without a doubt an attractive young woman.

"Care to tell me what's going on here?" she hissed at me, her voice deliberately low and presumably to prevent Phyllis Kilbride overhearing.

"Client confidentiality," I answered, just knowing that I was pushing my luck.

"Don't give me any of that shite! Are you screwing her?"

No beating about the bush with DC Burns then, I thought to myself and decided that I was fed up being the fall guy, that I'd wind her up a bit. I half smiled at her.

"Don't really think it's any of your business, is it DC Burns."

"It bloody is if her husband turns up dead, you twat, because then you become the number one suspect."

Shit. That wiped the smile off my face, I can tell you. Hadn't considered that one. I leaned heavily on my stick and saw her eyes ever so briefly glance down at my gammy leg, than back to my face.

"No, strictly business. I turned up here this morning just as she'd had a rammy with her daughter, I mean her stepdaughter," I corrected myself. "Found her in the condition that you saw her. Tried to ask her a few questions and she tried it on with me," I replied, feeling a bit self-conscious admitting this to Burns. She smiled at my discomfort.

"From what I heard there she'd offered you your Nat King and you knocked her back? Now that I find hard to believe. Given your apparent reputation and history by him," she nodded to Coleman who was apparently trying to calm the irate Mrs Kilbride, "I'd have thought a drunk, semi-naked woman would have been fair game to you, Mister Logan."

I slowly shook my head and smiled back at her.

"You seem like a bright and astute young detective officer DC Burns. As you said, given my reputation with women and my history as your neighbour there," I also nodded towards Coleman "likes to bandy stories about me about, there's no way I'm going to put myself in a compromising position, particularly with a client, or probably former client now," I sighed.

"So you're off the case then?"

"Can you see her retaining me after this debacle?" I replied.

"You're probably right, but before you go anything you want to share with me?"

I wasn't patronising her when I told Burns she seemed to be a smart young detective and it did occur to me at this juncture, very briefly I have to admit, that maybe I should share with her my run-in with Jackie Dewar and his interest in Martin Kilbride. Sort of get myself some back-up if Dewar did indeed try to carry out his threat about blasting me in the good leg, but that might in turn lead to more questioning and likely at the police station, with Burns and probably Coleman urging me to make a formal complaint. In turn, of course, it might also lead to Burns digging deeper about Martin Kilbride and discovering that somewhere near Stirling, some place with a name like Gar or Gunnick, Kilbride had a second getaway home. I had a flash of thought that this was information I'd prefer to keep up my sleeve. How I was going to use it, I wasn't yet certain, but I figured my next move would be to speak with his daughter, Sheila.

I realised Burns was staring at me, awaiting my response to her question and I decided to feed her something.

"For what it's worth, Missus Kilbride isn't quite the woman I first thought she was. More London cockney than Essex, I'd say. Maybe a bit of history there, before she married Kilbride. And the banks froze their joint account, so she's apparently no ready income. Added to that, the relationship with her stepdaughter is, as I said, fractious. Apart from that, I'm no further forward," I shrugged my shoulders as I lied to her.

Burns relaxed, unfolded her arms and shoved her hands into her trouser pockets, crossing her legs at the ankles as she leaned back against the car.

"You're right, of course, about Phyllis Kilbride. The original missing person report included her full details, so I did a bit of checking on the PNC and also with the Met Intelligence. Seems she lied about her age," and smirked, "a woman's prerogative, though, I'd say. She's actually five years older than she claimed, but not in bad shape as likely you've already noticed," she half smiled at me. "As far as I'm aware, Martin Kilbride's her fourth husband, something else she lied about on the MP report. And she's a bit of history too with the Met police, albeit a number of years ago. She's had two warning for soliciting and one minor conviction for fraud. She was described in her police report antecedents as an actress, though I doubt she's ever really trod the boards of the Old Vic or any other theatre for that matter."

"Sounds a bit like the women I used to meet at the dancing," I quipped, relaxed now I was sure that Burns wasn't going to press me for further information. She glanced down again at my leg.

"You'll not have met many women in the recent past then? Maybe you should have taken advantage when it was offered."

"Thanks, but I'm saving myself for the right one this time," I replied and added, "will that be all then, officer?"

Burns nodded. "Don't think I'll be seeing you again Mister Logan, now that you're off the case, so cheerio and good luck," she said.

Curiously, I believed she meant it and felt just a twinge of regret that I'd lied to her. I watched as she walked back to join Coleman who was still trying to calm the loud and increasingly abusive Phyllis Kilbride, whose arms were now flailing wildly, and then I turned and headed towards my car.

I got back to my office well before midday and turned on the computer. While it warmed up, I switched on the kettle and made myself a strong black coffee. Black because again I'd forgotten to get milk. I also realised that my stomach was aching, though not from Scorcher's punches, but from hunger. It didn't help that my throat was parched and right then, I could have used some of Phyllis Kilbride's vodka to help me get through the day. Well, that and some painkillers. Funny though, that while the ache in my leg is always there and reminding me to grimace every time I put my foot down, it didn't seem as important right at this minute as getting to the bottom of Martin Kilbride's disappearance. And on that issue, I smiled to myself; I believed I was now ahead of the game. I didn't relish another trip down the flight of stairs, but figured I'd get a croissant as well as milk and treat myself to a proper breakfast.

I exited the close and the first thing I saw was Sheila Kilbride, Martin's daughter, standing beside her parked Mini and watching me from across the road.

She was dressed, as I'd seen her this morning and quite a sight in her short, grey dress and wide red coloured belt, but now with her hair lying loose to her shoulders. To say I was surprised wouldn't really describe it. She half waved at me then crossed between two parked hackney cabs, both of whose drivers appreciatively watched her walk across the road. I could see the envy in their eyes when she approached me.

"Mister Logan," she hesitantly began, "I'm sorry about this morning. I know that you must think I'm awful…."

It seemed she was about to cry and that's me all over of course, a sucker for women in distress.

Sucker I said. Try and concentrate, please.

"Look," I made the decision, "we can't talk here. My office is up there, first floor, green door needing painted. It's not locked. Why don't you go on up, I'm just going to get some milk and breakfast. Some croissants. I'll be but a minute," or ten, I thought, the time it takes me to climb those bloody stairs.

She smiled, stemming the tears that threatened to erupt from her and involuntarily glanced down at my leg.

Why do all the women do that I wondered?

"No, I'll get those things. I'll meet you up there," she said in a voice that brooked no argument and turned to cross the road. I remembered then and shouted after her, asking her to get me some painkillers. She turned her head and nodded and I watched her walk to the door of the dairy. I saw the taxi driver's also watching her and with good reason. She is quite a stunner.

Ten minutes later, I'm sitting in my office chair, checking area maps on the computer when she enters and wordlessly, places a plastic bag on the desktop. I indicated the two mugs of steaming black coffee on the small side table and she brought them over, placing one down in front of me and opened the bag, saw me nod and poured milk for us both and again reached into the bag to hand me a paper tissue wrapped, freshly baked, lukewarm croissant. Thankfully, as an after thought and at my request, she'd also got me a packet of twenty-four, strong, non-prescribed Co-codomol painkilling tablets.

She was now more composed than she'd been on the street and I guessed she'd taken the time to calm herself.

"Have you found out where he is yet?"

I smiled at her and I knew. Right there and then, I knew.

Sheila Kilbride had no fears for her father's immediate safety, simply because she knew where he was.

"Shouldn't you be at work?" I asked, then realised I didn't even know if she was employed.

"I got the day off," she replied, "told the head teacher I wasn't feeling well."

"Sorry, I didn't know you worked in a school."

"I'm a teacher, primary three class. In Kelvinbridge," she replied. "Private school."

Of course it is, I thought. I couldn't see the elegant Miss Kilbride subjecting herself to teaching the plebs in an inner city school.

"The reason I'm here," she began, "is that I want to pay you off. Tell you to stop looking for my father. The police are involved now and I would much rather they handled the inquiry. I realise," she glanced about the office "that it's probably not unusual in your line of work, Mister Logan, to be dismissed during your investigation, so I'm really here to settle the bill."

She stared hard, as though trying to intimidate me, challenging me to argue with her.

I finished the croissant and dabbed with the tissue at my lips, then slowly took a drink of the coffee. That, I can tell you, made me feel a lot better and I stared back at her, knowingly smiling because I'm a smart arse and about to surprise her.

"You can't sack me because you didn't employ me. Your stepmother contracted me to find you father. She is the only one that can request I quit my inquiry. Is that what you're telling me? That your stepmother sent you here this morning to cancel my services? Or is it that you're worried that I might find your father? Maybe seven miles west of Stirling in a little village called Gargunnock? In a getaway holiday home, not far from the local church?"

She had the good grace to blanch at that and her lower lip trembled and I realised I was spot on. I'd hit the jackpot.

Okay, I'm starting to sound a little overbearing now, but truth be told, after Phyllis Kilbride's drunken revelation earlier this morning about the holiday home and with a little research on the computer, it wasn't hard to put two and two together. This wasn't a hardnosed woman used to dealing with the law or criminals. This was a frightened young daughter, fearful for her dad and I decided to calm her down and get the full story.

"Do the police know?" she asked, dabbing at her eyes with the croissant paper tissue.

Now, no matter how bad I've been or get and as I've said before, I always, but always carry a spare, clean, linen handkerchief in my pocket and this I offered to her.

Her shoulders slumped and she began to twist the handkerchief in her hands.

"Nobody knows, except I think, you and I. That's correct, isn't it?"

She nodded and sighed, almost in relief.

"How did you find out, about where my dad is, I mean?"

I decided not to go into details, but simply told her I acted on information provided by her stepmother.

She looked aghast, then furious.

"That bitch! That sluttish cow! I'll kill her!" she ranted as she stood up.

"Sheila!" I bawled at her. "Sit down."

That stopped her and stunned, she slowly sank down into the chair.

"Let's start at the beginning," I said, "are you certain nobody else knows of your dad's whereabouts? Absolutely certain?"

"Yes, I mean no," she replied. "Nobody knows. He begged me not to tell anyone. He's so frightened," then she burst into tears, sobbing her heart out.

It did occur to me to get up and comfort her, but to be honest, I'd had enough of the Kilbride women for one day, so sat and waited till she'd composed herself, then pointed to the small toilet if she wanted to freshen up.

Freshen up? Maybe not the place I'd normally recommend, but while she'd been fetching the breakfast, I'd taken the precaution of pouring a half a bottle of bleach down the loo to try and kill what remained of the sickly odour that seemed to permeate in there. A couple of minutes later, she returned to her seat, her eyes red but no longer weeping.

"Does the name Jackie Dewar mean anything to you?"

Her eyes opened even wider and I just knew that no matter what she'd previously told me about denying having heard the name, she knew exactly who and what Dewar is.

"He's the man, the thug, that's looking for dad," she replied in a flat voice. "Do you know him?"

"Yes, but do you know why he's looking for your dad?"

She'd began to recount the story that I knew had been told to her by her father and trusting him as no doubt she did, she believed that story to be true.

According to Sheila, Martin Kilbride told his daughter that in his profession as a chartered accountant, he was employed by Dewar to handle a number of business transactions, but several days previously had discovered that when liquidating Dewar's assets, the money was diverted from the account set up by Kilbride for Dewar, to an offshore account in Jersey, over which Kilbride had neither authority nor control. In essence, the money was stolen online. I figured from what Sheila said, the plan had been that Dewar would simply thereafter transfer the money to an account in the name of his supplier and therefore need never have to actually handle the cash. But without the account details and password, the money was lost to him. These details, Dewar obviously believed, could be had from Martin Kilbride. Her father had also apparently taken the precaution of warning his daughter how dangerous and violent Dewar was.

"How much money are we talking about here?"

"Dad told me in excess of six million pounds."

Now it was my turn to be startled.

Bloody hell, no wonder Dewar was anxious to get a hold of Martin Kilbride. He thinks' the bugger's stiffed him for six million quid. I swallowed hard, thinking that this was getting a bit out of my league and, yes, it did occur to me to phone my old mate Mickey Farrell and get him, forty armed members of his team and the Parachute Regiment round here pronto to protect my one good leg!

Jesus, I sat back in my seat, six million quid! And I was worried about an earner from Kilbride's wife. I needed to tie up some loose ends.

"I found your dad's car, the Saab, burned out in the forest at Polkemmet. Who did that?"

She blushed and half smiled.

"I followed dad in my Mini. We knew that car had a tracking device in it somewhere, in case it gets stolen. You know, an insurance thing. Dad isn't very technically minded and I don't know the first thing about engines, so we'd no idea where this thing was in the car. I followed him to that place, where you found it, I mean. He was in such a panic, worried in case Dewar or his thugs got him, he decided to burn the car, eliminate all trace of it, but I don't think we made such a good job of it, not if you were able to find it."

"And his phone?"

She smiled at that.

"I've seen these programmes on television, how they can trace you through your phone. You know, James Bond stuff and the like. I bought dad a pay as you go phone, so he has some form of communication, in case they find him," she shuddered slightly. "That's why we threw his own phone into the car, when we burned it."

"You didn't make such a good job of either the car or the phone," I dryly told her. "The phone was receiving calls after you dumped it in the car, but the battery has discharged now, so that's not a problem, but the car will likely be found in time and it's easily identifiable from not just the plates, but the engine and chassis numbers too."

I could see that Sheila might be a pretty, bright and articulate young woman, but when it came down to practical matters, I couldn't envisage her getting her head under the bonnet of a car.

Thinking of my scrappy Focus, who am I to judge, you might ask.

"Tell me, who else knows of this holiday home?"

"The cottage?" she pursed her lower lip, "As far as I'm aware, just dad, Phyllis and myself. Unless of course dad told anyone else at work or the golf club, but I can't be certain. I do know that dad and I are the only ones that use it and I haven't been there for years. I'm sure he'd have mentioned it if he'd let anyone use the cottage. Dad uses it every other month as a bolthole when he goes walking in the Campsie Fells. Phyllis," she almost spat the name out, "came with us once, not long after they married, but when she saw the size of the village and that there was no social circle that suited her, she didn't go again."

"What about the boat, the Elizabeth? Any idea where she might have gone, who might have taken her?"

She shrugged her shoulders.

"That wasn't dad or I. I've no idea who took the boat," she replied, her brow furrowed as she shook her head.

"Might Phyllis have had it moved somewhere, do you think?"

"Unlikely," she almost sneered, "Phyllis is strictly a big boat cruise in the sun, person. Can't think of her ever having any interest in the boat."

Something bothered me about the boat, but right then I couldn't put my finger on it. It also left me with a loose end, but meantime, something else bothered me too.

"The money, you said, had been stolen online. I understood that these financial transactions between accounts were encrypted, that when the cash is being transferred between the accounts, only the transferee has the relevant security codes and passwords to access these accounts?"

"That's what dad told me," she replied, "but someone has somehow gotten hold of this information."

I recalled that working within the CID, I had access to all sorts of programmes that operated within the parameters of the police intelligence community, most of which required their own passwords to access. Of course, anyone cleared to operate these systems were warned under Data Protection law of dire consequence if they revealed their passwords or permitted unauthorised users to access these systems. Users were also discouraged to write down or record these passwords, where others might discover them. And rightly so, you'll likely agree, but provided of course you don't have half a dozen passwords to remember, some of which change monthly. Human nature being as it is, most of us do write down or somehow record our passwords and this, I suspected, if Martin Kilbride's story were true, was how he came a cropper, so to speak.

"I'm going to need to meet with your dad," I told her, "and for his sake and his health, probably the sooner the better."

She baulked at that and I could see it in her eyes. Just how far could she trust me.

"Look," and I was thinking on my feet here as I leaned forward on the desk, my hands upright in the surrender position, "your stepmother tried it on with me when I called by this morning…"

"What, you mean, sexually? No way," her eyes lit up with delighted shock, "go on, tell me more."

"That's irrelevant," I sharply replied, "but what is relevant is that because of her behaviour," I lied, thinking that being the upright, good guy wouldn't do me any harm, "I no longer work for her, but I am available to help your dad. But for a fee, of course. I don't work for nothing and remember, I do have contacts within the police," silently praying that Mickey Farrell would be pleased with what I had to offer him, rather than pummelling me for not giving it up before.

She bit her lower lip and screwed her face in concentration.

"I can phone him, see if he'll meet with you…."

"Then I suggest that you do it now. I don't think there's any time to waste, particularly if a man like Dewar is hunting your father."

I know that was a rotten trick, scaring the poor girl and burdening her with her father's safety, but what you have to remember is that I still needed to make a living and having been turfed off the inquiry by Phyllis the good time girl, helping Martin Kilbride save his life might be the only chance I'd have to earn a wage from this debacle.

She nodded, reached into her small shoulder purse for her mobile phone and went to the office door. I must have expressed curiosity.

"I'm just stepping out into the landing. He'll want me to tell him who you are and I don't want to do it in front of you," she explained, almost apologetically.

I nodded and waited.

She returned almost five minutes later, her face a little flushed.

"He's not pleased that you know where he is, but said that if I trust you, then that's good enough for him. So, we've to meet him at the cottage at 11am tomorrow morning."

She stood and stared hard at me.

"I can trust you Mister Logan, can't I?"

"John. My name is John. And yes, Sheila, you can trust me. I won't be the cause of any harm to your father and I'm sure he'll be safe for now, I promise."

We agreed to meet at nine, the next morning at my office and as I watched her from the office window walk to her car, I was to find out later, it was a promise I couldn't keep.

I'd hardly got my backside on my chair when the desk phone rung and surprise, surprise, who should be calling me but my new partner, Jackie Dewar.

"DS Logan," he drawled into my ear "thought I'd give you a wee buzz and catch up, like old friends should. How's it hanging, Johnny boy, eh?"

Throughout my life, I'd hated being called Johnny. Now, there's nothing wrong with the name Johnny, it's just a quirk of mine. John I was christened and John I prefer.

"What can I do for you, Jacqueline?"

I heard the sharp intake of breath and knew I'd scored a point.

"Funny bastard," he snapped down the line, then almost as quickly asked, "what did Kilbride's daughter have to tell you, eh?"

I felt my blood go cold. Either he or one of his minions was watching my office. I heard plates rattling and noisy conversation in his background. A restaurant. Someone else was watching the office and had phoned him, I decided.

"Like you, Jackie," I soothingly replied, "she's very concerned for her father and surprisingly, when I mentioned your name to her, she seemed to recall her old dad having spoken about you. So, what exactly is your relationship with Kilbride, then?"

Almost as quickly as he'd angered at my derisive comment, Dewar had calmed down.

"It's strictly business, Johnny boy and nothing for you to worry your head about. Just worry about your good leg," he snorted in my ear, "and concentrate on finding him for me, eh. Might be an earner in it for you as well. Maybe a couple of grand? I mean after all, you are in business aren't you? Just like me. And Johnny boy, time is cracking on, okay, eh?"

"I hear you Jackie. Stay in touch and I'll see what I can find out," I glibly lied and replaced the handset.

Exhaling quietly, I sat back in my chair and thought of what had just passed between us.

The offer of a reward told me that, if nothing else, Dewar was getting desperate, that he needed Kilbride found sooner than later. Whether or not Kilbride had the bank account information Dewar needed had nothing to do with me. That was Dewar's problem. I also reasoned that Dewar's haste probably meant that the drug deal Mickey Farrell told me of, that had been brokered for Dewar by Billy Crawford with the Columbian Cartel, must be very close indeed.

You might think, was it worth two thousand pounds to me to give Dewar the address, or at least the village, where Kilbride was hiding out? Was I tempted? Course I was. I could simply have had Dewar or one of his flunkies meet me with the cash and once it was in my grimy Judas hand, gave him the information and walked away without any further involvement and the added bonus of keeping my good leg intact. So why didn't I? Was it because of the young, worried and let's face it, very pretty Miss Kilbride? Because I'd made a promise that she could trust me? Or did some part of me remain a cop, a drug squad officer who just didn't like to see types like Dewar make money from the misery of others?

I'm not quite sure what prevented me from handing Kilbride over, but I knew that I felt a little better for it. Physically, not much because I still ached with pain and opened the Co-codomol. I popped four tablets from the blister packaging and threw them back with the remains of my now cooled coffee. No, I felt better morally, a word I hadn't attributed to myself for some time. However, I would need to think of something to tell Dewar.

I inched over to the window and from behind the faded green curtain, peered down into the street.

Now who should be lurking on the opposite corner, but my old friend Scorcher Lamond, pretending to read a newspaper, while furtively glancing up to my window.

Time for a bit of fun.

"Hello, Stewart Street police office, can I help you?"

"I don't wish to give my name officer," I replied in what I hoped sounded like a falsetto Edinburgh accent, "but there is a rather intimidating man standing in Osborne Street at the corner with King Street. He seems to be watching the children from the local school passing and I do believe he has tried to engage some in conversation. I just think it's rather odd," I finished, and then hung up before the guy could ask any questions.

It didn't take long. Within five minutes a patrol car with two young policewomen turned into Osborne Street, then raced to where Scorcher stood. The cops were out the car and big as he was, poor Scorcher was stunned to find himself turned against the wall, adopting the position, as it were, hands flat on the wall, feet kicked and spread wide. While one officer patted him down, the other was on her radio, probably checking him out for warrants or whatever. I also saw that in her other hand, discreetly tucked against her trouser leg, she held her drawn extendable baton.

I have to say that I thought for two seemingly young lassies, these girls knew their job.

Scorcher turned his head and stared at my window, the venom in his face obvious. I took the hint and cramming the Co-codomol packet into my pocket, left the office and shuffled as quickly as I could downstairs to my car. I glanced up the street and saw that one cop, apparently satisfied Scorcher was no threat, gesticulating with her thumb in the time honoured manner of fuck off and don't be hanging around here again.

Scorcher caught sight of me opening the car door and that one look was enough. Next time, there would be no quarter given.

CHAPTER 8

I drove home towards the flat and reflected on my day so far. I'd learned where Kilbride is in hiding, his wife is a fraud, Jackie Dewar is growing increasingly desperate and the time for the drugs being delivered by the Columbians is seemingly imminent.

So, I smiled and I wondered, how could I use all this information my financial advantage?

After a quick shower and change into a bottle green polo shirt and clean chinos, I cooked myself a boil in the bag pasta meal and washed it down with a glass of milk. Tempted though I was to grab a can of lager, I'd my second appointment that evening with Alex Haldane and didn't want to turn up smelling of alcohol or mints. From her own tragic experience, that lady would spot any ruse a mile off. For desert, I popped four more Co-codomol. God alone knew what damage I was inflicting on my poor liver and kidneys, but my tolerance to pain was getting lower by each passing day. I only wished it had been the stronger medication that Julia Goodman previously prescribed for me.

I grabbed my old black coloured windcheater jacket and was almost at the door when I occurred to me that maybe a wee precaution might be wise. Cautiously, from behind the curtain in the darkened lounge, I checked the street for any sign of Dewar or his crony, Scorcher Lamond, but it looked clear. At the front door, I listened for a few minutes and opening the door, almost sighed with relief that the close foyer was empty. I got to my car without incident and drove through the evening traffic to Coplaw Street, arriving five minutes before my appointment time.

It was Jimmy of the Scooby-doo slippers who again opened the door to me, but no smile on this occasion. Just a wary glance and perhaps a little surprise that the nutter had returned. To his credit, he allowed me in without comment and showed me to the same room, where this time Alex Haldane was already seated behind the desk.

"Wasn't certain you'd come back, John," she smiled, as though pleased to see me. She was wearing her hair tied back in a French plait, again no make-up, but with skin as clear as hers, she didn't really need any, and a lemon coloured blouse. As she stood to shake my hand, I saw she wore tight, denim jeans.

"I'm being blackmailed by my doctor to attend here, remember?" I grinned awkwardly at her.

She returned a smile and lifting what looked like the same cardboard file from our previous meeting, opened it and took from it a single page.

"I wrote down a few observations from our last meeting," she began, offering me the page, "would you care to read them or do you trust me enough that they'll be correct?"

"Who are these observations for?"

"Well, at a point when you believe that you've made progress, we can discuss my initial observations and compare the notes from the first meeting to decide how far you've moved on; improved, so to speak."

"So, what you're saying is that I decide if this counselling is working?"

Believe me, at this point I too was slightly confused.

"In a sense, yes," she replied. "I can only listen and advise you, John. You are the only one that can help yourself. I can't stop you drinking or taking your medicines or whatever poison you consume to make you feel better. I guess the physical pain must sometimes be overwhelming, but in the two hours we spent together yesterday evening, it didn't take me long to realise that you are a strong man. Maybe a lot stronger than perhaps you give yourself credit for. I can understand," she smiled again and run her tongue over her upper lip, "why Julia Goodman has taken such an interest in you. Like it or not, I believe you are one of life's good guys."

I saw she was a little embarrassed, making this comment, but I didn't take the page from her and I can't really explain why. Maybe it had been so long since I'd actually had the opportunity to trust someone that something inside me, some inner need, wanted to believe in this woman.

Now, you're thinking that I'm getting all soppy on you, aren't you?

But it wasn't that.

I think I'd realised that Alex Haldane didn't want anything from me. At our last meeting, she'd bared her soul to me. Without emotion, she'd broken down her life into a few, tragic sentences, made me realise that pain isn't always physical. Trusted me with her sadness and heartache and convinced me that nothing is insurmountable. Perhaps even made an old cynic like me believe that there's always a way back.

I took a deep breath and shook my head.

"I'll read it another time," I shrugged and spent the next two hours moaning the face off her about my feelings and how I felt life had did me dirty.

But with a little humour, of course, because that's just my style.

It was dark when I returned home and I did a full circle in the car round my block, looking for anyone or anything that might indicate I'd unwelcome visitors awaiting me. I also cursed myself, having forgotten to phone and ask the building factor to replace the broken light in the close entrance.

Apart from a couple of drunks, wandering down the road from the nearby pub and loudly extolling the recent victories of Glasgow Rangers, the street was deserted. I parked the car fifty yards from my entrance and approached the darkened close, my stick held firmly and teeth clenched tight, but on this occasion there was no Scorcher waiting in ambush and I got safely into the flat. Securing the front door against surprise callers, I made myself a weak coffee and had the blister pack of Co-codomol in my hand before I realised what I was doing. I looked longingly at the pills and considered what Alex and I had discussed within the last hour. I shook my head and made a deal with myself.

Two tablets, but no alcohol.

Seemed fair and let's face it, at least it was a beginning.

The following morning was, I saw from the bedroom window, overcast with rain clouds threatening to unleash the heavens on a dull and grey Glasgow.

Curiously, I felt fresh and relaxed and realised I'd slept well. I dressed for the weather in casual trousers, plaid shirt and warm, light brown coloured V-neck sweater and grabbed a coffee, strong this time, and guiltily washed down four Co-codomol. Well, I reasoned, it might be a long day so I'd be better preparing myself for the pain that was sure to come later.

Traffic was predictably heavy as I drove towards the office for my nine o'clock appointment with Sheila Kilbride and I hummed along with some of the songs played on Smooth Radio by my favourite early morning DJ's, John and Sharon.

Early morning parking in Osborne Street can be a bit of a nightmare, but once again, I was lucky and eased the Focus into a space near to the entrance to my building. As I got out of the car, I saw Sheila Kilbride's Mini parked a little further along the street. She wasn't in the car so I presumed she'd be at my office door.

Don't think I'd forgotten about Dewar and Scorcher. Those guys were now constantly on my mind, so a little cautiously, I made my way up the flight of stairs and almost with relief, found the only person waiting there was Mister Zao.

"Good morning Mister Logan," he half bowed, "any news for Zao?"

I unlocked the door, wondering where Sheila was and invited him in. He shuffled past and turned to face me.

"I'm still working on it, Mister Zao, but I've no real news to give you right now."

His lined face was ashen, his clothes crumpled more than usual and he looked like he'd not slept.

"Tai Pei, she not come home last night. Again. That two nights, now. No phone call, nothing. I very worried," he said.

I wouldn't say I'm a particularly tactile person, but I reached out and my hand and rubbed his arm.

"Mister Zao, I promise you I'm making progress. I'll try to find something out for you today, okay?"

He stared tight-lipped at me, nodded his head then said, "You do something and find something out," he repeated, "or Zao must act himself. Understand?"

I understood and he turned to leave just as Sheila Kilbride arrived at the open door, a little breathless and carrying a paper bag that indicated she'd just come from the dairy across the road.

"Sorry," she stammered, her eyes darting between me and Zao, "have I interrupted something?"

Zao stared at her, then turned to me and said, "Today, Mister Logan, you do something today or Zao act."

He shuffled past Sheila without a second glance.

I ushered her in and turned towards the kettle, having already smelled the hot croissants from the bag and realising that I was hungry. We sat munching the food and drinking the coffee, but I knew she was anxious to set off.

At her age, she didn't need much preparation to face the day. Dressed in a loose tan-coloured sweater, black coloured, denim jeans and with her hair tied back, I saw she hadn't bothered with make-up. She'd brought a light, navy blue waterproof jacket to combat the impending rain and wore stout, walking shoes on her feet.

Ten minutes later we set off with her driving, having insisted we travel in her Mini. I balanced the thought of the discomfort in a small car against the expense of the petrol and allowed her to win the argument, then was pleasantly surprised to discover the modern Mini was a lot roomier than I'd remembered, so got into the passenger seat without too much struggle. The journey out of Glasgow was a lot easier than the poor sods had getting into the city, as we passed the lines of queuing traffic on the opposite carriageway.

Sheila proved to be a competent driver and we passed the time with her telling me of her childhood and growing up, firstly in Edinburgh where her mother had died after a short battle against cancer, then the marriage to Phyllis, whom her father had met on one of his business trips to London; then moving to Kirkintilloch just as she finished her A level exams, a move that took her from friends and all that she'd previously known.

"He was bedazzled by Phyllis," she bitterly recounted, "and when she insisted we make the move from Edinburgh to get away from what she called old memories, he just gave in to her. As he always did. Changed jobs and everything. It was like starting anew," she sighed.

"So, John, what's your story?"

I smiled and gave her the potted version, injured in the line of duty, blah, blah, blah. So that's how the journey continued until we arrived at the quiet village of Gargunnock.

Apart from a few elderly women, standing chatting outside the local Cooperative, the place seemed deserted and she turned off what can only be described as the one main road and into Stark Street. I saw that one side of the street was bordered by mid terraced, one storey houses while on the opposite side was a row of what seemed to have once been farming community detached and semi-detached workers cottages, each in turn set back behind a low brick perimeter wall.

Sheila pulled up outside a detached cottage near the end of the street.

"Here we are," she announced.

I managed to exit the Mini with some dignity, and looking at the cottage, saw a brightly painted red door with a similarly painted window frame on each side of the door. Oddly, the curtains of both windows were closed and in the greyness of the morning, I noticed through a crack in the curtain of one window that the inside light seemed to be switched on.

Sheila pushed open the low, red painted gate that squeaked at the metal hinge and led the way up the short, garden path. She turned and smiled as she tried the door handle and it swung open.

"Stop!" I barked at her, causing her smile to fade and saw alarm cross her face.

"What is it?"

"Something's not right."

Instinct had kicked in and the proverbial hair on the back of my neck had stood up, usually a good indicator that all was not well. I tugged at Sheila's arm and pulled her back from the doorway, then cautiously used my stick to push the door open.

"What's wrong?"

"Why," without turning, I softly replied "would a man in fear of his life leave his front door unlocked?"

I stood almost frozen to the spot, my mouth slightly open and my head cocked to one side as I listened for about thirty seconds, for any noise from within, but there was complete silence. I entered the small, narrow and dark hallway and could almost hear my heart thumping in my chest. My mouth had gone dry and holding my stick in right hand in front of me as a prod, I used my left hand on the wall to balance and guide me. The light from the open door behind me showed the way through to what looked like a rear kitchen. There was two doors', both to the left and right side of the hallway.

The right hand door was slightly ajar and I sneaked a glance inside and saw a bed, the covers thrown back and some male clothing lying discarded on the bed and the floor. Don't ask me how I knew, but I was certain the room was empty.

I turned my head slowly towards the front door and saw Sheila staring at me, wide eyed and opened mouthed, her hands held together across her chest in fright. I raised a cautious finger to my lips to warn her to be silent, then motioned that she was to remain where she was and turned back toward the closed door on my left. If anyone is behind the door, I knew, they'd be aware now that I was in the house.

"Mister Kilbride?" I called out, suddenly realising my mouth was dry, "My name's Logan. John Logan. I'm just coming into the room now," and pushed the door open wide.

Now, I hadn't just been a drug squad officer all my service. Apart from time in uniform walking the beat, I'd cut my teeth for six years in divisional CID, dealing with all sort of crime ranging from simple theft to the capital crime of murder, so it's fair to say I'd a modicum of experience dealing with violent crime. That's why when the door opened and I sniffed the sickly, sweet smell of dried, arterial blood and another smell that I dredged up from my suppressed memory, I knew that something awful had occurred in that room.

The main light and a small, two bar electric fire were both switched on and Martin Kilbride, who I recognised from the photographs I'd seen, was lying face down and fully dressed, on the carpeted floor, arms and legs akimbo and his head turned towards me. His eyes were opened and he had died with his face registering surprise, as though disbelieving what was happening to him. The back of his salt and pepper hair was matted with blood that had also seeped into the carpet around him, framing his head in a halo of death.

A pale green hand towel was lying beside him and also coated with blood and, I guessed, presumably been used to wipe clean the murder weapon. I heard a gasp behind me and turned to find Sheila Kilbride, white faced and speechless, her hand pointing to her father, her face chalk white.

I made to grab her as her legs buckled beneath her.

That's when she screamed.

As I've said and you'll know by now, not being the most able limbed guy myself, it took all my strength to bundle Sheila from the room and half carry her to the kitchen at the rear of the house. In truth, I didn't know what I was going to find there, but was relieved there was no more dead bodies. I got her sat at the wooden, kitchen table and she collapsed across the table, weeping inconsolably. I searched the wall cupboards and found an opened bottle of Glenfiddich, poured a generous measure into a tumbler and made her drink it. She gasped as the fiery liquid hit the back of her throat and dribbled some from her lips, but it did the trick and though she was still in shock, she sat up, breathing heavily.

"Is he really dead?" she sobbed, the tears and mucous from her nose running unchecked.

I nodded and half bending over her, gave her shoulders a squeeze.

"But, who, why…."

She was lost, for the moment and all I could do was almost force her to take another gulp of whisky and can I just say, I wasn't beyond needing one myself. It had been quite a while since I'd been in the company of violent death.

But I refrained, knowing that right now I needed to think, needed to assess what had happened here, and why. My mind was turning over faster than a bookie's hands at Ayr racecourse and something wasn't right. Something was definitely wrong.

The first suspect for Kilbride's murder had to be Jackie Dewar, that somehow Dewar had tracked him down to this cottage. But it niggled me and I couldn't work out why?

No matter, it would come to me, I knew. At some point later in the day, the week or whenever, it would come like a flash.

You know that film or piece of music or guy or book that you can't quite remember the name of? No matter what you do to recollect, whether it's going through the alphabet or asking your spouse or pal?

Then, sometimes at the oddest moment, shopping, brushing your teeth, driving, watching TV or whatever, it comes to you. The very detail that you couldn't quite recall.

Well, I'm a bit like that. If I can't remember at the time, I usually give up, knowing that eventually it will come back to me. So I moved on and decided to deal with the matter in hand.

"Wait here," I told her and returned to the front room.

The first thing I did was switch off the electric fire as the heat being generated had turned the small room into a sauna and believe me, between the smell of the blood and Kilbride's loosened bowels, I was gagging. I stepped back into the hallway and took a deep breath, placed my clean handkerchief over my mouth and nose and stepped back into the room to critically examine the dead man.

Careful to avoid kneeling in his blood, I saw that he'd been struck across the back of the head more than once, maybe three or four times I thought, with what seemed to be a rounded weapon, whose circle was roughly the diameter of a fifty pence piece. Pieces of bone had splintered and were mixed with the blood and brain matter. What was curious, I thought, was these seemed to be the only wounds, though I wasn't about to turn him over or anything to make a more thorough examination. A sustained and violent assault, as the subsequent forensic examination would likely conclude.

Pushing myself upright, I returned to the kitchen and found Sheila still sat at the table.

"Have you phoned the police yet?" she mumbled.

"No time for that," I replied, "we need to get out of here. And right away," I added.

She looked confused.

"But my dad," she cried, "we can't just leave him here, we need to tell someone."

I'm not a bully by nature, no matter what the bitch of an ex-wife might have claimed, but right then I wasn't having any argument and I realised that she was in no fit state to listen to reason.

"Sheila," I snapped back at her, "the people who killed your dad might now be looking for you. The first thing I need to do is get you away from here to somewhere safe. Whoever killed your dad," and I didn't mention I suspected Jackie Dewar, "needed information from your dad and they might suspect that you now have that information. Do you understand? You might be in danger."

I decided to play the emotional card again and, taking her chin in my hand I stared into her tear-ridden eyes.

"Look, love, your dad obviously loved you and wouldn't want any harm to come to you. He'd only want what's best for you, for you to be safe. Okay?"

She nodded, but clearly felt guilty about leaving her father lying dead in the front room.

I stepped back and took the glass she'd used, doused it under the tap and wiped it clean with a dishcloth and didn't forget the whisky bottle either.

"What you doing?" she asked, her face betraying her bewilderment.

"The police will receive an anonymous call later this afternoon," I told her "but we don't want them to know right away that we've been here, so I'm cleaning my prints off what I've touched."

"What about my prints?"

"They'll expect to find yours here because, after all you visited your dad here, didn't you?"

She nodded and stood up, swaying slightly as the whisky I'd made her swallow kicked in. Obviously not much of a drinker, I thought. Her face turned a pallid colour and I knew then she was about to throw up.

I steered her into the small, but serviceable bathroom off the kitchen and held her hair back from her face as she vomited into the enamel bowl, her body wracked by the heaving spasms.

"Sorry," she muttered in apology as I wiped her face with a wet facecloth.

Making sure I wiped down enamel bowl and handle I'd touched, I supported her into the hallway towards the front door, pleased I'd had the good sense to close the door where her father lay. She hesitated and then, as if coming to a decision, lifted her head and shrugged me off, then swayed slightly to the door.

"Wait," I told her and checked that the street outside was empty, but of course there was no way of telling if anyone was watching from behind curtains. That was something I'd just have to chance. At the driver's door, I took the car keys from her hand.

"You've been drinking," I half smiled at her, but she realised anyway she was in no fit state to drive.

It had been quite a while since I'd driven a manual car, but once learned, never forgotten. The problem wasn't with the gears; I worried that my gammy left leg might not be good enough to operate the clutch. No option, I decided, let's find out.

After crunching the gears half a dozen teeth-grinding times, I got the hang of it and once on the main roads, it got that bit easier.

Sheila sat silent and still in shock, her head turned away from me as she stared unseeingly out of the passenger window.

"You know something," she finally said, her voice breaking with accusation. "You know who did this."

I knew she was again about to cry and decided to tell her the truth. But for the moment, it would have to wait. First, I had to get her somewhere safe. My place was definitely out of the question. Dewar already knew where I lived. It would need to be somewhere she couldn't be found.

I asked if she'd any close friends and it turned out she'd a boyfriend and being such a beauty, why it never occurred to me there would be at least a couple of young guys pursuing her, I don't know. Turned out her and Gavin McPherson had been an item for almost one and a half years.

She directed me to drive to the west end of the city and finally to Cowan Street, a small thoroughfare that connects the parallel Bank Street and Otago Street, not far from Glasgow University. At her direction, I parked in a resident's bay and she produced a permit from the glove box.

"Gavin's a lecturer at the Uni," she explained, "and sometimes I stay over."

"Is he at home now?"

"Should be, but no matter. I've got a key."

I locked the Mini and handed her the key, then followed her into the tenement. Like me, Gavin lived in a ground floor flat and almost immediately answered Shelia's knock on the door. I guessed he'd seen us arrive through his large, front room window.

Taller than me by about three inches, he was probably in his late twenties, had a
shock of fair hair, wispy fair beard and wore thick lens glasses. He was dressed in
a faded and well-worn Scotland rugby top and shocking pink Bermuda shorts with
palm trees and leather sandals on his feet. Did I mention he was built like the side
of an outhouse?

He reached forward to give her a peck on the cheek, all the while staring curiously
at me, then stood aside to let us through the door.

Maybe it was the aftershock, maybe it was just the sight of him, I really don't
know, but Sheila threw her arms around his neck and burst into tears. The big guy
was dumbstruck, but simply stood and held her, all the time saying nothing, but
staring at me. Self-consciously, I half nodded and walked past him to the front
room and gingerly sat on the stressed leather settee, conscious the unaccustomed
activity with the Mini's clutch pedal had brought about more than a little pain in
my gammy leg.

The room, I decided, was almost as bad as mine, with books piled everywhere.
Most of them seemed to be about social science. A few minutes later, Gavin came
into the room, alone.

"Sheila's just freshening up," he explained, "Mister, eh?"

I tried to stand, but the stick was a give away, so he waved me back down and
reached out his hand.

"John Logan," I introduced myself from my sitting position, while trying not to
grimace at his powerful handshake. He exhaled and had obviously decided to wait
for Sheila to return before asking for any kind of explanation. That gave him time
to ask if I wanted coffee.

By the time Sheila returned to the room and sat beside her boyfriend, her face red
from having scrubbed her tears away, Gavin had produced three coffees in
matching white mugs that sat on the low wooden table in front of us.

I'd already learned from Sheila that she trusted Gavin, that I could tell him
anything relating to the time her stepmother had hired me through to the finding
of her father's body this morning. I didn't bother about minor details such as the
flirtatious Mrs Kilbride being a drunk and a con artist. But I didn't know him and
that meant I didn't trust him, so I was as concise and formal in my recounting of
the story as I could be.

"And the police are unaware that Martin's been murdered?" he asked, sounding
aghast.

"Not yet."

"So, who does know, about Martin I mean?"

"Four people know," I replied, "the killer, Sheila, me and now you."

I could see his mind working overtime and likely the question at the forefront of it
was, did this knowledge in some way implicate him? You'll know by now that I'm
not any kind of expert in human relationships, after all with my marital failure,
how could I be? But as I stared at him and Sheila in turn, my guess was that
Sheila Kilbride was more in love with Gavin than he was with her.

"I need Sheila to be safe, till I try and work this out," I pressed him, "will you be able to keep her here until I can work out some sort of strategy?"

"Of course," he replied, reaching out to pull her towards him, and holding her hand, "Nobody need know that she's here."

Then he asked, "When do you propose to inform the police about Martin's murder?"

"Probably some time this evening. I'll make a call to the local force in Stirling, anonymous of course. That'll set in motion a murder inquiry and the local guys will then contact the cops here in the city for the purpose of establishing background details. I'm guessing that the Stirling cops will keep the inquiry, but might use the local guys here to track down family and friends, business colleagues, anyone who has had recent contact with Martin. They'll obviously look first for a motive and that'll mean they'll backtrack from the time that he was reported missing. I'll be roped in, having been hired to find him, so can expect a visit and will be interviewed to provide a statement and an alibi."

"An alibi," he interrupted, "does that mean you might be a suspect?"

"Everybody's a suspect to begin with," I replied, "until they're proven to be no longer of interest. Thereafter the inquiry will be collecting statements and putting together a picture of his movements and, more importantly, who knew of the cottage and who recently visited it."

I saw his face turn ashen and he turned to Sheila.

"You and I," be blurted out, "we were there just a few weeks ago."

He turned to me.

"Does this mean I might be interviewed too, as a possible suspect?"

Ever so slightly, I saw Sheila draw away from him, her hands now in her lap and I guessed that maybe she was seeing a side of Gavin that she hadn't previously suspected. I felt sorry for the young woman. She hadn't just lost her dad today, but I figured she was about to give her boyfriend the heave-ho, too. Her day was just getting worse. In reply to his question, I shrugged my shoulders.

"The police will fingerprint the whole house and any fingerprints they lift will be used to identify, interview and either obtain a suspect or eliminate those persons whose fingerprints they've got on record. Those they can't identify, they'll try to track down as either suspects or, as I said, for elimination purpose. If the police have your fingerprints on file, they might knock on your door to interview you, or alternatively, you can contact them and offer your statement rather than have them track you down."

He seemed to consider my suggestion, and then asked me, "What would you advise?"

A nagging thought struck me.

"Have they got your prints on record?"

He had the good grace to look sheepish and half turned towards Sheila, apologetically telling her about a party, then the drugs bust, all before he met her, he insisted. "Just a group of friends on the campus," he continued. "A little bit of pot, nothing major. But someone in the group had some charlie, a couple of grams

…so we all got charged with possession, but luckily, I only got fined. The thing is, I didn't declare it on my application to work here, at the Uni. You must see the position this puts me in?'"

From the corner of my eye, I could see Sheila shaking her head, then abruptly, she stood up and reaching over, handed me her car key.

"Mister Logan," she said in a deathly calm voice, "could please wait for me in the car?"

I glanced at Gavin who, taken by surprise, had also stood. I pushed awkwardly up from the low settee and without a word, walked out of the flat and across the road to the Mini and got into the driver's seat. A couple of minutes passed, then I watched as Sheila dragged open the tenement front door and hurriedly walked across to the car.

Gavin stood at the door, mouthing something, but I couldn't hear what he said. Sheila got in, angrily slammed the door and said "Drive please."

I started the car and drove off, turning right into the one-way system on Bank Street, then almost immediately stopped and parked across two empty bays.

"So, anywhere else you might feel safe?"

Her head down, I could see she was quietly weeping. Shit, I angrily thought, what the fuck do I do now?

I watched as she reached across for the parking permit and snatched it from the dashboard, before ripping it into little pieces.

"Well, I'll have no further need for that," she snarled through her tears.

Then it struck me. Hide in plain sight. I smiled at her and started the car.

You might wonder what I'd planned and to be honest, I cursed myself for not thinking of it sooner. The one thing I gambled that Sheila Kilbride was bound to have in her purse was the very thing currently denied me.

A bank Visa card.

I drove the Mini to the Tesco superstore in Anniesland and walked with her through the store as she bought the bare essentials for a woman who would be out of the house for a few days. Toiletries, a couple of changes of underwear, a cheap, but practical change of clothes, some magazines and a small, travel holdall to carry her purchases. Those paid for, I then drove the Mini to the Hilton Hotel near to Charing Cross and told her to book into the hotel for at least two nights, not to worry about using her own name because if she was paying by Visa, it would seem odd using a false name and paying with her own credit card. While she booked her room, I parked her car in the underground car park, then met with Sheila in the foyer to return her keys.

"Will I be safe here?" she anxiously asked.

"Jackie Dewar has a lot of influence in the city and quite a few people owe him favours," I replied, "but even he can't watch everywhere. The guy in charge of security here is an ex-cop, Peasy Byrne, a former detective officer and all round good guy. I've had a word and told him that your ex-boyfriend has threatened you.

I'd suggested you hide out here for a couple of days till the boyfriend cools down, so not only will the reception desk be monitoring any callers that might ask for you, but Peasy will be keeping an eye on you, too."

I wasn't comfortable lying to Peasy, a former colleague from divisional CID days and one of the few who didn't condemn me, but I didn't wish to put Peasy in a situation where he might feel duty bound to contact the inquiry team, when Martin Kilbride's murder becomes public. I gave him my house and office number and asked that he contact me if anyone asked for Sheila or anything that struck him as suspicious.

"I can't believe I'm hungry," she said to me, "can we eat here? My treat."

I would have preferred hitting the bar because my leg continued to badly ache, but agreed that some food might be in order.

I hadn't realised it was now early evening.

After dinner, I walked her to the lift in the hotel foyer and gave her a paper napkin that I'd scribbled my mobile, home and office numbers onto.

"You'll make the call, to the police, I mean? I don't want my dad lying there too long," she said, tears forming in her eyes.

I promised her I'd make the call as soon as I returned home, then made her promise that no matter who it is, on no account was she to phone anyone and disclose where she is, not even to answer incoming calls unless it was from one of my three numbers.

She nodded and made her lonely way into the lift.

Using some of the cash Jackie Dewar had flipped at me, I caught a taxi to my office.

CHAPTER 9

I told the taxi driver to drop me off at the corner in Osborne Street and watched in the fading light for a few minutes for any sign of Dewar's team and then, satisfied that the surrounding area was clear, limped over to the Focus. Driving home, I tried to shake off the image of the dead Martin Kilbride and then it struck me. He had no facial injuries, nothing that suggested a beating. To be perfectly clinical about it, just a straightforward bashing to the back of the head. Nothing in the room suggested a struggle. His face in death had seemed surprised, as though the assault was completely unsuspected.

Yes, I know what you're thinking, of course it was bloody unsuspected, but what I'm trying to say is that Kilbride apparently didn't consider that the person who murdered him intended to do him harm, he didn't consider his killer to be a threat! Of course, I smacked the steering wheel with the palm of my hand, my mind racing.

Not for one minute did I believe that Jackie Dewar would not have exacted some sort of revenge on Kilbride for stiffing him for the money. Even if Kilbride had willingly and without protest, surrendered the account details that would have led to the money, that sadistic little prick Dewar would still have taken pleasure in either himself or Scorcher Lamond working Kilbride over.

Yet there was no trace of that, nothing. No bruising, no broken face bones, no fractured limbs. Nothing.

Someone else killed Kilbride, someone that he trusted, of that I was now certain. I also theorised that unless Kilbride had contacted his killer and revealed where he was, and I doubted that theory, then the killer knew where to find him. That begged the question, who else had known of the address, other than Sheila, her very recent and former boyfriend Gavin McPherson and of course, the scheming Missus Kilbride herself, Phyllis the Vamp as I had come to think of her.

All I had to do now was figure out whom, why and for what?

I'd remembered earlier that morning to call the tenement factor and was pleased to see he'd replaced the close light bulb. Then again, it probably helped reminding him that as I was disabled and lied that he'd be in contravention of the Disability Act if he didn't get it sorted.

I boiled the kettle for a coffee and considered a couple of Co-codomol, but a picture of Alex Haldane popped into my mind and I resisted. It wasn't an easy decision, I have to admit, but I gritted my teeth and sat down with the coffee and prepared in my head to make the call to the police at Stirling, the call that would inform them of a dead man in Gargunnock.

I thought about the call first and knew from experience that my call would go through to a switchboard that would likely have a Call Related Data system, whereby they could trace the number calling them. I decided that instead, I'd pick a more rural station and pass the message that way, guessing such a station would have a landline only and no fancy switchboard. My laptop provided all the station phone numbers around the Stirling area and I picked one at random. At the risk of boring you, I dialled the 1471 number to prevent call-back, then the police number of a suburb station in the outskirts of Stirling.

A world-weary sounding female voice answered and once more using my falsetto Edinburgh accent, I quickly told her to get pen and paper and then informed her that if the police cared to call at the address in Stark Street, Gargunnock, they'd find a murdered man.

"Is this a joke?" she sharply retorted.

"No joke love, so over to you," and hung up on her.

I breathed a sigh of relief that it was done and sipped at my coffee. The woman, I guessed, would be thinking that indeed it was a joke, but protocol would kick in and shed probably pass the message to the divisional control room who, in turn would action a patrol car to investigate the address.

Alex Haldane. Shit! I was supposed to attend my third continuity meeting this evening, but that was over two hours ago.

Ah well, couldn't be helped, I sighed, surprising myself at my own disappointment.

I thought about Jackie Dewar and wondered what his reaction would be when it became common knowledge that Martin Kilbride had been found murdered. No Kilbride, no account details. No account details, no payment for the shipment of cocaine. And of course, I reflected, Dewar wasn't to know that the account details Kilbride had or was supposed to have, were useless, that the money had already been diverted to God knew where.

Talk about a can of worms.

Problem was, what was Dewar expecting from me and what would be his reaction when he learned Kilbride was dead.

Unconsciously, I stroked my good right leg.

Dewar obviously believed that Kilbride had stolen the money himself, so would he think Kilbride had passed on the details of where the money was to be had, maybe to his wife or daughter? Would they both now be at risk?

I might sound to you to be hard hearted, but frankly I couldn't give a flying rat's arse if Dewar visited Phyllis Kilbride. That was her lookout, but his daughter Sheila. That was another story. Sheila Kilbride was undoubtedly innocently unaware of her father's shenanigans and, call it old fashioned chivalry or what you will, no way was I letting that bastard get his hands on her. I knew that Sheila Kilbride trusted her father, believed what he had told her, but I also guessed what he had told her was a partial lie. I didn't doubt for a heartbeat that Martin Kilbride knew exactly what kind of business Dewar was involved in and was complicit with Dewar in hiding the proceeds of his drug running business, what the police these days call an OCE, an organised criminal enterprise. Problem was, how deeply involved had Kilbride been?

Thinking more of it, I realised that with the apparent money involved, if what Kilbride told his daughter was correct, he must have kept records of transactions, companies or businesses where the money was laundered and likely, in this age of technology, on a computer somewhere. In short, a money trail. I knew that such information would be of extreme interest to the police, who for a number of years have unsuccessfully tried to close Dewar down. And if the police could connect Dewar to the transactions, it might even lead to a prosecution.

The obvious place to try and find these transactions would of course be Kilbride's place of work, the supposed reputable accountancy firm of Boyle and Spencer, but I remembered the cool and aloof Alison Carlisle, the office manager who had fobbed me off when I last called there and knew there was no way she'd entertain a visit from me. I wondered if I could persuade Sheila to try her luck as the grieving daughter, see if she could somehow get into her father's office. No telling what she might find there, I thought. The only hiccup in my plan was that if everything is on computer file, she'd need passwords and there is no way that I could think of round that problem.

The front door knocked and surprised, I involuntarily knocked against the table, almost spilling my now cooled coffee. I glanced at the clock and saw it was almost eight o'clock.

Dry mouthed, I stumbled to the door and reached for the pickaxe handle I kept behind the coat rack and peered through the spy hole.

It wasn't as I feared, Dewar and his sidekick, but Alex Haldane. I watched as she reached again to knock on the door.

I took a deep breath, replaced the pickaxe handle and opened the door.

"Alex, what a surprise. Come in, please," I smiled through tight lips, standing aside to let her enter. Mentally, I cursed my luck, knowing the front room looked like a bombsite and I dreaded to think what state the toilet was in.

Dressed in a knee length, green coloured waxed coat, her hair bundled under a mans tweed cap and hands thrust into the coat pockets, I smelled a faint wisp of scent as she brushed past me, also seeing she wore lipstick. She turned expectantly and I pointed to the front room.

"Bit of a surprise," I said, the curiosity probably evident on my face.

She stood in the middle of the room and I saw her glancing at the table where my mug sat and then I knew.

"I was a bit concerned when you didn't show tonight," she began, her hesitation evident.

"You thought I might be on a painkilling, drunken binge," I grinned at her.

"Something like that," she smiled in return and did I detect some relief in her voice?

"Coffee?"

"Eh, yes, please. Just milk," she replied and took off her cap, shaking her hair that fell to her shoulders.

"Take your coat off, sit down," I invited her and went into the kitchen to boil the kettle, silently praying she didn't want to use my bathroom.

"Can I use your bathroom?" she called out to me.

Bugger. Why is it women always need to look in a mirror when they arrive somewhere?

I spooned coffee into two fresh mugs and when the kettle had boiled, returned to find her sitting on the couch, her hands in her lap and placed the mugs on the table.

"Live alone then, John?"

"That obvious, eh?"

"There is some advantage I suppose. Try being my age and living with your mother," she replied.

An awkward silence fell, then she said "I should explain, why I'm here, I mean. It's just that Julia Goodman has sort of made me responsible for you. Kind of made me feel that your success depends on my support. When you didn't show tonight, I worried that maybe the last two sessions had been too much for you, baring your soul like you did and sharing your problems with me. I thought maybe I'd pushed you too far, that perhaps you weren't as ready to talk as I had thought. I didn't want you to give up, didn't want you to think that I'd pressured you. I had to just make sure you were okay."

She paused and run her tongue over her upper lip.

I grinned at her.

"What?" she smiled at me.

"When you're nervous, you do that," I pointed at her mouth, "run your tongue round your upper lip."

"I do not," she laughed, a little self-consciously.

"Yes, you do," and laughed with her.

She sipped at her coffee.

"So," I asked her, "is this a common occurrence, making house calls?"

"Only when the client deserves it," she replied.

No answer to that one, I thought.

"I took four Co-codomol this morning," I admitted. Right out of the blue, I confessed and somehow felt a little better for it.

"Anything since?"

I shook my head. "No tablets, no booze and yes, to be absolutely frank, I could use some of both right now but," I stared at her, "your face kept popping into my mind and made me feel guilty."

"I don't know whether that's a backhanded compliment or an accusation," she softly laughed.

To my surprise, state of the flat aside, I was pleased Alex had called by and was starting to relax when again, the front door knocked.

Peering through the spy hole with some apprehension, the last person I expected to see was detective Helen Burns and a small, redheaded uniformed female cop. I opened the door and she pushed past me and walked into the front room. I stumbled after her, followed by the cop and saw Alex had gotten to her feet, her face showing surprise at the obviously irate woman bursting through the door.

"Who's this?" demanded Burns.

"Hold on a minute," I replied, "you can't just barge into my flat like this. What the...."

"I take it you're not Sheila Kilbride," Burns said, staring at Alex, "so I'll ask again, who are you?"

Alex, puzzled, glanced at me.

"John?"

"Her name is Alex Haldane," I explained, "she's a friend. Now what the hell do you..."

"So tell me, Mister Logan," Burns interrupted and turned, her eyes boring into me, "what do you know about the murder in Gargunnock of Martin Kilbride?"

And that's how I find myself, handcuffed to the front and sitting in the rear of a marked police car beside the female cop, her male partner driving and Helen Burns in the front passenger seat. I couldn't imagine what Alex Haldane must've thought, recalling her stunned expression. I had of course no option but to leave her there, in my flat and without explanation because no way was I saying anything to Helen Burns, not till I learned exactly what she knew. I also realised that from what she'd said in the flat, she'd not found Sheila Kilbride.

I remembered what old Mister Zao had told me a few days previously, that there was a police leak, that somebody was providing Zao with information and that's how he was able to give me Billy Crawford's address. I also remembered that Mickey Farrell had told me that somebody, presumably working for Dewar, had liberated a kilo of cocaine from a supposedly secure police evidence room. No, the police leaked like a sieve and I wasn't telling. No way.

"Where we going?" I asked.

Burns turned and faced me. Her eyes betrayed their scorn and distaste.

"Baird Street police office, where if you screw the nut and answer the questions correctly, you just might be able to cut a deal."

"Why the handcuffs?" I held my arms up.

She smiled, but not in a nice way, believe me. More sinister is how I'd describe it. "Because, Mister Logan, you've quite a reputation for hitting women so I couldn't take any chances now, could I?"

I sank back in my seat, aware that policewoman beside me had turned and was staring at me. Great, I thought, all I need to do is fart in the wrong direction and this wee toe rag will set about me in the back of the car. We turned into the rear yard at Baird Street and into a parking bay. I waited till the policewoman got out her side and opened my door.

What I didn't expect was to be grabbed by the collar and physically hauled out and unceremoniously dumped onto the wet concrete.

"Sorry, Helen," I heard the cop smirk, "he was resisting."

I didn't complain, there was no point. Burns statement in the car made it clear that as a wife-beater I was fair game for any fly punches or kicks.

The male cop, I was pleased to hear, didn't hold with what his smaller partner did and hauling me to my feet, he dusted me down and without comment about his partners actions, led me through the security door and into the charge bar.

Now, surprise surprise, but who should I find waiting there for me but my old chum, DS Eddie Coleman. There was evil anticipation in his eyes and without a word he walked off. But I knew I'd be seeing him later.

Burns and her uniform pals processed me with the duty Inspector as a detained person, allowing them six hours to question me, and then I was led along the familiar corridor to an interview room. Coleman had taken off his jacket and sat behind the desk, notepad in front of him and beckoned me to sit.

Burns thanked and dismissed the cops and closed the room door, then sat in the third chair, behind me.

"Funny how things always seem to turn about, eh Logan?" he began.

I glanced at the dual tape recording machines, but neither was switched on. I didn't like this and figured whatever I said might not be how it was written down. Let's face it, the police have in the past been accused of telling porky pies. That's why tape recording was introduced.

"Don't know when you joined Coleman, but these days I'm entitled to a lawyer. Just as the Inspector noted in his computer at the charge bar, so maybe you should wait, eh?"

He smiled, an action that made him look even menacing than he was.

"This time of night? Now, where would we find a duty lawyer," he sneered.

"Aye, that's right, I forgot," I sneered right back, pretending to be braver than I really am, "you never really got to grips with learning the law did you, you ugly bastard."

His face turned white at the jibe and his fists clenched. I decided to hit home and taunt the bastard again. You might ask why, but it was just perverse pleasure on my part. I really don't like Coleman.

"Look," I showed him my handcuffed hands, "'this is usually how you interrogate your prisoners isn't it you cowardly shit. Fancy your chances do you?" and made to stand, but Burns was on her feet and forcibly shoved me back down into my chair.

"Logan!" she tried to warn me and to be honest, I should have listened.

"This is how you like your prisoners isn't it, Coleman? Unable to fight back. Just like the wee lassies that you're so keen on fondling."

That did it. That sent him over the edge. With a wild shriek, he lunged across the table at me and even though I was expecting it, he still managed to hook me to the left jaw with his right fist. I fell backwards, taking the chair with me and leaving him spread-eagled across the table, screaming abuse and scrambling with both hands to grab at me.

Jesus, I thought, he's really lost it!

From my position, lying with my back on the fallen chair, tasting blood in my mouth and looking upwards at the ceiling, I saw Burns hit the panic alarm bar on the wall and then step over me to grab at Coleman.

"Eddie! Eddie!" she was shouting at him, "Cool it, for fuck sake, calm down!"

The door crashed open, but the way I was lying, it smacked into the back of my head with such force that I was immediately dazed and right then, all I did was want to go to sleep.

I came to, I'm guessing, maybe ten minutes later, lying on my back in what I recognised as the medical room. Burns hovered over the top of me, anxiety etched on her face. The duty Inspector stood behind her, equally anxious and I supposed he was worried that any injury to a prisoner or detained person while in custody and when he was in charge, might reflect badly on him. The only consolation was I was no longer wearing the metal bracelets.

"Logan," Burns asked, "how do you feel?"

Not one to miss an opportunity, I replied, "How do you think I feel, having been belted in the mouth and then battered by a door?"

Burns, her back to the Inspector, gave a sharp intake of breath and slowly closed her eyes and I knew right then that she'd not mentioned Coleman using me as a punch bag. I managed to turn my body and sit on the examination bed, slightly dizzy, my legs dangling over the side and raised my hand to examine the back of my head. I winced as I touched a lump, but thankfully, no bleeding.

"I want to see both you and Coleman when you're done here, DC Burns," hissed the Inspector and left the room.

"Thanks a fucking bunch," she snarled at me.

"What, I get punched by that pervert, you call the cavalry who knock me unconscious and I'm the bad guy?"

"You wouldn't have been hurt if you hadn't wound the bastard up!"

"And I wouldn't have needed to if you'd interviewed me in my flat instead of dragging me across the city to this shitehole!"

"It's your own fault for not getting in touch with me, for not keeping me in the loop!" she hissed back at me.

"I would have done if you'd given me the chance to get things sorted before you got on your high horse and dragged me here!" I shouted back at her.

Then, to my utter surprise, she grinned at me, folding her arms and leaning back on the wall.

"Fondling wee lassies? Where did that come from? I know he's a bit of a letch, but wee girls? I haven't heard that one before."

The dizziness began fading and God, what I'd give for a strong painkiller, but on this occasion for my head, not my leg.

"Have you not wondered why he's been passed over all these years for promotion?" I sighed. "Couple of years ago, back when I was divisional CID, two uniforms working in the Blythswood Square area in the Central division walked into a lane and found Coleman with a wee drunk, teenage girl. Her jumper was up, her bra undone, her tits out and he was fondling her. The cops thought it was a prostitute and her customer, until the wee lassie said here's two of your pals. That got them curious. Seems Coleman had told the lassie he was a cop searching for offensive weapons and that he suspected she had a knife in her bra."

"She believed that?" replied a doubtful Burns.

"She was drunk and said that he'd flashed his warrant card. I wasn't there, but that's how the story goes. And we both know that being a cop doesn't mean that you can't be a pervert too."

"Oh aye," she replied with feeling, "I've met one or two of those in the recent past."

"So DC Burns. Martin Kilbride's murder. What do you want to know?"

We returned to the interview room together, but fortunately this time, without Eddie Coleman. Burns sat opposite me taking notes as I recounted the events from when Sheila Kilbride visited my office, but inserted a little lie, claiming that Sheila had told me about the cottage at Gargunnock rather than admitting that I'd worked it out from what Phyllis Kilbride had said. I didn't want Burns thinking that I'd known about Kilbride's location when I'd last spoken with her and Coleman, at Kilbride's home, figuring she might not be as sociable as she is now.

I also admitted that it was me that had phoned the local cops to report the murder, but somehow I guessed that Burns already knew this.

She pressed me for the whereabouts of Sheila, but I emphatically refused to tell her, knowing that she couldn't coerce or threaten me with the law. I wasn't holding out on a killer, just a prospective witness.

Now it was my turn to ask a few questions and reminding Burns that I had the opportunity to make a formal complaint about my treatment, suggested it might be prudent to consider answering them. With ill concealed grace, she admitted that when the call had arrived from the Stirling police about Martin Kilbride's murder, they'd already had her details as the officer in the missing person inquiry. She'd not had the call but five minutes when Sheila's former squeeze Gavin McPherson had phoned in from his home and decided to tell all.

"Not a guy I'd like to go for a drink with," she commented. "He couldn't fire you and Kilbride's daughter in fast enough. Made her out to be a heartless wee cow, leaving her dead father lying in a pool of blood. Said he'd dumped her straight away then begged me to keep his name out of any murder investigation because he didn't want his employers at the Uni knowing he'd been mixed up in such a sordid incident. Then," she shook her head, "had the bloody nerve to ask me if there might be a reward from Crimestoppers for his information."

"Anything else I should know?" she cocked her head to one side and stared at me.

I was tempted then, really tempted, to tell her about the connection between Kilbride and Jackie Dewar, but the murder inquiry was really the Stirling cops responsibility. If anyone should be told about the Kilbride-Dewar partnership, it should be Mickey Farrell.

I stared back at her and lied to her face.

"No, nothing comes to mind right now."

And just then, as my luck has it, the door knocks and once again, my world goes apeshit.

CHAPTER 10

"Well, well, well," said Mickey Farrell, his bulk taking up most of the doorway, "what kind of bother have you got yourself into this time, Logan?"

"You are?" said Burns in her icy, coldest voice.

"This is DI Michael Farrell, drug squad. DC Helen Burns," I introduced them like some kind of social secretary.

"How is it going, doll?" asked Mickey, whom you'll have gathered was not the first signatory to the political correctness charter.

Burns turned ashen and I thought she was about to explode, but retained her temper and asked, "Can I help you sir?"

Mickey shut the door behind him and grabbed the third chair, turning it round to sit cowboy style.

"You're the lassie dealing with the MP Martin Kilbride that got himself murdered over by Stirling?"

Burns warily nodded, not sure where this was going and likewise, but with a sinking feeling in my stomach, didn't know either.

"And this clown," he nodded to me, but continued to look at her, "has some knowledge of the murder?"

Again, Burns nodded then said, "Do you have an interest in the inquiry, sir?"

"Mickey, call me Mickey. Can I call you Helen?"

That took her aback and she stuttered, "Yes."

"Aye, well Helen, my old pal Logan here, you'll know he was a former drug squad man? And I good one too, I can tell you, until some bastard nearly shot his leg off. That's the gammy one there," he said unnecessarily, pointing at my left leg.

"Anyway, I digress. A few days ago, not having seen John here for quite a while, do I not get a surprise when he turns up at a location where I've got my team planted outside a targets gaff, down at the Riverside. They new apartments, you know the ones?"

Burns slowly nodded, her interest now peaked and I could see Mickey was getting into the story.

"The target was one William Crawford of this parish, a right scummy lowlife if ever there was one. Worked for a major player called Jackie Dewar. Do you know the name?"

Burns again nodded and I could see she was puzzled, as was I.

"Now, Logan here was working for a wee Chinaman, the landlord of his office, is that right John?" he turned towards me.

I nodded as he turned back towards Burns.

"Turns out the daughter of this wee Chinaman was shacked up with our Billy and the Chinaman didn't like his daughter getting shagged by a lowlife drug dealer. Good looking wee lassie, too. Her father must've been in the horrors knowing what his daughter was up to," he said, shaking his head. "Anyway, when our John here drives past the location, his car looks out of place and the registration number is recorded on the surveillance log. But turns out one of my boys recognises John and tips me the wink, so in the spirit of comradeship and not wanting my good friend to get caught up in the shite I work with, I delete the number from the log. Kind of hang my balls out for somebody to kick them, if you pardon the expression."

I have to say that Mickey was getting a bit vocal at this point and I had a sudden feeling that maybe I should have visited the loo a while back.

"I even visit John, bring him a fish supper and a couple of cans and have a wee social evening with him, don't I old son?"

Miserably, because I know this isn't going to end well, I agree.

"Now, Helen, you must be asking yourself, where is all this leading to?"

"I am getting a bit confused and wondering how it's connected to my MP, sir…I mean Mickey."

"Right, where were we? Oh aye, so there I am this evening at the squad office, reading the printout from the Stirling cops about the murder of a Martin Kilbride who frankly, at this point means nothing to me, and the forensic attachment that details the injuries to his head, presumably from some type of carpenters claw hammer. The printout identifies Kilbride as an MP from Kirkintilloch and you Helen, as the inquiry officer. Still, so far nothing to do with me," he raises his hands into the surrender position. "Then less that an hour later, lo and behold, the daughter of the wee Chinaman, you remember her don't you Helen," he asks with feeling, "phones 999 and screams that she needs the police. The cops arrive in a blue light hurry and my guys that are staked out nearby, follow them into the flat to find the wee Chinese girl hysterical and Billy Crawford lying face down, his head caved in at the back with what seems to have been, you've guessed it," he grinned humourlessly, "a carpenters fucking claw hammer!"

He stopped to draw breath and yes, I definitely needed to go to the loo.

"So, I'm thinking, because being a fucking Detective Inspector," he roared at me. "That's what I get paid to do!"

He takes a deep breath and calm now, continues. "This guy Kilbride from Kirkintilloch, murdered with a claw hammer. The very next day, my target Billy Crawford, murdered with a claw hammer. Now being me, I think that's really coincidental, so I go back and fetch the printout from the Stirling cops, get your name Helen and decide to give you a phone, just in the off-chance that the cases are connected. But when I call the office here, you're not immediately available and why? Because," he turned and stared at me, "you're interviewing a suspect for the Kilbride murder, a John Logan from Minard Road. My fucking pal! The same pal that I covered for when he drove by the now recently murdered Billy Crawford's place!"

Slowly, I lowered my head and covered my ears with my hands.

"What do you think, Helen?" he asked, "That it's a coincidence or do you think John here might have something to tell us?"

I raised my head and stared at them in turn.

"You might want to send out for fish suppers," I said. "We might be here for a while yet."

I know that you'll be aware of the old saying, like caught between a rock and a hard place or from the frying pan into the fire or even back to the wall. None of these describe how I felt right then. Staring at Mickey and Burns in turn, I knew I'd no option but to give up everything I knew. Well, nearly everything because sick or not with worry, I wasn't handing over Sheila Kilbride to anybody, not even my old pal Mickey. Him I trusted, but I didn't know who in his squad he'd task to get Sheila protected and I didn't forget also that it was someone connected with his squad who had stolen the seized kilo of charlie for Jackie Dewar. Oh, and one other item I neglected was Phyllis Kilbride's drunken attempt to bed me. I was in enough trouble and didn't need Mickey's humiliating sarcasm too.

So I began at the start, from the first phone call that set me on Martin Kilbride's trail, visiting Kilbride's office and being curtly sent away with a flea in my ear by the ice-cold Alison Carlisle, but finding Jackie Dewar and his sidekick Scorcher Lamond also visiting the office.

I interrupted my story to ask Burns if her pal in the Fraud Squad had discovered any paper trail link between Dewar and Kilbride?

"No," she replied with a shake of her head, "but you have to remember that if she made any inquiry other than using her contacts in the financial and business sectors, to probe deeper she'd have to consider applying for a warrant and without being able to provide the evidence to justify the issue of a warrant, she's on a loser right away. So the short answer again is no, nothing that she could dig up."

I continued with my finding Kilbride's car burned out and that, I saw, provoked a disapproving glance from Burns. Then I admitted learning from Phyllis Kilbride and not Sheila, as I'd earlier told Burns, of a house in Gargunnock where he might be hiding out. That earned me a scowl this time. I also included the nocturnal visit from Dewar and Lamond and the minor beating I'd taken and included the threat of what would occur if I didn't locate Kilbride. As I recounted the story, I saw Mickey's fists tighten and was a bit heartened, imagining what he'd like to have done to the pair for beating his crippled mate. So maybe he hadn't completely fallen out with me I hoped. Really, really hoped because let's face it, I've so few friends left I can't afford to be losing another one.

With some reluctance, I admitted that Dewar offered me ten grand to find Kilbride, hoping they'd believe that a good guy like me wouldn't stoop to such depths. It didn't escape me that neither made any comment nor agreed that indeed, I was a good guy. I continued and related the meeting with Sheila Kilbride, our trip and arrangement to meet with her father and the gruesome discovery of his body. I could see they were both keenly interested in my description of the murder scene, grisly though it was and expressed professional curiosity in my actions.

Mickey nodded in approval that I hadn't apparently contaminated the locus too much, but still of course believed I should have called it in right away.

"Tell me, Crawford. Was he lying face down? Battered on the back of the head, you said?"

Mickey nodded. "Yeah, why?"

"So presumably he'd turned his back to his killer?"

"Again, yeah, I suppose so," he shrugged his shoulders.

"Which might indicate Crawford knew his killer, didn't think he was in any danger or felt threatened. And was the murder weapon there or had it been wiped and is missing?"

"No hammer, assuming the forensic boys are correct. Bloodstains on a tea towel, from the kitchen," Mickey's eyebrows turned up, realisation dawning. "I'm guessing that's how you discovered Martin Kilbride?"

Time passed and I fielded their questions, keeping as close to the truth as I dare.

"What about the wife," Burns slyly slipped the question in like a dagger between my ribs, "the spouse is usually red-hot favourite in most murders. What's your assessment of her, seeing that you've likely had the most contact with her," she coyly asked.

I realised that Burns is recalling the naked Phyllis at the door, hollering after me and probably suspected there was more to that visit than I was disclosing.

Mickey had a puzzled expression and his eyes narrowed; no doubt suspecting there might be more to what I'd already said about the foxy Phyllis Kilbride aka Phyllis the Vamp.

"I'm thinking Kilbride was her meal ticket. I don't believe she's a woman that can get to where she is on her own ability. From what I've gathered and what you discovered," I pointedly replied to Burns, "she's had a succession of men in her life and worked her way through and up the food chain. Had she been somehow involved in Kilbride's murder, it's likely she'd had kept a low profile, been happy to report him as a missing person to you guys and left it at that, let the normal turn of events occur and maintained her silence. And, at the right time, simply played the part of the grieving widow. Engaging me to find her husband was a step too far, if she was somehow involved in all of this. No, I can't be absolutely certain, but I don't figure Phyllis Kilbride to be involved."

"But let's face it, Logan," Burns replied, "hiring you to find her husband wasn't exactly like hiring one of the larger and more reputable private investigation firms with access to all sorts of resources. You're not exactly Magnum PI," she chortled.

Now, I have to admit, that stung. True, but still a kick in the balls, if you see what I mean.

"However," she nodded, "I have to agree with your assessment of her. From the little I had to do with her, I'd say she's cunning, manipulative and undoubtedly a user of men, but setting something like this up, taking on Jackie Dewar? No, I don't think she's got the capability. Unless of course she has a partner?"

"We can't rule that out," I agreed.

Finally, Mickey clasped his hands behind his head, leaned back in his chair with one leg crossed over the other and asked me for my take on the situation?

"Seems to me," I slowly began, knowing I'd have to recall all this if asked later, "that Kilbride worked for Dewar laundering his money, agreed?"

They both nodded.

"Billy Crawford, from what you told me," I glanced at Mickey, "brokered the cocaine arrangement while he was visiting Palma and has suggested the deal to Jackie Dewar. Dewar's obviously jumped at the chance of a large shipment and instructed Martin Kilbride to liquidate all his assets into cash at an off-shore account, such an account to be made readily available to pay for the cocaine. All the bold Jackie had to do was, in exchange for the cocaine, provide the account and password details to his supplier. But somewhere in-between this simple arrangement, the new account and password details were stolen from Kilbride and the money diverted to the thief's account."

"Fair enough," Mickey slowly nodded his head, "but what's the connection between Kilbride and Billy Crawford? I don't get that one."

I shook my head.

"The only mutual link between those two is Jackie Dewar," I replied, "but I don't think Dewar killed Kilbride" and explained why. "As for Billy Crawford, he'd likely be the contact between Dewar and the Columbians, so there's no reason to murder him. And as far as Kilbride's daughter Sheila is concerned," I added, "it's possible that Dewar might consider she has the account details from her father, so I'm not telling anyone where she is until you guys get this mess wrapped up."

I have to say, it sounded a lot tougher than I felt. Burns cocked her head and a smile played on her lips.

"You know that you're also the one connection between the two dead guys," she reminded me, "so who's to say the DI and I might not consider locking you up as the prime suspect?"

I swallowed and tried not to look nervous.

Mickey stared thoughtfully at me, then said, "Crawford was killed about five o'clock this evening. The wee Chinese girl was in the shower. He was supposed to be in the kitchen cooking dinner. She didn't hear a thing, apparently. Came out of the bathroom into the lounge and there he was, dead on the floor. Where were you at five this evening?"

I sighed with relief.

"With Sheila Kilbride, having dinner. She'll be able to alibi me for that time."

"Then tell us where to find her and we'll get a statement," Burns smoothly replied.

I grinned at her. "Only when you guys have got this thing sorted and I know she's safe."

"We might still lock you up for perverting the course of justice at the Kilbride murder or maybe even concealment of a body," she responded, "so why shouldn't we charge you?"

"Maybe because if I'm still out there and nosing about, I might have another visit from Mister Dewar and if we now presume he's aware Kilbride's dead, who knows what he might need me to do or tell me?"

"He might also take off your good leg, you stupid bastard," Mickey leaned forward, suddenly angry and I hoped, with some concern for my well-being.

"Risk I'll take," I replied with more bravado than common sense and turned to Mickey. "Old Zao's daughter, Tei Pai," I remembered, "where is she now?"

"Couldn't get much sense out of her," he replied, "so had the uniform take her to the Royal Infirmary. Shocked, she was and it seemed obvious she'd be of no use the state she was in. Thought it better to get her seen by a doctor. I've a uniform cop with her, trying to get a statement, but I don't think she'll be able to tell us much."

"Will you detain her?"

"Not much point," he shrugged, "we can always speak to her at another time."

"Would you mind if I gave her father a call, told him where to collect her?"

"Fuck me," he burst out, "you give us the run-around Logan and now you're looking for favours?"

"Oh, all right then," he conceded, "save me the trouble of having a cop staying with her."

"And that's it? We're just letting him go?" said Burns, very miffed indeed.

"What else do you what to do with the gimpy bastard," he replied, "and besides, he's right enough. If he's loose and on the street, Dewar might still have a use for him and," he stood, toweringly threateningly over me, "I'll be the first to know, won't I, me old pal?"

I weakly grinned and decided not to push my luck.

Burns returned me to the charge bar and asked the civilian support officer to fetch the Inspector.

"That other business," she began, "with Eddie Coleman. How do you want to handle it?"

I could see the challenge in her eyes, knowing that if I pushed it she'd have no option but to side with the twisted bastard, both of us aware that any allegation of assault would mean an investigation. It had been my experience that regardless of innocence or guilt, these things usually stick to a cop's record and can influence future promotion.

"Tell you what, give me a lift home and we'll call it quits," I replied.

The Inspector signed me out of the station with palpable relief on his face that I had no intention of making a formal complaint about my treatment. At one point, I actually thought he was going to shake my hand.

In the car, I took the opportunity to use my mobile and phoned old Zao, telling him his daughter could be collected at the Royal Infirmary and yes, she was fine, if a little shocked, adding that there would be a police officer who would wait till he arrived to ensure she was okay and no, she wasn't under arrest. Yes, I agreed, I'd see him tomorrow.

Burns drove for the most part in silence, but I could sense something was nagging at her. We turned onto Pollokshaws Road and she couldn't contain herself any longer.

"So, who was the woman when we arrived at your flat?"

"Alex?" I replied, my voice oozing innocence, "Just a friend."

At the back of my mind, just a tinkle of a thought, I wondered if there might have been a hint of the green goddess, Jealousy. Could it be possible, I briefly wondered, that Helen Burns had a wee fancy for me? Unconsciously, I shook my head, sneaking a glance at her profile.

My first meeting with her had impressed upon me that she was a good-looking woman, certainly younger than me by at least ten years, but I couldn't see the attraction that she might have for a guy like me. Not that I'm self-effacing, simply facing the fact that right at this time, my life is shit.

But, as I've said before, what do I know of women?

She stopped right outside the close and turning, with a half smile on her face, asked, "Should I walk you to the door?"

Now, this is where I got it really wrong.

"Why, do you want to come in for a drink?" I replied, my face and my voice expressing obvious surprise that she fancied me.

It was the stare that gave it away, the stare that seemed to suggest I needed certifying.

"No," she replied, "to protect you in case your pals are waiting for you with big sticks, you fucking idiot."

I'd forgotten, albeit briefly, about Dewar and his minder.

I admit being a little petulant when I declined her offer and she let me get out of the car, almost helpless with laughter at my stupidity, before driving off.

Sure enough, there was no reception party within the close, not that I expected anyone to be hanging around, given that it was almost two-thirty in the morning. Wearily, I let myself into the flat and still smarting from embarrassment at having so misread the situation with Burns, bad-temperedly banged the door behind me. I limped into the kitchen and found the note from Alex Haldane, beside the kettle. She apologised for not hanging about and was worried that I was okay, asking if I'd call her when I got home, no matter what time it was.

Something struck me as strange, then I realised the kitchen had been tidied, dishes washed and put away. I left the kettle boiling and found Alex had set about the front room too, all neat and shipshape. Seemed that she'd whiled the night away not just worrying about me, but doing a bit of domestic too. I read her note again and considered a phone call might waken her, so sent a text message instead.

To my surprise, I got a reply right away, telling me she was glad I was home safe and that if I wished, she'd see me tomorrow at six at the Centre.

I sat back on the couch and smiled, thinking it was nice that somebody worried about me and then made the mistake of closing my eyes, for just a minute or so I thought.

CHAPTER 11

The sun streamed through a crack in the curtains and I groaned, but not so much from my aching leg than the crick in my neck from having fallen asleep on the couch. Not forgetting too that my head still ached from being battered by the interview room door. My coffee lay cold and untouched on the table, but that didn't deter me from having a mouthful, if nothing for else to remove the taste of dried blood in my mouth that had resulted from Coleman's punch. All in all, I was in a sorry state.

Stiffly I made my way into the kitchen to boil the kettle before heading for the bathroom, my bladder urging me to hurry. Not an easy task when you're limping and staggering half asleep. My shoulders drooped. Seemed Alex had been in here too and I cringed a little, remembering the state it had been in prior to being hauled off by Burns and her petite, uniformed thug.

The kitchen clock said eight-twenty. My first thought was phoning Sheila

Kilbride and checking she was okay, but figured I'd leave it till nearer nine, give me time to get cleaned up and I'd call her before setting out for the office. Shaved and showered, I dressed in a clean, bottle green shirt, no tie, dark grey flannels and my black patent shoes. The weather seemed to be holding so I decided to risk it and wore my dark grey sports jacket.

I still had a few quid from Dewar's kind donation and decided to grab a couple of rolls for breakfast, from the dairy opposite the office.

Before leaving the flat I swithered on whether or not to pop some Co-codomol and decided on two, washed down with a glass of freezing cold water. Two, I figured, was better than four and a distinct improvement on the last few days.

I hadn't made it to the car when my mobile burst into life. The calling number, I saw, was withheld.

"Morning Johnny boy," said the familiar, sleazy voice, "pleased to hear the filth let you go."

I'm usually careful who has my mobile number and couldn't understand how Dewar had gotten hold of it, but I'd work that out later.

"How's it hanging, Jackie," I replied, trying to sound more confident than I actually was.

"I'm fine and dandy, Johnny boy and probably a lot better than those legs of yours. I'm hearing that you found my old mate Martin Kilbride, eh? Was it you that did for him I'm wondering, maybe trying to cut yourself a wee deal with me, eh? Maybe thinking that the information he had is now yours, that you could strike a bargain, eh? Is that it, Johnny boy? Trying to stitch up your old pal Jackie, eh?"

You know, normally I'm tolerant of people with speech defects and such like, but this habit he had of finishing a sentence with "eh" was really getting on my tits.

"Actually, it's you the cops are hunting Jackie. Seem to think that you killed Kilbride."

"Not me Johnny boy," he laughed, "I've got an alibi for the time he was killed, eh. Solid and irr…irfoot…ifr…"

"Irrefutable," I finished for him, "but tell me Jackie, how do you know when he was killed?"

That seemed to stump him and there was a definite pause before he replied.

"Just what I heard, eh, Johnny boy, just what I heard from a wee bird, eh?"

"Did this bird also tell you about Billy Crawford getting himself murdered?"

"And who is Billy Crawford," he smoothly replied, "and why should I be interested in him getting killed, eh?"

There was no sense in me revealing to Dewar what I knew of his relationship with the now deceased Crawford and I knew then that Dewar had a source in the police, someone feeding him information, someone who had told him the when and where of both Martin Kilbride and Billy Crawford's murder. Someone who provided him with enough detail to arrange his alibi for Kilbride and likely Crawford's murdered too, enough at least to ensure Dewar wasn't going down for either murder.

"So, what do you want from me, Jackie, now that Kilbride's been found?"

"He had something of mine, Johnny boy, information, eh. An account number as well as a password for that account. Somebody has this information, maybe even you," I could almost hear the threat in his voice, "and it could be worth something to me."

"How much are we talking here, Jackie?" I grew a little bolder.

There was a sharp intake of breath and I suspected Dewar was trying to remain calm.

"How much is your life worth, Johnny boy, eh?" he replied with venom.

I had him now, dangling and uncertain.

"If I have the information, we'd be discussing terms Jackie, but as I don't have the information yet," I tempted him, "maybe we should discuss a finder's fee. Say, fifty grand?"

Another pause and he replied through what sounded like gritted teeth.

"No police involvement, stay away from them. Get me the information and you'll have your fifty grand you fucking weasel!" then abruptly cut me off.

Now, don't imagine for a minute that I believed that even if I could obtain the details for Dewar, he'd pay me fifty thousand pounds. No, more likely if I was to find the account and password details, an arrangement would be made to meet me in a dark and lonely place, beat the shit out of me until I bled from every orifice then leave me somewhere my body would never be discovered.

Daft I might be, stupid I most certainly am not.

Except, of course, maybe where women are concerned.

The Focus, my fingers crossed when I realised the petrol gauge was again sitting in the red, started first time and I made my way through light traffic to the office. Halfway along Eglinton Street, the mobile phone in my jacket pocket rung, but the two traffics cops sitting in the four by four in the adjacent lane was enough of a deterrent to persuade me to let it ring out. As soon as I stopped in Osborne Street I checked the mobile and saw a missed call from a number I didn't recognise and called back.

Sheila Kilbride answered on the second ring.

"Are you all right," she asked, a little breathlessly.

"Fine. Just arriving at my office. And you, you okay?"

"Just stepping out the shower," she replied.

I tried not to think what she looked like, stepping from the shower, but failed miserably while wondering if she'd called because there was a problem?

"I was just wondering if you'd any news, any kind of update for me?"

That explained it. She was likely going stir crazy wondering what was going on.

"I've reported your father's death," I told her, using the word death rather than murder. "The police in Stirling are working on the case and have contacted the local cops here. I spoke with them last night," preferring not to tell her it began with me handcuffed, "and they in turn will deal with this local end of the inquiry. They'd like to speak with you, but I'm not certain that right now, it's a good idea telling anyone where you are. I believe there might be a leak among the local cops and I'm certain that someone is feeding information to Jackie Dewar. I'd prefer that you remain at the hotel, probably get food sent up and stay in your room for now. That okay with you?"

"Okay. Have you heard anything from Phyllis? I mean, I know that I've told you I'm not her number one fan, but is there a likelihood she could be in danger? From this guy Dewar, I mean?"

Frankly, as I've already said, I couldn't care if Phyllis Kilbride was in danger from Dewar or not, but though I considered it unlikely, sighed that I'd give her a call and warn her not to open the door to any strange men. That will probably put a dampener on her love life though, I unkindly added.

She sounded uncertain with my decision, but agreed that she'd stay where she was for the meantime anyway and asked me to stay in touch, then hung up.

Two rolls and bacon in hand, I pushed open the office door to find some mail waiting for me among which, to my surprise, I discovered an envelope and note from Phyllis Kilbride and a cheque for one hundred and fifty quid; my previously agreed retainer and obviously posted the first day I called on her and before her drunken seduction attempt. No matter, I kissed the cheque; it was going into my account anyway, to blow off some cobwebs and prayed that Kilbride's bank would honour it. Stuffing the cheque into an inner jacket pocket, I set about demolishing the rolls and put on the kettle to boil.

"Mister Logan, so good to see you happy," said Zao's quiet voice from behind me at the open door. Boy, but can that wee man move silently. Once my heart restarted and I'd scraped myself back down from the ceiling, I replied, "Collect Tei Pai for the hospital without any problem then, Mister Zao?"

"Oh yes indeed. Tei Pai now on way to stay with my sister in London. She care for Tei Pai for little while now," he replied.

Shit, I thought. Mickey Farrell won't be pleased about that, particularly as it was me that suggested Zao collect his daughter.

"Zao here to thank you, Mister Logan. Zao very happy that gweilo shit Crawford not now hurt my daughter. Zao keep promise. You no pay rent to Zao for," he stopped to think, "five months."

Had I been an honest man I might have confessed that it really had nothing to do with me, that the death of Billy Crawford was for me, good fortune. However, never having been one to look a gift horse in the mouth, I graciously accepted Zao's kind offer.

Zao bowed and was about to leave when something occurred to me.

"Mister Zao, the last time we spoke here in the office, you suggested that someone, probably a police officer, was giving you information. Someone that owed you a lot of money. I helped you get back Tei Pai," I blatantly lied, "so maybe you can tell me something about this person, a man maybe? A police man perhaps?"

I waited and could see that I'd put him on the spot. He shuffled uncomfortably and licked his lower lip.

"I not tell name," he said at last, shaking his head, "I cannot do that. He needed money for daughter. I sometimes lend money in exchange for tip-offs. I have friends who like to place small wagers, you understand?"

Yes I did understand. Illegal gambling dens. Becoming more common in the city centre and I guessed Zao, with his various properties, provided the venues. Mister Zao continued to surprise me in all sorts of ways.

"He give me information, not big stuff, little things. Where police might take interest in certain streets and buildings. Times they might wish to knock on certain doors, you follow me?"

"This policeman, he also told you about Billy Crawford and the drug squad watching him, didn't he? And that Crawford worked for another man, Jackie Dewar?"

Zao nodded. "He say Crawford little fish to big fish, but I not know name Dewwa," he shook his head. "I not interested Dewwa. I only interested Crawford," then slyly smiled, "but you deal with Crawford and for that Zao plenty grateful. Let's call it six months, and grinning hugely, turned and left as silently as he had entered.

Then it struck me. Zao thought I was responsible, that it was me who killed Billy Crawford.

While I realised that Zao was not prepared to give up his police source, I also presumed that he or she must still be in place and wondered if it was the same cop that was providing Jackie Dewar with information.

I'd already suspected it was a cop and not a civilian employee of the police, figuring it was unlikely that a civvy would be privy to information about raids. No, it was more than likely a cop. I knew that while it was rare, it wasn't uncommon for cops to turn to the dark side. Sometimes it was money or for sex or even convincing himself or herself that to get a little information, you had to give a little in return. On the odd occasion, it was family, whether helping or protecting, but no matter the reason, it is straightforward betrayal. Betrayal of the system, betrayal of the public and betrayal of colleagues. No other way to cloak it. I knew I could drive myself crazy trying to work out who Dewar's source might be and it was probably likely I didn't even know the cop, let alone have the information to identify him or her.

The desk phone rang.

"Morning, Logan," said Helen Burns, "so how are you today?"

I could still hear the laughter in her voice and gritted my teeth.

"Very well, thanks for asking, so, what can I do for you?"

"Just checking that no bogeymen caught up with you last night. Have you heard from Phyllis Kilbride at all?"

"She's likely the last person I want to speak to, why?"

There was a definite pause on the line, as though she was choosing her words carefully.

"Coleman and I went to the house yesterday to officially inform her of the death of her husband, but didn't get any reply at the door. I tried the landline, but again got no reply. Do you have a mobile number for her?"

I shuffled in my desk drawer among the bits of pieces of paper and produced the scrap of paper on which Phyllis Kilbride had jotted down her mobile number, and then read it carefully to Burns.

"Do you think something might have happened to her or suspect she might have taken off?" I asked.

"Don't know," replied Burns "but I'm taking another turn up to the house if I can't get her on this mobile."

Quickly, I thought about it and besides her needing a change of clothing, figured this might be the ideal time to have Burns interview Sheila Kilbride. If nothing else, it gets my alibi sorted for Crawford's murder and if the police suspect the same killer, by context also alibis me for Kilbride's murder.

"Why don't I bring Sheila Kilbride to meet you at the house? Give you the chance to interview her too. You were wanting a statement from her anyway," I reminded Burns.

"I'd have preferred to interview her at Baird Street," she sombrely replied, "but okay. I'm needing to see the wife anyway, so whether or not I get her on the mobile I'll meet you and the daughter at the Kilbride house."

We agreed one hour and she abruptly hung up.

It was only a few minutes after the call that I remembered, apart from my old mate Mickey Farrell who I believed to be above suspicion, I recalled having given Burns a business card with my mobile number on it. That made her the only other cop to whom I'd given the number and besides, with her access to all sorts of information it wouldn't be too difficult to obtain my home address and it's highly unlikely Dewar could have found that out himself, not unless someone told him."

With a start, I realised I might just have discovered Jackie Dewar's source of police information.

Two suits carrying briefcases stepped to one side as Sheila Kilbride exited the lift, both taking a few seconds to give her admiring sidelong glances.

And no wonder, I thought.

Her dark hair was loosely bundled up into a pile and clasped on top of her head, showing her shapely neck. Wearing an oversize navy blue hooded top and skin-tight jeans with black trainers and carrying a small plain black shoulder bag, she looked cool and relaxed, like an off-duty model. It was only when she got closer I could see the tension in her eyes. She nodded to me and walked to the reception desk where I saw the young blond guy almost race his female colleague to smilingly take Sheila's key from her. Walking toward me, I took perverse pleasure from the faces of the males in the large foyer, obviously wishing they were me.

"Do you think this is a good idea, John?"

"You've got to face Phyllis at some point," I replied, as we entered the underground garage area, "and maybe better to do it with me in support. Besides, it will also give you the opportunity to collect some of your clothing."

"You don't think I should return home then?"

"Not for the time being. Another day or so at the hotel might not go amiss. You have the funds?"

"That's not an issue," she replied, "dad settled a generous annual allowance on me, as well as my teaching salary."

I didn't miss the small sob that escaped her, when she mentioned her father and let her get into the Mini without another word.

She drove at a sedate pace and I guessed she was reluctant to meet with Phyllis. Turning into the driveway of the house, I saw the CID car parked outside the door. Coleman was lying back against the car while Burns was at a lounge window, trying to peer in and rapping with her knuckles on the glass. She turned at the approach of the Mini and strode towards us as Sheila pulled up.

"Sheila, this is DC Burns," I stiffly got out of the car, and introduced them. "I didn't bother looking at or introducing Coleman."

I could see that the curtains were drawn on all the downstairs windows.

"No answer then?" I asked Burns.

She shook her head.

"I tried the mobile number you gave me," she replied, "and I'm almost sure I can hear it ringing from inside the house."

"I have my house key with me," volunteered Sheila and made toward the front door.

Some inner sense told me it might not be a good idea for her to enter first and I placed my free hand on her shoulder to stop her and took the house key from her. Sheila gave up the key without comment, but with a puzzled expression, while Burns glance indicated she had the same idea.

The door was unlocked by me then swung open by Burns and she and Coleman wordlessly entered, leaving Sheila and I standing on the porch.

I heard Burns calling out Phyllis Kilbride's name, but didn't hear a response.

A minute or so later a grim faced Burns nodded for me to accompany her, but raised her hand to Sheila.

"Might be a good idea if you'd wait in the car, Miss Kilbride. There's nothing here for you to see," she said.

Sheila, her eyes wide and lower lip trembling, numbly nodded and turned towards the Mini. I limped after Burns into the front lounge as Coleman was drawing back the heavy curtains. The light flooded in and the sweet smell of dried blood hung heavy as dust mites danced in the spacious room.

Phyllis Kilbride lay where she had died; face down, the back of her blonde hair matted with congealed blood. Dressed in a light pink coloured tracksuit, the trousers bore a stain at the crutch where in death her bladder had released the contents. It seemed apparent she'd been dead for some time, probably since last evening if the closed curtains were an indicator of the time. Her face was slightly turned towards the piano, her eyes open and staring blankly at the destruction that lay on the floor. I saw the framed photos that had previously sat atop the piano, had been swept and scattered to the floor and now lay broken and some destroyed in what could only have been a wanton act.

The dead woman's left hand stretched towards the photos, her fingers almost claw like as if in death she had reached out for them. One casual shoe had slipped from her right foot and lay beside her ankle. Coleman, completely ignoring me for which I was grateful, had a phone in his hand and said to Burns that he'd call it in, get the forensic and casualty surgeon to attend and made quickly towards the front door.

As Coleman was the senior police officer on site, I knew that the first actions of any police at a serious incident, and in particular murder, would be pored over by both prosecuting and defence lawyers at a subsequent trial and I just knew he was getting himself out of the house, thereby lessening his chance of contaminating the murder scene and being later asked awkward questions. In essence, taking the easy road out, for his statement would simply read attended, saw and got out the house. Cynically, it also occurred to me that the perverted bastard might be making a beeline for the emotionally distressed Sheila Kilbride, maybe hoping to catch her at low ebb.

I stood back and watched as Burns, her attention devoted to her job, carefully stepped among the debris at the piano. I watched her pull on a pair of thin, blue coloured rubber gloves.

"Can't see what she's been struck with, but my guess would be a hammer, just like her hubby and that guy Crawford," she straightened up and said.

Don't forget, I had this woman down as a possible tout for Jackie Dewar, so warily watched everything she did.

"There's the mobile," she pointed to a phone lying on the floor near to the fireplace.

"Why would it be on the floor?" I asked.

Burns turned to look at me, her eyes narrowing in thought. "The way she's lying, head towards the phone, maybe she had it in her hand when she fell and it's bounced over there. What do you think?"

"It's possible if she's had it in her hand, she was perhaps going to call somebody," I suggested.

Through the window, I could see Coleman at the Mini, his hand on the roof as he leaned forward to speak through the driver's window with Sheila.

"I see your partners taking this in his stride," I said.

Burns ignored me, picked up the mobile phone and examined it. "Shouldn't you wait till that gets photographed before you start handling it?" I asked.

"I'll not tell if you don't," she grinned in response.

I watched her flip through the phone menu.

"The last three calls are from me," she said "and the last outgoing calls is to..."

"Bugger!"

"What is it?" I asked.

"Two nines."

"Two nines? So, she must have been on the verge of calling the emergency services, presumably the police."

Burns laid the phone back on the floor where from she'd lifted it.

"Check the back door and windows," I suggested. "If there's no forced entry and the front door is a standard security lock, she has let her killer into the house. That, like the other two murders, might indicate she either knew her killer or had no reason to be alarmed or frightened."

I bent slightly at the dead woman's face well, as best I could given that I'm using a stick and without losing my balance.

"Can't see any injury other than to the back of her head, can you?"

Burns shook her head and went to check the rest of the house.

I walked round the body and stared down at the broken framed photographs, shaking my head at the waste. But the more I stared, the more some thought niggled at me. I looked hard, but the irritating thought persisted. Something just wasn't right, something I'd seen, but in my mind, wouldn't click into place. I hate it when I get like this, remembering the joke told to me by an older, nearly retired colleague and that I was always repeating that the best thing about dementia was forgetting you had it. I sighed with frustration as Burns returned to the lounge.

"All tight and shipshape," she said.

Shipshape? I can't explain why, well, couldn't explain just then, but that one comment was provoking another memory and I almost shouted in frustration. I'd just have to give up and wait for the old grey cells, as Monsieur Poirot keeps telling us, to kick in.

Coleman startled us both, rapping on the window and indicating we should come outside.

"That's the casualty surgeon and the DCI with the team, on their way," he told us, his hands thrust deep into his anorak pocket.

"You," he nodded to me, "should take your bit of fluff down to the station and we'll get a statement from you both later."

I dearly wanted to tell the arse where to shove his station and fully aware that as senior officer present, any comment should be addressed to him. Instead, I turned to Burns.

"Sheila Kilbride has had more than her fair share of shocks recently, so if you don't mind, I'll bring her to the station at a time that's suitable to you both."

I could see Coleman open his mouth to protest, but in fairness to Burns, she beat him to the punch.

"Agreed," she replied. "We'll make a tentative appointment for tomorrow morning, nine sharp at Baird Street. I'll speak to the Detective Chief Inspector and tell her that she's in no fit state to be interviewed right now. But Logan," her eyes bored into me, "don't let me down here."

"What about Mickey Farrell? Will you give him a bell too?"

"Likely the boss will have him attend here, so I'll update him when he arrives."

I nodded and left Sheila's house key with Burns, then walked to the Mini's driver's door and told Sheila to squeeze over to the passenger side. I could see she was on the verge of tears. Without argument, she slid across and I threw my stick into the rear seat and manoeuvred into the car.

I didn't take Sheila back to the hotel, but instead took her to the Lismore pub, a famous and popular hostelry on Dumbarton Road, where I made her drink a double brandy. She coughed at the first sip, but then sank the rest in one gulp. Me? I had a diet coke, persuading myself it was because I was driving rather than the real reason, that I really needed a strong drink. And I hadn't forgotten my leg, because it sure as hell was hurting and reminding me that I was overdue some painkilling relief. I popped two Co-codomol and drew a curious glance from the elderly barman.

"Is it the same person who killed my dad, do you think?" she asked me, loud enough for the elderly couple sitting at an adjacent table to give us a curious and bewildered stare.

"Probably," I replied.

"God knows," she spluttered, "I couldn't stand Phyllis, but why was she killed? Was she working with my dad for this man Dewar?"

The old couple lifted their drinks and prudently moved to a table further away, the wife discreetly having a wee backward glance, no doubt thinking she'd better remember what we looked like in case she had to later provide the police with a statement.

"I don't know why she was killed," I said, "but my gut reaction is that she was murdered to shut her up. That implies that she knew something, or at least the killer thought she knew something. Either way, she had to be silenced."

"Does that mean the person who killed my dad and Phyllis," then almost as an afterthought, "that other man, might think I know something too?"

She began to tremble and I briefly considered a comforting hug, but thought that it might seem a bit like an older guy trying it on with a good looking young bird, so decided on another brandy and pointing to her empty glass, gave the barman a nod and a wink. He nodded back and turned to the spirits optic on the wall behind him.

"Whoever is committing these murders," I began, "is doing it for a reason. That reason began when your dad had the account and password details stolen from him. The killer seems to have somehow connected the other man, Billy Crawford, with your father and then killed him. In the killers mind, your stepmother seemed to represent a problem...."

I stopped just then, something forming in my mind, some idea.

"What? What is it? You know something," Sheila stared at me, almost accusingly, "you've worked something out, haven't you?"

"I don't think, in fact," I corrected myself, "I'm certain that Dewar isn't involved in these murders. It doesn't make sense that he'd kill your dad without first getting the account details from him."

The barman arrived with the brandy that he placed in front of her, taking the opportunity to ogle at her and display a perfect set of brilliant white, false teeth.

"There you are miss," he said, "I'll get the money from your dad later."

That firmly put me in my place, I thought as I scowled at his retreating back.

I decided to level with her, even though I knew that I was about to plunge another knife into her already broken heart.

'"Look, you're not stupid. In fact, you're a lot brighter and more astute than you pretend to be, so here's the truth of the matter."

I then gave her an overview of the situation as I saw it. She looked horrified, yet I suspected she had already guessed most of it.

"In his profession as an accountant," I continued "your father oversaw Dewar's financial transactions and organised the transfer of Dewar's assets to cash and thereafter to this bloody account. But somebody got wise to the whole affair and diverted the money to an anonymous account, where it now lies. And that person is probably the killer, tidying up loose ends as they go along."

The more I retold the story, the more I began to convince myself.

"Dewar is as much a patsy in this affair as was your father. He's so bloody stupid that he's still convinced that he can threaten or connive the account details out of anyone connected to your father and that's what makes him dangerous, but no, I don't think he's the killer. I'm guessing the killer, for want of another name, was probably well known to all three, that's why all three didn't feel threatened when the killer arrived at each address."

"So it's possible," she looked horrified, "that I know who the killer is?"

My mobile phone burst into life and interrupted me.

"Logan?" asked Helen Burns, "where are you?"

"Glasgow city centre," I lied.

"Still with Sheila Kilbride are you?"

"Yes, for the minute."

"The boss is having a fit and kicked my arse for letting you guys leave the murder scene, so bring her back to Baird Street please. She wants all statements done and dusted by this evening. And Logan? Be prepared to answer some questions yourself, okay?"

"Right," I slowly replied and ended the call, "wondering what questions Burns was on about."

"Drink up," I told Sheila, "we've an appointment with the police."

CHAPTER 12

On this occasion visiting Baird Street, I used the front door and informed the attractive, dark haired female civilian bar officer that Miss Kilbride and I were there to meet with DC Burns. With a dazzling smile, which I idly thought made a nice change from being hauled out of a vehicle, she directed us to take a seat. A short time later the security door buzzed and Helen Burns bid us follow her.

From previous visits, I knew the layout of the building and recognised when she took us toward the lift that we were headed for the recreation room that also doubled as a major incident suite. Knowing the area of Glasgow that is policed by the officers of Baird Street and the high incidence of major inquires that result from the various shootings, stabbings and murders, I very much doubted that a ping-pong ball was ever struck in that room.

Mickey Farrell, for once looking as dour as an Aberdonian that's lost fifty pence, greeted us in the corridor outside the room and shepherded all three of us into an interview room.

"The boss's pissed at her," he thumbed towards Burns, "for letting you guys go in the first place, so don't fuck DCI Massey about, excusing my language miss," he nodded towards Sheila, then almost as an afterthought, "and sorry for your loss."

That's Mickey all over, I inwardly grinned. Curses and compassion all rolled into one big bear.

Sheila had the good grace to smile in appreciation.

The door opened and Eddie Coleman walked in.

He didn't even look at me, but said "I've to interview Miss Kilbride here."

"If you think I'm letting a fat fucking paedophile like you near this lassie," I roared and stepped towards him.

I know, I'm crippled and not much use anymore in a set-to, but just give me the opportunity to get my hands round this perverts throat, I almost pleaded.

Mickey Farrell grabbed me by the arms in restraint.

"Aye, quite right," Mickey agreed, glaringly warningly at me "given that the young lady has suffered the terrible loss of both her parents, maybe DC Burns here could take her to the cafeteria for a coffee while she notes her statement. Okay with you Helen?" he turned towards Burns, ostensibly asking her, but the decision made.

"But the DCI said…." Coleman blustered, then turned towards me, his face reddening, "What did you fucking call me?"

"And I'm certain that the DCI will sympathise with my decision, given the circumstances," soothed Farrell, slowly releasing me and backing away but still, I couldn't help but notice, standing between Coleman and me and in a position to grab me again.

Burns shuffled Shelia almost unseen, past Mickey and out the door. Coleman, still seething and with hate in his eyes, followed them out.

Mickey turned towards me with a smile.

"Well, that seemed to go well, don't you think?"

"Who's the DCI in the case?" I asked him.

"DCI Lynn Massey. A good guy, if you get my drift. Honest as the days long and very competent, but doesn't take prisoners."

I knew of Massey and had some vague memory of her being involved in a shooting in the city, a couple of years previously. A high profile murder case that led to an armed stand-off when a suspect had shot a cop, then been cornered on a rooftop.

"So, who's interviewing me then?"

"Well, since Billy Crawford got himself murdered my team is seconded to the murder inquiry, so sit yourself down, me old mucker," replied a grinning Mickey, "you've got the best of the best."

So I sat down and for over an hour, Mickey laboriously took notes, most of which he already knew from our conversation the previous evening. The note taking was predominantly about the finding of Phyllis Kilbride's body and being Mickey, who as I've already said can't hold his water let alone keep a secret, he gave me as much information as I gave him. I learned that indeed, it was a hammer that had killed her and no, the weapon wasn't found. A blood soaked towel was found in the downstairs cloakroom, presumably used to wipe the hammer clean. The fact that the killer had taken the hammer indicated to me one of two things. Either the killer feared that some forensic evidence attached itself to the hammer that might incriminate the killer and intended disposing of the hammer elsewhere or, more likely, the killer wasn't finished dealing with the loose ends.

The hair on the back of my neck went up.

As far as I figured, that left one very vulnerable loose end; Sheila Kilbride.

"Where are you stashing the wee lassie, then John?"

"Mickey, you've got a jackal in your outfit. Somebody walked a kilo out of your production cupboard and back to Jackie Dewar, so I'm not prepared to give out anything that could endanger her."

I knew the big guy was offended, deeply offended in fact. But as I've said, though I trust Mickey, I've no control over his tongue or who he has on his team.

"Speaking of which, Mickey," I leaned across the desk as if in confidence, "have you any suspects for the theft of the cocaine?"

He sighed and looked at me.

"You'll remember the system, John. The cupboard was used to stack all sorts of stuff, including drug seizures, bottles of booze for the odd piss-up when we'd a successful operation, sleeping bags for the guys that pulled overnighters or couldn't get home. It wouldn't have surprised me," he grumbled, "if there was the some retired guy hiding in there. Do you remember where we kept the cupboard key?"

I did remember. The key was always kept in the bottom drawer of the clerk's desk, the clerk usually being a uniformed guy who through sickness or injury was temporarily located to the drug squad for a few months. There had been a signing in or out book, for items stored in the production cupboard, but I didn't recall anyone ever taking it seriously.

"Well, that's all changed now," he said. "Since the theft the storage of productions has been drastically updated. Everything is logged in and out, inspected weekly and they're even talking about a sort of biometric system, whatever the fuck that is. Nothing gets in or out without a senior officers authorisation. Bloody nuisance it is too," he whined.

I asked him again.

"But do you have any suspects?"

He chewed his lower lip and stared hard at me.

"Why you so interested?"

"Because somebody is feeding Jackie Dewar information about the murders and that information includes my mobile number, of which you are one of the few who has it, and my home address."

"Now wait a minute," he exploded out of his seat, "you don't think that I..."

"Course I don't, you idiot. Do you think I'd be telling you this if I did?"

"Aye, right enough," he replied, his eyebrows knitting together and sat back down.

"How well do you know Helen Burns?"

"I don't know here at all, well, not till I met her last night," he said.

"So, she's not been one of your squad or based at your office when the coke went missing?"

Mickey's eyes narrowed.

"Why would you suspect her?" he challenged me.

"I can't think of any other cop that has my mobile number and let's face it. If she wanted to, she could quite easily find out where I live. And she has all the facts about the murders and would be able to keep Dewar updated about what's happening."

"Admitted, yes, but what would be her motivation? Money? Or do you have something else about her that's niggling you?"

"No, it's just a gut feeling and it wouldn't be the first time I was wrong."

"Well, if you've no evidence John, don't be bandying this allegation around. That sort of idle gossip could seriously damage a cop's career and that young lassie seems to have her head screwed on the right way. I have to admit, before you dropped this on me, I'd even considered asking her if she'd any notion about joining my squad."

"I hope that her prospective recruitment is based on her ability, DI Farrell and not her obvious good looks."

And you know, I do believe he almost blushed.

Mickey had some inquiries to follow through and apologising, left me back at the reception desk at the station main door, telling the civilian bar officer to keep her eye on me, that I was inclined to wander without my carer. The woman laughed with him and buzzing Mickey through the security door, turned to me and asked if I wanted a cup of tea? Thanking her, I refused but was grateful when a few minutes later, she come from behind the bar and brought me that mornings newspaper to read. It also gave me the opportunity to admire her shapely figure. It was another thirty minutes before Burns and Sheila joined me.

"Thanks for coming in, Miss Kilbride, if we need any more, I'm sure that Logan here will make arrangements for you to call back at the station," she pointedly stared at me.

As we walked to the car, I asked if she'd divulged to Burns where she was staying?

"She did ask, but I told her that you were worried about my personal protection and so I requested that my address could be care of you, for the time being."

"Good answer, well done," I smiled at her.

"And she gave me my house key back, said that their forensics had completed their inquiry at the house. I've a bit of a sore head," she grimaced, "could I have one of your aspirin things?"

"That'll be the brandy catching up with you. Come on, we'll find a cafe and get you a cuppa to wash the tablets down with."

Like the gentleman I profess to be, I held open the passenger door then limped round the front of the car to the drivers door. As I pulled the door open, I glanced at the building and there, two flights up, I saw Helen Burns at a window staring down at me, a mobile phone in her hand.

Seeing Burns like that spooked me a bit and I decided that rather than risk stopping at a city cafe, I'd drive straight to the hotel. I drove down the ramp to the underground car park and then took Sheila to the hotel bar, ordered a pot of tea for two and popped two tablets into her hand. We sat for a half an hour and went over what she'd told Burns, but I couldn't fault her on her statement. She seemed to have been straight down the line about everything, her limited knowledge of her fathers dealings with Dewar, her assisting him to hide that included torching his car and her distress in finding him murdered.

I could see that it brought back the horror as she recounted it.

She had admitted to Burns her dislike, bordering on hatred for her stepmother, but hadn't wished her dead. She also had told Burns of her fear that she might be targeted by the killer, stressing that she had no knowledge of any account details that her father supposedly had. Idly, I wondered if my suspicion about Helen Burns was correct and would this information find its way to Dewar and would he believe it? More importantly, would he consider that Sheila Kilbride wasn't worth the trouble locating?

Once more, I watched as she collected her key from the hotel reception desk and walked her to the lift. It didn't escape my attention that the security manager, Peasy Byrne was loitering nearby and he gave me the slightest of nods.

I collected the Focus from the underground car park and aware that I'd my appointment at six with Alex Haldane, decided to first call at the bank round the corner from the office and cash the cheque burning the hole in my pocket. I parked in Osborne Street and, my leg really aching now, took my time strolling round to the bank.

The ferret faced woman, hair tightly bound in a bun on top of her head and wearing the standard bank uniform, reminded me of a film I'd once seen where the Gestapo used a woman to torture a member of the resistance.

"You need to fill out a form," she crisply instructed me, pushing a pad towards me that required several boxes to be ticked and resembled the police Home Office Road Traffic form number one, universally known as the HORT1.

"Bugger!" I cried out loud.

The woman was startled and glared at me.

"Not you, sorry, I mean…."

I took a deep breath, my mind working overtime and scratched the details on the form.

Of course, the officious bugger took her time, regardless of the queue behind me, most of whom blamed me for the hold-up, but I took no notice.

I'd other things on my mind.

Fortunately, the cheque went through without any trouble and with seven twenties and two five pound notes in my pocket, the world seemed that little bit brighter.

Did I consider that a woman now murdered had paid me the money I'd just collected? And did I have any sense of right or wrong? Did I hell. As I've said before, money's got no conscience and besides, the money in my pocket might even help catch Phyllis Kilbride's killer.

I hurried as fast as my leg would permit me back to the office and oblivious to the pain that was saving itself up to hit me later. I almost fell in through the front door and, now out of breath, rummaged in the desk drawer.

It was there where I'd flung it.

I snatched up the phone and dialled the number.

Mickey Farrell answered on the second ring.

"What you want, reprobate?" he cheerfully asked.

"The time the coke was stolen," I asked, my breath coming in spurts, "who was the CID clerk?"

Mickey was caught wrong footed.

"Can't remember exactly," he replied, "there was a few over the course of the last couple of years, but if it's important I can maybe find out?"

"Do that Mickey and get back to me on my mobile. Soon as you can, buddy."

"Does this mean the lovely Helen Burns with the damned attractive bosom is off the hook then?"

I smiled and knew then that Mickey had a romantic interest.

"Just get back to me when you can and I'll let you know, okay?"

"Will do," he replied and hung up.

I sat at the desk, my head in my hands.

Mickey took ten minutes to call back with the name.

I hadn't really needed Mickey to confirm my suspicion, because I knew or at least had a good idea of the name of Dewar's informant, but how the hell was I going to deal with it?

I was in a bit of quandary. I didn't know whether or not to pursue my suspicion there and then or go ahead and meet with Alex Haldane. Finally, I decided to phone her and sound her out, before I made my decision.

"Don't tell me," she answered the call, "you've been hauled in again by the cops and identified as Bible John, the mass murderer?"

"Hello to you too, Alex," I grinned at the phone, "and you got it in one."

"Really?" she laughed, sounding surprised.

"No, but I do have a wee problem. I've a guy to meet and it'd better be done this evening and likely means that I'll miss my appointment with you."

"You're not," I could hear her hesitation, "I mean, if you'd rather call off….if you think the meeting's is a mistake…."

"Nothing like that, honest, it's genuinely work. Look," and I knew I was really chancing my arm here, "I should be done for sometime after eight, say nine tonight to be on the safe side. I know it's unlikely you'll still be at your office. What time do you eat or have you already…"

"When I've got appointments, I rarely eat before nine, why?"

Now, you have to understand, I was making this up as I went along and realised there was every chance I was going to fall flat on my arse, but faint heart and all that.

"Well, you know where I live and on that note, thanks for clearing up."

Jesus! Thanks for clearing up! Did I really say that! I took a deep breath.

"I was wondering if maybe, after your last appointment, you'd perhaps…." get on with it, I urged myself, "….maybe like to pop by for something to eat? We could talk then, if you like?"

The slight pause seemed to last forever.

"Chinese would be nice," she said, "something with chicken."

I found I was smiling and hadn't realised I'd been holding my breath. I quietly exhaled.

"Right then, see you some time after nine then, bye."

I was still smiling.

But then I remembered, I'd another call to make and that call would most certainly wipe the smile from my face.

CHAPTER 13

I drove the Focus, now with a half tank of petrol thanks to my financial windfall, to the McDonalds car park in Possilpark on the north side of the city. Night was falling and apart from the regular queue at the drive-thru, there was no more than six or seven cars parked at various bays. Two of the cars were occupied by teenagers, one with young guys the other with young girls, eating their food, loud music blaring from the open windows of one of the vehicles and good-naturedly cat calling to each other.

An immaculately clean black coloured BMW saloon was parked at the rear of the car park, the driver sitting alone in the vehicle.

I drew alongside with the driver's doors adjacent to each other and wound down my window.

"Thanks for coming to meet me, Wally," I said.

Wally, wearing a light coloured sweater over his police issue polo shirt, nodded and even in the dark I could see he was pale faced.

"How did you know, John?"

"I didn't for certain. I have a mobile phone, but I'm very careful to whom I give the number. I had only given the number to two cops, my mate Mickey Farrell and to Helen Burns that operates out of your office. I couldn't understand how someone like Jackie Dewar had gotten hold of it or how he was so well informed about the murders that happened, and then I remembered. What I'd forgotten was that I called you after you'd scribbled your mobile phone number on the HORT1 form, so my number must have been recorded on your phone as an incoming call. All you'd have to do was save the number."

He nodded and I knew I was correct.

"What I don't understand is why you'd tout for a scumbag like Dewar? The coke that was stolen from the drug squad production room," I reminded him, deliberately keeping my voice even, "Mickey told me that during that period, you were undergoing more chemo and temporarily assigned to office duties as the squads CID clerk. I'm guessing, Wally, it was you that took the coke to deliver to Dewar. I just don't understand. What kind of hold does he have on you that you'd rat out your own mates, your own colleagues? Put yourself in a position where you might end up in prison?"

He arched his back and slowly swivelled his neck, as though relieving some pressure then turned his head towards me.

"Who else knows?"

Yes, it did occur to me that Wally might not take kindly to being found out and might in desperation think he would silence me, but I'd taken the precaution of telling Mickey of my suspicion, so no matter what this meeting outcome was, Wally was in really, really deep shit.

"Mickey Farrell, so you might want to get yourself some representation. Maybe consider handing yourself in rather than have them arrest you, be ahead of the game, so to speak."

We sat in silence for a few moments and I'm thinking he's considering his options, one of which I hoped wasn't murdering me for exposing him.

To my utter and complete surprise, he lowered his head and began to softly weep. I didn't disturb him, just let him cry as the kids across the car park continued to noisily laugh and jest with each other. I watched as he took a deep breath and composed himself; wiping his eyes and his nose on his handkerchief.

"You must think I'm a dirty rotten bastard," he said at last.

"Well, to be honest, when Dewar and his sidekick Lamond punched the shit out of me on my own doorstep, I wasn't too enthralled by whoever had given them my address, Wally. I just didn't suspect it might be you."

"I'm sorry about that, really sorry. Dewar promised that he'd not hurt you. I wanted to believe him, but I suppose that I knew he was lying. I'm sorry, John," he said again.

"I just don't understand why, Wally?"

He sat still for a minute and then began speaking in a voice so low I had to strain to hear him.

"You remember my daughter Janice? And the kindness you showed her and me?" I nodded.

"She's a good girl, stayed off the smack after you dealt with her dealer and with the help of her counsellor, put herself through college. She's working in a nursery now, assistant manager."

I could hear the pride in his voice.

"The time she was on drugs, I told you that she was badly addicted and needed help to get off and you did help. For that I'll always be grateful and that made it more difficult, betraying you, John. But I'd no choice, you see. Janice has turned her life around, even got herself a nice young man and he's hinted about them getting married. She told him, about her drug habit I mean, but he sees her as she is now, not as she was and that's to his credit. A good man, a nurse at Gartnavel Hospital."

He stopped to compose himself again.

"Dewar came to me a while ago, when I was working with the drug squad as you said, acting as their clerk. He had photographs of Janice," a sob broke from him, "with men. She looked unconscious in most of the photos, out of her head with the smack. You can't imagine how vile they were," angry now, "the sort of photographs no father should ever see of his child!"

His eyes closed with the horrible memory of what he'd seen and told me that Janice was unaware of the existence of the photos.

"He threatened to put them onto the Internet, told me that he'd send copies to men's magazines, the filthy type that real men don't buy, you know? At first it was just a bit of information, when and where the squad were next hitting houses. I thought maybe I could convince him to hand over the photographs, but I was being naive, I know that now. Then he told me to steal the bag of cocaine. It wasn't too difficult. The cupboard was accessible to everyone and their granny and there was no real inventory check. I'd had it away and it was over a week before it was even discovered missing. I lived in terror that they'd find out it was me and waited for the knock on my door, but apart from providing a statement to the rubber heels, nobody really questioned me in any depth."

He stopped for a breath and it was then I thought that he really didn't look well.

"I hadn't heard from Dewar for some time and I'd thought he was leaving me alone. Then last week, he phoned me to find out what I could about you, your phone number, where you lived, anything. I don't know why, but I believe he seemed to think you were some kind of threat to him. He posted me some photos of Janice, just to remind me to stay onside. God forgive me, you were one of the few people in the job that stuck by me through my illness, helped my Janice and I did this to you," holding his head in his hands and said "I deserve what's coming to me, deserve it all."

"So what now, John?" He turned towards me. "Where do I go from here?"

Something about the way he was holding himself, about the way he was speaking, triggered a memory. I recalled when he'd stopped me the few days previously and how sickly he'd seemed to me.

"You're still ill, aren't you Wally?"

He nodded.

"The cancer spread to my pancreas. I'm riddled with the fucking thing and it's still spreading," he half laughed. "A month ago, the consultant at the Beatson Clinic told me that I'd a few weeks, not months, so I'm biding my time waiting for the call-up from the big boss."

"Why are you still working?" and then I realised. Wally hadn't declared to anyone he was dying. The mad bastard was literally working till he dropped.

"My thirty years is in," he smiled, as though in relief at an accomplishment, "and I can go anytime. I just didn't expect to die on the job, not like this anyway and to be honest," he smiled, "I've not really got anywhere else to go."

A daft idea struck me then. The craziest idea that I'd had in a long time and believe me, I've had a few and I know, just know that you'll think I'm the softest, most forgiving, stupid bastard that walked God's earth.

"Does Janice know you're terminal?"

Wally shook his head.

"She's that happy now with her young man, Simon's his name," he smiled, "that I didn't want her worrying about me. She's my life, John. Always has been."

"And your thirty's definitely in, then?"

"Aye, like I said. Why?"

"So, if you were to retire tomorrow, you'd get your lump sum and pension rights?"

Wally looked confused, but agreed.

"And I suppose that lassie of yours, who is a total innocent in all this, would inherit your money and half your pension rights when you turn your toes up, would that be right?"

He slowly nodded and I could see that he was wondering where I was going with this.

I took a deep breath.

"Right Wally, here's the deal, but don't forget, I'm still very, very pissed with you. Tomorrow, first thing, you hand in your retirement form and name Janice as your next of kin on the form. If memory serves me right, the process shouldn't take more that a few days for them to bank your money and set up the pension payments."

Had I offered Wally eternal life, he couldn't have been more shocked. His pale face, if anything, turned even whiter and he tried to speak, but the words failed him.

"As for Mickey Farrell," because I guessed what was going through his mind, "leave him to me," I said with more confidence than I actually felt.

Wally was unable to speak, simply stared at me, the tears running unchecked down his cheeks.

Almost as an afterthought, I asked Wally if he knew a wee man called Zao, but he shook his head, no doubt wondering where that question came from. Seemed there was more than just Wally giving out information, I thought.

"One last thing, Wally," I said as I turned the key to start the Focus, "Under no circumstances, none at all, do you have any contact with Jackie Dewar. Nothing. Agreed?"

He hesitated, then I saw him nod and after that, with my own curt nod to him, I gunned the engine and drove out of the car park. That at least solved the mystery of how Dewar had obtained my personal details and the inside information about the murders, I grimly thought.

All I had to do now was convince Mickey Farrell of my deal with Wally Bartholomew.

Mickey's flat was located in an old, sandstone tenement in Chancellor Street, just off Byres Road in the west end of the city. As usual, parking was murder, but I managed to find a resident bay and shoved the blue badge on the windscreen in the hope that Glasgow's blue meanies, or traffic parking wardens to give them their rightful name, might show some compassion.

I pressed the close door button at Mickey's name and he buzzed me in then I struggled the two flights up to his flat. Mickey met me at the door, his face showing obvious surprise at my visit.

"So, what's the occasion?" he asked, "I don't think I've seen you darken my door here for over a year, at least."

I limped past him and caught the slight whiff of cologne.

"Is that after shave you're wearing?" then noticed he was wearing a smart, light blue polo shirt and dark blue cargo pants.

"What, am I not allowed to smarten up now and then," he gruffly replied, following me into the lounge.

Mickey's flat belies his generally scruffy appearance. To say he is fastidious just doesn't explain it. Nothing is out of place; no papers lying about, no old socks, no dirty mugs, nothing. Not a trace of fluff on the wine red carpet, not a speck of dust on the real wood mahogany furniture and the cushions are all plumped up as if daring you to sit upon them. It's as if an army of housewives has descended on the flat and scrubbed and disinfected it to its pristine condition and left it looking like an advert for a woman's magazine. In fact, I'm surprised he doesn't walk about wearing one of those paper suits and slip-on paper shoes so favoured by the forensics people at murder scenes.

Wait a minute, I thought, Mickey's playing soft music, not belting out the rock and roll that's previously led to arguments with his downstairs neighbour.

But, to be honest, it was the two wine glasses and bottle of plonk in the ice-barrel that gave it away.

"You've got a bird coming up here," I grinned at him.

He had the good grace to blush and then grinned back at me.

"Congratulations, Sherlock, now what the fuck are you doing here, apart from trying to wreck my new found love life?"

He was right, about the new found love life bit, I mean. As far as I was aware, Mickey hadn't been seeing anyone since Marie died. The big guy had taken her death pretty hard and been off work for a couple of months, trying to come to terms with his loss. In some way, I'd loved her too, but more like a big sister. I suppose what I'm really trying to say here is that I wasn't jealous of Mickey, more I envied him his wife, someone who he loved and in turn loved him, unconditionally. No kids, but whether that was by choice or otherwise, I never really had the bottle to ask.

"So again," he asked me, disturbing my thoughts, "what exactly are you doing here that a phone call couldn't have sorted out?"

I sat down on the edge of the leather settee, a bit worried about disturbing the cushion and in quick time, mainly because I saw him glance anxiously at the wall clock, related to him my meeting with Wally Bartholomew.

"And you've agreed that with him?" he thundered, "are you off your fucking head?"

"Look, Mickey, the guy's dying. He was caught between a rock and a hard place. His daughters career, her reputation and her relationship, possibly her prospective marriage was at stake. He didn't personally gain anything out of it. Everything he did, the theft, setting me up, it was all done to defend Janice. She's all he's got at the end of his life, knowing that in some way he's did all he could to protect her, saved her life from being destroyed."

Mickey paced the room, shaking his head.

"The theft of the coke, as far as the rubber heels is concerned, that's not going to get solved. Wally was a good cop for a lot of years, but fell just at the twilight of his career. Surely we can let that go, let him go, let his daughter bury him without shame or embarrassment, for both of them?"

"And nobody else knows about this deal you've made with him?"

"Only me and now you."

"Yeah, thanks for that," he sourly replied, then said, "Okay. But listen good, John. You might be out of the job, but I'm still serving. Word of this gets out then its charges of perverting the course of justice and prison time for us both. Understand?"

I nodded in understanding and got to my feet.

It was an awkward moment and I could sense the big guy was severely pissed at me for involving him in what the courts would deem a serious criminal offence.

I looked about me, but something wasn't right, something was missing. Then it struck me, the framed photo of Marie that usually sat on the coffee table, wasn't there. I guessed Mickey didn't want his date to feel uncomfortable, looking at her boyfriend's dead wife.

Then it struck me and I was again at the Kilbride house, remembering the framed photographs that had been swept from the piano, to the floor. But why? What did the killer intend?

"You've got that glazed look about you again," said Mickey, "what is it?"

I shook my head.

"Nothing that won't keep till tomorrow," I replied and nodded to the clock.

"Oh, aye," he said and showed me to the door.

"And John, before you go making decisions that might end up with me being arrested, please at least give me a heads up, eh?" then shaking his head, he slapped me gently on the shoulder and closed the door.

I hobbled back to the Focus, thankful to see there was no ticket and was adjusting the seat belt when the Hackney cab pulled up outside Mickey's flat.

As I pulled past the taxi, I saw a very attractive, dark haired and shapely woman, wearing a short dark skirt, loose fitting cream jacket and carrying a bottle of wine, smiling as she paid off the driver. I also smiled, recalling that the last time I'd seen the woman was behind the uniform bar at Baird Street police office.

The Smooth Radio disc jockey presenting the evening Motown show announced the time as nearing eight-thirty, just time for me to grab a take-away from the local Chinese and meet Alex at the flat, I thought.

Meal in a plastic carrier bag clutched in one hand and stick in the other, I'd just stepped from the brightly lit shop towards the Focus parked at the kerb when Scorcher Lamond came out of the darkness. One hand on my arm and the other at the scruff of my neck, he frogmarched me to the new model Range Rover parked behind my car.

"Jackie would like a word," he growled with a breath that reeked of cheap tobacco, but I'd kind of guessed that anyway.

Dewar sat in the driver's seat, caressing a lit cigar between the forefinger and thumb of his right hand, watching the smoke spiral towards the open window.

"How's it hanging, Johnny boy, eh? You've not got back to me yet, eh?"

"Nothing to tell Jackie," I replied, feeling kind of helpless and worried the meal might be getting cold when really, I should have worried more that I might get a kicking.

I decided to take the initiative in this conversation, but let's face it; there wasn't much else I could do.

"So tell me Jackie, was it you that whacked Kilbride and his Missus and Billy Crawford?"

I thought that Dewar might like the word whacked; kind of suited his idea of him being like an American gangster.

His face turned purple, if indeed faces can turn purple and he almost choked.

Behind me, Scorcher gripped my neck that little bit tighter and forced me against the car so that my chest was crushed and making it difficult to breathe.

"Are fucking crazy, eh?" Dewar snapped at me, and then glanced up and down the pavement to ensure nobody was within earshot. "When I get people whacked, they don't get found, eh!"

He took a deep breath and then smiled, but not in a nice way, I have to say.
"So, where have you got Kilbride's daughter stowed away, eh? Giving her one are you, eh?" he leered at me.
"She doesn't know anything, Jackie," I told him, my voice sounding as tired as I was feeling. "If she did, she'd have told the police and you'd be sitting in the jail rather than here, annoying me. If you discover who killed the Kilbride's and your man Crawford, then likely you've found the thief. And let's face it, the police have got a lot more resources to track down the killer than you have, so you'd be better facing the facts, Jackie, the money's gone."
This time, his face turned white and I realised that he needed something to hit out at, someone to hurt and guess what? I was the nearest candidate for his rage.
Now, we all know the famous and often repeated line that's attributed to Humphrey Bogart, the one where in the iconic film Casablanca, he says to Ingrid Bergman something like of all the bars in all the cities in the world, you walk into mine. Now, I don't know if I've got the quote quite correct, but you get my meaning.
What Bogart's really saying is that what are the chances of something happening when you either do or don't need it.
Well, guess what? From apparently out of nowhere, who should come along right then but two young cops, both wearing bright fluorescent Lycra tops, Lycra cycling shorts, cycling helmets and pushing their police issue mountain bikes. Now, when I was serving, I always thought that cops on bikes was a daft idea, but now? I could have kissed them both. Well, the young bird anyway, because her partner had a beard.
"Is there a problem here?" asked the male cop, wisely propping his bike against a nearby lamppost, his right hand hovering over the extendable baton on his belt.
His partner likewise laid her bike down and stood cautiously on Scorcher's blind side, her hand also on her baton handle. I smirked in relief, pleased because these two knew their stuff.
Lamond dropped me as though I was electrified and stood back, glowering at me.
"No, just old pals having a wee chat, isn't that right Johnny boy, eh?" said Dewar.
"Absolutely correct, Jackie," I replied, limping towards the Focus, "but remember what I've told you. You need to get your Range Rover MOT'd before you can get it insured and taxed, eh?" I called out as a parting shot.
Getting quickly into the Focus, I glanced in the rear-view mirror, chuckling as I saw the young female cop speaking on her radio and glancing down at the registration plate of the Range Rover, with Dewar out of the vehicle and apparently protesting to the male cop. I knew that having had this run-in with the cops, Dewar wouldn't dare pursue me to the flat. He'd remember and want revenge, but not tonight.
Two minutes later I was in Osborne Street and saw Alex Haldane, wearing her lengthy waxed coat, just arriving at the close entrance.

Alex had come direct from the office. Her hair tied back into a ponytail, she wore a loose fitting pink coloured, lamb's wool sweater with a knee length, flared denim skirt and black leather boots. I also saw she was wearing lipstick and to be honest, and not for the first time, I experienced a slight tightening in my chest. She is, I decided and without a doubt, a good looking woman. But what kind of chance could a guy like me have with Alex, I wondered? None, I miserably decided and concentrated on enjoying my time with her.

We ate as we talked, the food on the low coffee table between us, still warm in the tinfoil containers and picked at it with our forks. I shovelled food onto my plate and between mouthfuls, gave Alex an account of the circumstances that led to my being hauled out of the house by Helen Burns and her wee blonde assassin.

I didn't hold back, told her everything and was pleased that she listened without comment, from time to time nodding her head and saw her eyes narrowing at the more harrowing bits, when I recounted the finding of the bodies. You might wonder why I decided to disclose all the details to Alex, who to be frank, is a relative stranger. Can't say I fully understand myself, but what I do know is that I needed to talk, if only to go over everything again so that I might try and make sense of what I knew and what I presumed. I also burst to her about my deal with Wally Bartholomew and silently prayed that my instinct about Alex was correct, that she could keep her counsel and not be the cause of Mickey and me going to prison.

"This man Dewar," she said, "you're convinced he's not the killer of these three people then?"

"Not entirely one hundred per cent certain, but my experience and knowledge tells me that he's nothing to gain and of course everything to lose. Jackie Dewar needed a quiet deal with the Columbians, but now it seems that as a result of the murders, everybody and their granny is involved and in particular the police. It's not in his interest to kill anyone connected to the deal. Hurt them maybe, threaten them certainly, but kill them? No, I don't believe he's behind the murders."

"And the young woman, the daughter that you've got hidden at the Hilton Hotel. You think she's safe there?"

"For now, yes, and I'm sure that by tomorrow, having provided the police with a statement it's very unlikely that Dewar will approach her now. Even Dewar is aware that the courts take a very dim view of anyone who tampers with witnesses, particularly in a murder case and if he tries to contact her or has someone else act on his behalf, threaten or harm her or even looks at her the wrong way, he could be sent down for anything up to five years. No, I'll let her have one more night in the hotel and arrange to get her home tomorrow."

"That's if she wants to go home to that house," sighed Alex, "knowing that her stepmother was murdered there just a few days ago."

"Her decision," I replied, "but I'm keen to go with her to the house. There's something there that she can help me with."

Alex half smiled, a mischievous glint in her eye. She had finished her food and I watched as she dabbed at her mouth with the paper napkin and sat back on the couch.

"From what you've told me of her, it that a professional or personal interest you've got in her?"

"Yes, you're right," I teased her, "she's one cracking looking young woman, very sexy and bright too. But I prefer women, not wee lassies."

"And what kind of woman do you prefer then?"

I stared at her, speechless, not daring to put into words what I was feeling and smiled, because frankly that's all I could manage.

The house phone rang. Talk about being saved by the bell.

"John, its Peasy Byrne. The young lassie you asked me to keep an eye on? She's gone, left the hotel. Drove off in her car."

CHAPTER 13

Just then, right at that moment, I experienced panic.

Not that Sheila Kilbride was my daughter and no, damned attractive though she was, my attraction in women, and one in particular, lay elsewhere. I panicked because she was my responsibility and I feared that somehow, my assumptions that she was safe from Dewar had been wrong or that the killer had discovered where she was and somehow inveigled her to drive away from the hotel.

All these thoughts flashed through my head.

"When did she go, Peasy?" I asked, my throat suddenly dry and my head hurting.

"Not sure, John," he replied. "She hasn't signed out or settled the bill. The rooms still booked in her name and I've used my passkey to have a look in. Her things are still there. It was the evening porter, one of my guys; I'd told him to keep an eye on her car and check that it wasn't tampered with or anything. You know how easily outsiders can get into the garage beneath the hotel. He was doing his security rounds about half an hour ago and saw the Mini was gone. He remembered it was there about two hours ago, so that kind of gives us a time frame for when she left. Sorry, John, I can't tell you anymore than that."

I could tell from his voice that Peasy felt bad, that he'd let me down. But realistically, he wasn't Sheila's minder and he'd been good enough to do me a favour, especially after I'd lied to him about the reason for keeping an eye on her.

Alex stared at me, eyes wide open and her hand at her throat, aware that something bad had happened, but not interrupting.

"Peasy" I tried to sound calm, "can you tell me if she received any phone calls to the room? Maybe within the last two hours?"

"Hold on," replied Peasy and I heard a low, muffled conversation that made me realise he must be at the reception desk.

A minute later he told me that he'd spoken with the reception desk staff and that no, none of them recalled having placed a call through to Sheila's room.

I thanked Peasy, assuring him I didn't blame him and hung up, knowing that even though Sheila's actions were out of his control, he'd still feel bad about the situation.

"What is it?" asked Alex.

She'd heard my side of the conversation, so told her about Peasy and related his side.

"Could she maybe just have taken off? I mean, you did tell me that she complained of being cooped up in the hotel and wanting to get out. Maybe she just went for a drive. You know how young girls can be."

"I'm not an expert of young women, Alex," I barked, then immediately regretted it.

"Sorry," I shook my head, "it's just that I'm worried. She trusted me and now she's gone God knows where to."

"It's probably a silly question, but have you considered phoning her on her mobile?"

No, I thought, that'd be too easy, but it was worth a shot and checked the number on my mobile, but used the landline when I saw the mobile had little battery life left.

To my surprise, she answered on the second ring.

"Sheila!" I snapped at her, "where the fu….where the hell are you?"

"I had to get out of there John. Sorry, I know you'll have been worried. I've come home, to the house I mean. I just wanted to be here for a while."

"Stay there," I instructed her. "Lock all the doors and windows and keep your mobile in your hand. If you hear or see anyone or anything that you recognise or don't recognise, phone the police immediately, do you hear me? Immediately," I repeated.

I slammed the phone down into its cradle with more force than I intended, my anger dissipating with the knowledge that she was okay, but still worried that she was alone and vulnerable.

"Sorry, Alex," I stood and limped towards the door, "I need to go."

"I'll come with you," she replied, striding after me and reaching for her waxed jacket from the coat hook in the hallway.

"No," I said with more conviction than I felt, "it might not be safe."

"Tell me this," she stared at me as she shrugged into her coat, "do you like me?"

Now that question, I'll be up front with you, completely threw me.

"Eh, yes, of course," I stuttered.

"Really like me, I mean?"

I grinned self-consciously at her.

"Yes, I really like you," I agreed, knowing I was blushing like some sheepish schoolboy.

"And I like you. Really like you," she replied, aping my grin, "and remember, I used to be a nurse, so if you think for one minute that I'm letting you go out alone to somewhere you might get hurt and I'm not there with you, you've another thing coming. Now, do we go together or do we argue?"

With that, she snatched open the door and I watched her storm out. Shaking my head and still grinning, I followed her out of the close.

We decided to take Alex's car, a silver coloured Honda Jazz automatic and I watched as she drove carefully, but with confidence through the late night traffic that was mercifully light. When she spoke, I was pleased to see that she continued to peer ahead through the windscreen rather than, as some women do, turn to the passenger when they're speaking.
"Surely it's unlikely that the killer would know of Sheila returning home?" Alex asked.
"Probably not," I agreed "but if what I suspect is true, then the killer has murdered Crawford and Phyllis Kilbride to tie up some loose ends. They might guess that at some point, Sheila will return home and take the opportunity to strike then."
"But what is it that Sheila knows, I wondered? What information does she have that might connect the killer to the three murdered people?"
"Quite possibly Sheila herself might not be aware that she has some knowledge that could identify the killer, I just don't know," I tailed off.
If nothing else, the visit to the house with Sheila there, gave me the opportunity to test my theory that the apparent wanton damage to the framed photographs swept from the top of the piano, was a deliberate act that might have a bearing on the identity of the killer. Or so I hoped, I thought with all my fingers and my toes crossed.
"Right, slow down and prepare to turn in here," I pointed ahead at the darkened driveway, "and slow down again. Turn off your lights and take it easy," I whispered to her, though why I was whispering inside the car, who knows. I supposed it's because I was anxious that Sheila was all right.
Alex slowed the car to a waking pace and drove up the incline of the driveway towards the house, the only sound being the quiet of the engine and the noise of the tyres crunching on the red chips.
The Mini sat parked and unattended, near to the front door. The house was in darkness and with the only light coming from behind a clouded moon, looked cold and sinister.
Alex stopped the car and as she applied the handbrake I quietly opened my door.
"Wait here," I turned and whispered to her, "I'm going to phone Sheila from the mobile and have her come to the front door. I don't want to unnecessarily alarm her," I explained.
As I made to get out of the car, Alex grabbed me by the arm and leaning toward me, pulled me to her and then awkwardly kissed me on the lips, her mouth sweet and faintly tasting of chicken and noodles.
I was so surprised I grinned like a primary schoolboy.
"Be careful, John, and don't do anything foolish, okay?" she warned me, her eyes glinting in the moonlight with concern.
I nodded and got out of the car and limped towards the front door.

Opening my mobile phone, the light indicated the battery was almost exhausted. Damn, I thought, cursing my stupidity for not taking the opportunity to charge it when I'd been eating. But there seemed to be enough charge left for at least one call. I scrolled down and found Sheila's number and pressed the call button.

A few seconds passed and then I heard from inside the house, what was probably Sheila's phone ringing.

The phone continued to ring, then my battery died and the connection cut off. Fuck! Why didn't she answer, I wondered. I'd told her to carry her phone with her. Something was wrong.

I glanced back to the Jazz where I saw the silhouette of Alex watching me from within. Using my free hand, I indicated a door locking motion. She seemed to understand and I heard the audible click as the central locking system activated and then she gave me the thumbs up signal.

I looked at the house and wondered right or left and decided to go left, to the back of the house.

Stumbling and groping my way through overgrown bushes along a flagstone path that circled the house, I got round to the rear and saw the back door slightly ajar. By the faint moonlight, I could see what looked like shiny diamonds sparkling on the ground and realised a glass pane in the door had been broken, enabling someone to put a hand through and unlock the door. My breathing was laboured, my mouth dry, my hands sweaty and my heart was beating in my chest like a pile driving hammer. Holding my not so sturdy stick in both hands and wishing it were a nail encrusted baseball bat, I prepared to enter the house.

As you'll have gathered by now, Bruce Willis I'm not, so when the figure in dark clothing and what was likely a ski mask, burst through the door I was bowled over and went crashing onto my arse, the stick I had been prepared to wield, flying out of my hands and landing behind me. Not my best moment, I have to say.

I didn't know if I'd imagined it or not, what seemed to be a flash of silver, glinting in the moonlight as the figure passed me by. By the time I'd collected my senses and twisted round to prepare myself for a kick to the head, the figure was gone. Not a word had been said nor a noise made.

Sheila!

I twisted by body round and reached for my stick, managing with a little difficulty to get to my feet.

"*Sheila*!" I screamed into the darkened house, groping for a light switch by the door.

The blinding light dazzled me and I blinked rapidly, my eyes adjusting as I moved through a utility room into the large, expansive kitchen with its seemingly endless wall units and cupboards, switching on more lights.

"*Sheila*!" I screamed again and continued to scream her name, moving across the hallway and through the house toward the front room, dreading what I knew I must find, my eyes taking in a mobile phone lying in a corner on the floor.

"Sheila, it's me, John. John Logan," I shouted again, my head twisting and turning, searching for her and expecting to see a body.

Suddenly, there was loud banging on the front door and the continuous ringing of the doorbell. I fumbled at the catch, my fingers shaking and unlocked the door from the inside to discover Alex, wide-eyed and anxious.

She reached for me, holding me close to her, staring at my face.

"I saw the lights come on," she gasped, "are you okay?"

I nodded and turned away, escaping her clutch as I continued to shout loudly for Sheila.

"John?" said the soft voice.

Alex and I turned suddenly.

Sheila, wearing the hooded top and jeans, stood at the open door of a cupboard that was located under the stairs, her arms wrapped round her shoulders, her face white and drained and her body shaking. She burst into tears and ran towards me, clasping her arms about my neck and almost bowling me over, hysterically crying. I looked over Sheila's head to Alex, who smiled with relief and made the T sign with her hands. I pointed her towards the kitchen.

Slowly, supporting Sheila against my body, I followed Alex into the kitchen. While Alex busied herself with the kettle, I got Sheila sat down on a seat at the table and once more, my famous clean hankie came into play. Her body convulsing, I let her sob and managed to get down onto one knee, holding her head against my shoulder while I soothed her, stroking her hair and rubbing her back as I did my son when he was very little and had hurt himself. I felt her body relax, the tension easing from it and waited till she was ready, fighting the urge to ask her what had happened, knowing that her attacker was long gone by now. Alex touched my shoulder and placed two mugs of hot, sweet tea down in front of us.

Gently, I took Sheila's hands from my neck and placed them onto the mug, watching as she cringed slightly from the heat and, sighing as though she'd exhausted her tears, bowed over to blow at the top of the tea to cool it.

"Thanks," she whispered to Alex, standing over me.

"When you're ready," I quietly said.

It took her a few minutes and really, there wasn't much for her to tell. She'd become bored, sitting about the hotel room and decided to cheer herself up with a visit home, at the same time collecting a change of clothing. No, she said, she hadn't considered that there might be any danger to her.

"So what happened when you arrived here?" I asked.

"It was still daylight and I didn't intend to be anymore than fifteen or twenty minutes. I didn't think of it as a risk. When you phoned, I'd been here about a half-hour, longer than I'd thought. Time just seemed to pass so quickly. I got caught up deciding what clothes I should take with me," she blushed.

I guessed that being a young woman, fashion sense had overtaken common sense, but had the good grace to take heed of Alex's warning glance and kept my mouth shut.

"Go on," I urged her.

"Well, as I said, you'd phoned and it occurred to me that darkness was falling faster than I'd anticipated and you warned me to lock the doors and keep my phone in my hand. Honestly," she grimaced, "I was doing as you said. I checked the front door and was through in the kitchen, just about to ensure the back door at the utility room was locked when I thought I saw a man, someone dressed in dark clothes, in the bushes at the rear garden."

She choked off speaking, the memory frightening her and tightly clasped my hand.

"I was so frightened," she sobbed, then took a deep breath and exhaled slowly. "The kitchen was in darkness so I guessed he hadn't seen me and decided to hide because I knew you were coming to get me. I sneaked through to the hallway, but tripped over something, my own feet likely," she smiled, "and the phone went flying out of my hand."

That must be the phone I saw lying in the hallway, I realised.

"I didn't know what to do, to run out the front door or what. The frightening thing was, I didn't know where he was, not until I heard the smashing glass and realised he must be breaking in through the back door. It just seemed to happen so quickly and I run into the small cupboard where we keep the shoes and hid."

Sheila paused for breath and sipped at her tea.

"I couldn't hear anything. He didn't call out or anything and I couldn't hear any footsteps. At one point I thought I heard him shuffle past the cupboard door and I almost died of fright. Then I heard what sounded like a car and shortly after that you shouted my name. At first I thought it was a trick, that's why I didn't answer. I'm so sorry, John, I should never have left the hotel. Sorry," she lamely finished.

"And you've every right to be sorry, young lady," I rebuked her, but smiled as I said it.

That earned me another crushing hug and almost over-balanced me and I had to hold onto the table to prevent from falling onto the tiled floor.

"Better get this old guy up before he does himself a mischief," said a smiling Alex as she put one hand under my armpit and helped hoist me to my feet.

Sheila looked up at Alex, as if seeing her for the first time.

"I'm sorry…." she began.

"My name's Alex Haldane, I'm a friend of John's."

"Oh, I'm…."

"Sheila, yes, I know," Alex smiled again, then turned towards me.

"John, do you think we should maybe contact the police, tell them what happened here?"

"Of course," I agreed, "but first I'd like Sheila here to help me with something."

I led Sheila and Alex through to the lounge. Of course, Phyllis Kilbride's body had been removed, but the dark stain on the polished wooden floor would remain until professionally cleaned. I saw Sheila startle and her body shuddered at the sight of the stain and Alex came from behind her, her arm going about Sheila's shoulder in comforting support. That small act of compassion reinforced what I was beginning to understand, that I wanted Alex Haldane to remain in my life and, dare I hope, she might want me in hers.

Because the windows were tightly shut, the room retained the faint odour of dried blood and here and there, I saw patches of what seemed to be fingerprint dust, a bloody nuisance if it gets onto your clothing and the devil to get out. That's why most detectives wear cheaper, off the peg suits rather than the more expensive tailored suits, because during the course of a working week, divisional detectives usually find themselves smeared with blood, vomit, fingerprint dust and a hundred other nasty stains, some of which I don't even want to think about anymore.

The room, minus the body, was almost exactly as I'd last seen it and also included my point of interest.

What I had initially thought to be a wanton act of vandalism, the sweeping to the floor of the framed photographs and then their destruction, seemed to me to now be something more deliberate. I knew that the police photographers would have completed an album of photographs of the crime scene, so had no worries about picking my way through the debris by the piano.

I called Sheila to help me and, with some pain because my leg was really giving me grievance, bent down and began sifting through the photos.

She looked at me with obvious curiosity.

"I want you to carefully lift these photos and I know, some of the frames are broken," I replied to her unsaid question, warning her to mind her fingers on the broken glass, "and try to place them as you remember them, on the piano. Can you do that for me?"

"I'll try, she replied, eager to help, if a little puzzled at my request.

Alex stood by, watching as Sheila matched photos to frames and placed them on the piano, some lying down because they were broken and no longer fit to stand upright.

Some three or four minutes passed then Sheila declared that they seemed to be as she remembered.

I stared at the photographs and then turned to her.

"Is this all the photographs, Sheila? Are you certain?"

Her eyes narrowed in concentration and she stroked her lower lip with the forefinger and thumb of her right hand, concentration etched on her face.

"You're right," she turned to me, her eyes opened wide in understanding, "there's one missing. There's a photograph that sat here," she jabbed at the piano lid, excited now, "but it's gone, it's not among the rest."

"And can you recall what the photograph was?" I asked, trying to remain calm, but as nervously excited as she was.

"Of course I can. It was my dad, standing on the Elizabeth, his hand on the tiller. That's the photo that's missing."

"Think hard, Sheila, who else was in the photo with your dad, at the back of the boat?"

She closed her eyes in concentration and we listened as she remembered, telling

Alex and me of that warm, sunny day, taking the boat from the Inverkip Marina for a Sunday outing, the picnic basket filled with all sort of delicious foodstuffs. The sun beating down on her face as she lay on the decking, delighted to be away from school, yet worried and having discussed with her dad one pupil who frequently arrived with unwashed clothes and the occasional bruising to his face that could never quite be properly explained. Her dad, so relaxed, laughing and happy, joking that Phyllis was missing a wonderful time, yet sad that she just didn't appreciate the thrill of sailing a small yacht on the Clyde. Cajoling Sheila to take a turn at the wheel and finally, insisting she photograph him because he was the Captain and the crew, both of them, were at his beck and call.
"Both of you?" I asked. "Who was the other crewmember, Sheila?"
She stared at me and then, telling me the name of the crewmember who was with them on that bright and happy day, the whole shebang, murders and all, became a little clearer.

CHAPTER 14

Sheila searched her father's room and within minutes, found his small, electronic address book in his desk and from which she found the name and address that I was looking for.
I left the two women at the house with the instruction that they phone Mickey Farrell, tell him where I was going and to hotfoot it after me, preferably with cavalry, because I guessed I was on a time limit and I might just be that little bit too late.
I borrowed a protesting Alex's car, but not before she walked me out to it and almost squeezed the life from me before smothering me in kisses.
"Don't read into this, John Logan," she warned me, "you're still going to have to romance me with flowers and dinner before we go any further, okay?"
I promised that if she didn't mind being romanced by a gimpy guy, then I was her man.
Then she got a little more serious, telling me that we all carried a bit of disability and if I could cope with hers, then mine was no real problem to her.
I think just then I realised and to my own surprise, I was a little in love with her.
I drove quickly down the driveway, gunning the engine a little and headed westwards through the darkness towards the village of Rhu, situated about three miles east of the town of Helensburgh, on the banks of the Clyde. A few years previously I'd been part of a team involved in the surveillance of a drug dealer who had resided in Helensburgh, but kept a small dinghy he'd used for fishing in Rhu Bay, so I was reasonably familiar with the area and the roads round about it.
The Jazz is a lovely, dependable family car, but not used to a former police surveillance driver like me treating it like a Formula One vehicle and protested the abuse I meted out as I raced towards Rhu. I figured if not already too late, I'd

less than an hour before the tide turned and my quarry would be gone.

It was pitch black as I hurled the Jazz along the A814, pleased that at least Alex kept the fuel needle sitting above the halfway mark. Rain began to fall, though not the heavy pounding rain that is synonymous of the Clyde coast, but a fine drizzle of the bloody nuisance type that barely mists over the windscreen. I turned on the wipers at intermittent, but the rain was so fine that after a while, the rubber blades squeaked noisily on the glass. As I drove, my mind was turning over everything hat had happened since that first phone call from Phyllis Kilbride. As a police officer, I had always been part of a team or working to a specific plan or objective. But here I was, speeding along the coastal road in a borrowed car, hunting a multiple killer and making it up as I went along and to top it all, my bladder was reminding me that I needed to pee.

What the fuck am I doing, I wondered?

I was no longer a police officer, I couldn't arrest anyone and more importantly, not only was I possibly risking my life, but there was no wage at the end of it. That is, if I'm still alive, I grimly thought and prayed that Alex had contacted Mickey Farrell or at least someone who'd come to help.

I finally arrived in Rhu and turned into School Road, cursing the poor street lighting as I searched for number seventy-nine. The house was in darkness, as I expected and with all the curtains wide open, I guessed there was nobody home, a fact seemingly borne out by the garage being empty and doors lying wide open. Shit.

Nevertheless, I took a few minutes to get out of the car and sneak round the back of the house. There being no sign of life and in the darkness, I took the opportunity to pee.

I knew now where to go.

I drove at breakneck speed to the marina at Rhu Bay, killing my lights as I approached the entrance. I had little fear of being stopped by any cops in this backwater and at this time of night, traffic was nil. I stopped and parked the car outside the closed metal gate, but saw that the chain was pretty slack and permitted me to squeeze through the gap, no mean feat for a guy with a stick, let me tell you. The moon glistened on the water and apart from a couple of fading security lights that really did nothing, other than illuminate a circle of about ten feet around the area where they were situated, the place was in darkness.

The masts of beached yachts and some that bobbed as they rode the water at anchor, stood out against the blackness that was the Clyde. Two small jetty's run from the shingle down each side of the hard sanding and into the water, one for about fifty feet and another for a distance that looked to be about twice that length. I could see the masts and stern of a yacht tied up along her portside at the smaller jetty.

I crouched down low, trying to see any movement on the yacht, but it was too dark to make anything out, then suddenly, for an instance, a deck hatch must have been uncovered and a sliver of light escaped the cabin, but just as quickly was extinguished.

Now, I don't know if you've ever tried to walk or, in my case, limp quietly on shingle, but if you haven't, then let me give you some advice. Don't bother trying. It's the noisiest bloody under footing you'll ever have the misfortune to come across. But then again, why would you try to be quiet, unless like me, you're trying to sneak up on a killer.

I opened my mouth and breathed quietly through my nose to cut down noise. The faintest hum of an engine drifted towards me and I cursed. I was thinking tides and sails, but common sense should have prevailed. Most yachts of this size, I should have guessed, would also be equipped with some sort of power, likely a diesel engine.

You have to remember that I'm no Horatio Hornblower, more of a Captain Pugwash.

I realised the one advantage I now have was that anyone on the yacht would be distracted by the noise of the engine and less likely to hear me shuffling across the shingle. The closer I got the more detail I could make out. The yacht seemed to be about twenty-five foot long and the sails were curled against the mast so I was right, the boat was about to depart under engine power.

There was the faintest smell of paint or varnish, I wasn't quite sure and guessed that the yacht was no longer the Elizabeth, but likely now known by some other name.

So here am I, standing on the jetty and reaching across to take hold of the safety line strung along the port side the yacht and balancing myself to make the short step across the dark water and not for the first time I suddenly think, what am I going to do when I'm aboard?

I don't have a weapon to defend myself, other than my stick and there's no reason for me to be here. But to be honest, perhaps I was here because I wanted to again, just this once, be the old me, the detective that wanted to close the case. Prove to myself that I can still finish what I started. With one hand on a stanchion that supported the metal guard wire, I gingerly stepped onto the decking, remembering the fall of rain that had just ceased and regretting that I didn't have proper deck shoes or whatever they were called. One slip and I was either going over the side or at best, crashing to the deck.

I could hear someone rattling down below, but the port side portholes all seemed to be blacked out by curtains and I was unable to see into the cabin.

I saw a sliding hatchway, a closed cover that seemed to lead down into the cabin area and presumably from where I'd previously seen the beam of light appear. It occurred to me that if I could lock or jam it, I'd be safe and the killer would be trapped below deck. There were enough handholds on the boat superstructure and roof of the cabin available for me, so gently I laid my stick down and crouching, I made my way towards the hatch cover.

I was six feet from the cover when without warning it flew back into its recess and a brilliant shaft of light from the cabin completely dazzled me.

The figure that climbed up from the cabin was dressed in a black polo neck sweater and black ski pants and, turning to face me, seemed startled to see me. "Well, well, Mister Logan. Nice of you to drop by."

My eyes slowly adjusted to the blinding light and I could see the figure standing a few feet in front of me, outlined in silhouette.

"Nice to see you too, Miss Carlisle," I replied, "though by now I expected you'd have long gone."

I saw her glancing over my shoulder and furtively looking about, no doubt trying to assess if I was alone or accompanied.

"Is this a social visit or what?" she asked, stepping fully onto the decking, her right hand from the elbow down hidden from my view by the corner of the cabin arch.

"Just trying to tie up a few loose ends in my inquiry, Miss Carlisle. Yeah, a few loose ends, much the same as you've been doing."

She nodded and half smiled, having by now probably decided that I was alone and happy to talk while she worked out how to deal with me.

By dealing with me what I really mean is how to kill me.

"Loose ends," she repeated, her eyes narrowing. "I think I know what you mean. It's very brave of you, being a cripple and all, to come alone, Mister Logan. Or do you think that I'm about to simply put my hands up, flutter my eyes and come along nicely, as they say?"

From the periphery of my eye, I saw her right arm and shoulder tense and I knew, just knew, that she was holding the hammer.

I decided to press on, gambling that Alex had gotten a hold of Mickey or someone and tried to stall for time.

"Yeah, loose ends. Like did you have an affair with Martin Kilbride or simply steal the account number and password and how did you know that he was acting for Jackie Dewar? I don't quite get that one. Or Billy Crawford, where did he come into it?"

We've all watched TV shows where the good guy corners the bad guy and prior to the bad guy, usually unsuccessfully, trying to top the good guy, the bad guy always confesses how he did this or did that. Why the bad guy just doesn't simply kill the good guy without an explanation of his dastardly deeds, I never really understood, but hey, as a friend of mine who is a playwright always says, it's just television.

It seemed that Carlisle thought she had enough time to relate how smart she was to the good, but dumb guy, who on this occasion was unfortunately me.

"Billy Crawford," she almost sneered. "A real wanker if ever there was one. Met him in a bar in Palma and he bought me a couple of drinks. I thought what the hell, he wasn't that unattractive and had money to spend and besides, it was just a holiday fling, a simple diversion from my humdrum life, if you like. Wasn't too bad in bed either," she said, eager now to tell me how clever she is, "if a little unimaginative. But a boaster, telling me that he was going to be into a lot of money, that he had a scheme cooked up. Then one night I saw him at the hotel bar with two Latin types, evil looking bastards. Columbians, he later told me. Didn't really mean much to me at that time."

She shifted ever so slightly of the balls of her feet, but still her right hand remained out of sight.

"A few drinks later and in bed, I got him ever so excited," she almost smiled, "because I am very good in bed, Mister Logan and Billy, poor Billy," she almost pouted, "told me all about his deal that he was fixing up for a Glasgow gangster called Jackie Dewar."

Swallowing hard, she almost mesmerised me and I had the uncomfortable feeling that I was the mouse and she the cat.

"I didn't really give Billy a second thought when I returned to the UK, just considered him another idiot involved in the drug scene and it had nothing to do with me. So, imagine my surprise when a few weeks ago, who should call into the office to meet with Martin, but the mysterious Mister Jackie Dewar. Now, I'm not usually one to believe in coincidence, but my curiosity was peaked and so, using my feminine wiles and God given good looks, I persuaded Martin to have an after-work drink or three, during which he confided in me, as a colleague. He was an extremely unhappy man, married to that bitching cow and really just wanted to offload on someone. So after more drink, we arrived back at my place and," here she grinned, "as I said, I am extremely good in bed."

I stared at her, the blonde hair tied back into a ponytail with the sort of figure that most women strive for and I didn't doubt her, not for one minute. Funny, I thought as I shifted my legs ever so slightly, that even in moments of stress, the old male urge kicks in.

"You'll recall that I am," she smilingly corrected herself, "or was the office manager at Boyle and Spencer, so one of my jobs was Data Protection and the issuing of computer login details. For security purpose, the partners and staff make up their own individual passwords. So I was halfway there, having Martin's login details and all I needed was his password."

"Elizabeth," I rightly guessed.

She nodded her head. "Well done, Mister Logan, I am impressed. I tried Sheila first, then Phyllis, but then I remembered the drunken Martin confessing that he was still in love with his first wife, the dead Elizabeth," she sounded almost surprised, "and so got there in the end."

"But," I interrupted her flow, "you guessed that he would eventually work out that you logged onto his profile and would know it was you that diverted the money to an account presumably set up by you?"

"Correct," she beamed. "I couldn't take the risk of being exposed and so," she sounded almost apologetic, "poor Martin, ever so trusting Martin, had to go."

She almost made it sound that he'd taken a holiday.

"How did you know about the holiday home?"

"That was easy," she gushed. "In Martin's account profile, I saw he'd a second mortgage and it wasn't difficult getting the information of the address from the lender. Not when you work for an accountancy firm and explain that the information is required to comply with the Money Laundering Regulations."

"Billy Crawford was another loose end, I suppose. He'd remember telling you about the deal and if he discovered you worked with Martin...."

"Absolutely right," she interrupted, her enthusiasm evident for her own cleverness. "Billy had to be dealt with as well. Poor, Billy, got the shock of his life when he opened the door, because he was already entertaining someone else," she giggled, her right hand still hidden by the corner of the hatchway.

"And the photographs on the piano, when you murdered Phyllis. You remembered that you had been photographed on the boat here, coiling the rope," I indicated the stern behind her. To my disappointment, she was shrewd enough not to turn her head away. "You couldn't risk being identified as having knowledge of the boat or being socially involved with Martin Kilbride."

"Again, very good, Mister Logan," she smiled, "you have been doing your homework. Phyllis wasn't stupid. A completely selfish cow and a gold-digger and very, very sly. When I visited her she seemed to suspect I had been involved in some way with Martin and believe it or not," she leaned slightly forward in an almost conspiratorial manner, "I enjoyed knocking her head in. Does that surprise you?"

"No," I solemnly shook my head, "that doesn't surprise me Miss Carlisle."

"Do you know she tried to call the Police?"

I nodded, "And," I continued "that's why you tried to get rid of Sheila, the daughter, because you thought maybe not now or next week or next month or even next year, but sometime in the future, she'd remember you being on the boat. Remember your friendship with her father and maybe put two and two together, maybe just enough to cast suspicion your way. Sheila was a connection to you, a loose end and you deal with loose ends, don't you Miss Carlisle? But how did you know that Sheila would be returning home tonight? Who told you?"

"Nobody told me," she scoffed, stressing the word 'told' like I was some sort of idiot who didn't comprehend, "I waited for hours each night in my car, watching the driveway, knowing that eventually she'd have to return home. I have tremendous patience, you see Mister Logan, one of my attributes. But I'd almost given up, when lo and behold I saw the car arrive. I couldn't see who was in the car and didn't know if she was alone or not. When I broke in, I couldn't find her and then shortly after that, you arrived Mister Logan. How very clever of you."

That's all I needed, being complimented by a psychotic nutcase.

"But why the boat," I asked, "what advantage is there in stealing the boat?"

"I have my deckhand certificate, which is why Martin and I first developed our...friendship, shall we call it," she replied, "so sailing this lovely old thing won't be a problem and I really need to get to Guernsey. I'm off work with stress, you know," she continued, as if seeking sympathy, "and I don't want to be recorded going through an airport. On my salary, I can't afford to buy a yacht, so the Elizabeth is now the Fair Maiden. And let's face it," she almost giggled, "it's not as if poor Martin will be using it again, will he?"

That explained the faint smell of paint and I realised then she was crazy, not just bad, but really, really off her fucking head.

"So that's where the money is, in Guernsey?"

At that, her head turned slightly as though listening, her eyes still locked to mine. I knew she was thinking that even though it had been just a few minutes, she should be departing; shoving off if you want to be nautical about it, right away. Her right arm dropped to her side and I saw it for the first time.

A shiny, aluminium coated carpenter's hammer glinting in the light from the cabin and with a black vulcanised grip.

"So that's it, then," I nodded to the hammer, "that's what you used to murder three people?"

"Four people, Mister Logan. Four people, if we count you," and raised the hammer above her head as she suddenly and swiftly came at me.

I backed off, using the cabin roof to propel myself backwards as the hammer swung down towards my head. I raised my free right arm and the shaft caught me on the forearm, not enough to break the arm, but painful? You've no idea! I stumbled back a few more feet and she slowly came after me again.

"You can't stop me now, she whispered through gritted teeth, "Not after all I've worked for. I won't let you," and swung again at my head.

I'd reached the corner edge of the cabin roof and fell to my left, my back against the mast. Still, she came after me, looking for an advantage to strike at my head. "Don't suppose you want to make a deal?" I grunted, trying to stall her and again taking a blow to my right forearm, but this time it was the head of the hammer and yes, did it ever fucking hurt.

I half fell, half stumbled round the mast and knew that my back was now to the starboard side, the water glistening below.

Alison Carlisle was a young, strong and athletic woman and possession of the hammer not only gave her an unfair and overall advantage, but bear in mind that she was up against a guy who has difficulty retaining his balance… and that's when I'm sober.

I realised the only chance I might have, the only way I was going to save my life was to try and get her on the deck, then get her in a clinch and hold on, fight rough and tumble, head to head, cheek to cheek, if you get my meaning. I felt the wire guardrail at the small of my back and she lunged once more at me, the hammer swinging down towards my head.

Call it luck, chance or sheer desperation, but I gritted my teeth and pivoting on my good right leg, swung my gammy leg towards her, but in doing so, the wet decking and my leather-soled shoes came into play.

I felt myself crashing down on my back to the deck and sort of half bounced off the wire guardrail, landing heavily with the breath being knocked from me. Just as the very act of falling took me by surprise, Carlisle was swinging forward and my now outstretched legs crashed into her shins and knocked her feet from under her. With a grunt as the air also expelled from her body, she collapsed along side of me and the hammer, spinning from her hand, struck me on the forehead above my left eye, but fortunately for me, the momentum wasn't as bad than it might have been had she'd still been wielding it in her hand. Still, the blow was enough to render me stunned.

Both of us now prone at the edge of the decking, in panic and self-survival, I dazedly tried to grab at her, but she pushed away and, without realising what was happening, slipped backwards head first, over the side of the boat.

I heard a short yelp and a splash as she hit the water.

My right arm was numb from the beatings she had inflicted with the hammer and I used my left hand to pull me to the edge, the blood from the wound on my forehead mixing with the soft rain, now streaming down my face and blinding me. In horror, I saw that when rolling over the edge of the boat, the bottom of Carlisle's ski pants had snagged in a cleat, one of those capstan things that is used to secure ropes when docking the yacht. She hung by her left leg over the side, her right leg dangling uselessly and her head and shoulders beneath the water, her arms flailing as she desperately tried without success to get some purchase, find something to hold onto, to pull her head up and clear from the water. Twice, she managed to raise her head and I saw the terror in her eyes, reaching for me, spluttering as she tried to speak, her eyes begging me to help as the water cascaded from her mouth, before she sunk again beneath the water.

Frantically, I reached with my one good hand to pull at the material, to try and free the leg of the ski-pants from the cleat, but her weight, my rapidly weakening state and the strong material combined to defeat me.

I tried to shout for help, but was overcome by nausea and realised I was losing consciousness.

Again, for what I think was the third or fourth time, I can't be certain, Carlisle forced her head from the water, the fear evident in her face, her long blonde hair cascading about her, vainly reaching for her left leg, then for the final time sank beneath the cold, oily surface and I saw her body go limp, a few bubbles rising to the top and marking her last breath.

My head felt like a ton weight and I let it sag to the deck. In the faint distance I thought I heard the sound of a siren, the good old blues and two.

"Fucking typical," I mumbled to nobody in particular, then passed out.

I woke and almost immediately was conscious of something over my mouth. I fumbled, but a hand brushed my fingers away and opening my eyes, well, my right eye really because my left eye was covered over with something. A figure in green fumbled with something covering my mouth, an oxygen mask I later learned and I heard him tell me not to move, that I was in an ambulance and that I was going to be okay. I blinked against the bright light and tried to lift my left arm to take the mask off, but a hand gently held my arm firm and the man, the paramedic, soothingly told me that I needn't speak, just nod or shake my head in response to his questions.

"Mister Logan, John," he said, "Can you hear me?"

I was vaguely aware of his face peering down at me swaying slightly as the ambulance battered on or rounded corners.

"We're taking you to the Southern General Hospital. You've got quite a bad head injury, concussion at the very least," he told me, "I'm just going to shine a wee light into your eye, so don't worry."

No problem, I think I slurred, because really, all I wanted to do was sleep and that's about all I remember.

CHAPTER 15

If you know the general area that I've spoken of, you might wonder why the ambulance crew decided to take me past a couple of casualty wards that were nearer and the longer distance onto the SGH, but it seemed the knock I suffered to the head from Alison Carlisle's hammer had given the young paramedic some cause for concern and he made the decision to get me as fast as possible to the country's finest neurology department.

I don't recall much more other than when about thirty-six hours later, I'm wakening in a single bedroom on the sixth floor of the hospitals Neuro wing, my head bandaged, my throat parched and feeling like shit. It was daylight and the sun streamed through the Venetian blinds making a striped pattern on the dull, yellow painted wall, opposite my bed. Turning my head caused me a blinding pain above my left eye and my bandaged right arm ached from where it had taken a pounding. But I'm alive, I thought, so things aren't that bad.

I must have been awake, I don't know for certain, say fifteen or twenty minutes when a young nurse with a wide smile and Caribbean accent, wearing the standard white trouser uniform and a disposable plastic apron, popped her head round the door.

"My, sleepy lad, you back with us now? Bet you want a drink of water, eh?" she said as she filled a plastic beaker from a jug and tipped my head forward.

Let me tell you, nothing tastes quite like water when you're feeling as I do.

The nurse, Jocelyn I later learned, gently laid my head back on the pillow and dabbed at my lips with a paper tissue to wipe off the dribbled water.

"Can you tell me…" I started to say, but she interrupted me by placing her forefinger on my lips.

"Hush there, me sleepy lad," she grinned at me with a mouthful of shiny teeth, "you got lots of questions I bet, but rest now and I see you when you waken."

I didn't intend to fall asleep, but the next thing I know is that it's night-time, the blinds are drawn and Alex Haldane is sitting in a chair beside the bed, reading a magazine.

"Hi," I said, smiling at her and feeling a damn sight better than I had previously.

Alex placed the magazine on the bed cover and for a few seconds, just stared at me, her lower lip trembling and eyes brimming with tears. She pretended to scowl and shook her head.

"Can't let you out of my sight for an hour and you end up in here," she said, then slowly raised herself from the chair and with some awkwardness, leaned over to hug my neck.

I quietly gasped as she half lay on my sore right arm, but the pain was worth it and I felt her body shake as she gently sobbed. The emotion of the moment was interrupted by my very own angel Jocelyn, who like a whirlwind chose just then to come into the room carrying a basin and with a towel slung over her shoulder.

"Missy," she smiled at Alex, "you give me five minutes with your man and I'll have him smelling sweeter than he does now," and started to pull the plastic curtains round the bed. Alex patted my cheek and nodded, still too upset to speak and left the room.

"You've got visitors, my sleepy lad, two police people outside. You okay to speak with them now?" asked Jocelyn, her eyebrows raised at me as she expertly began to give me my bed bath. I guess had I said no, they wouldn't have gotten past Jocelyn.

And yes, it's true what people say, all modesty is left at the door when you are admitted to hospital.

Turned out my police people were Mickey Farrell and the senior investigating officer in the murder inquiries, Lynn Massey, a strikingly good looking woman, with copper coloured hair that fell to her shoulders and wearing a thin pinstriped-skirted skirted suit.

After introductions, she said, "Gave us quite a scare, John. For a few minutes after we arrived at the boat, we thought you might have been victim number four." Massey took the chair and Mickey leaned against the wall, pretending to glare at me.

"I understand that the knock to your head resulted in a serious concussion and that initially, the doctors here considered you might have internal bleeding on the brain," she told me.

"No fear of that, then, because his head is a lot thicker than most and his brains are in his arse, too," interrupted Mickey, trying to sound scornful, but failing miserably and I knew there was sentiment behind his comment.

Without me realising it, Massey got me talking and I learned that she knew of my involvement up to and including the time I'd attended with Sheila Kilbride at Baird Street police office. From that time forward, I related everything I'd done, whom I'd spoken with, the whole gambit and left nothing out. Lynn Massey, I quickly realised, was a smart and shrewd detective officer and it was plain why at a relatively early age, she'd achieved her rank. She listened without interruption, other than to clarify some point or other, nodding or shaking her head in understanding as I recounted my part in story that included her skidding across the decking and rolling off the yacht, into the water. It didn't escape my notice that Massey's eyes narrowed at that part.

At the end, when I described how Alison Carlisle had drowned, she asked me, "And there was nothing you could have done to save her, nothing at all?"

I paused, again running the incident through my mind and questioned my own actions.

Could I have saved her, I wondered? Did I really, really try as best I could? Or, was I unconsciously aware that had I managed to free Carlisle from the cleat that trapped the leg of her ski pants, would she have been grateful or more likely, swum to the jetty and climbed back aboard the yacht to finish me off?

"No, I didn't have the strength to free her," I replied, shaking my head, "and when she'd struck me with her hammer, she'd unknowingly but effectively disabled me from helping her."

Massey slowly nodded her head as though in understanding.

"Were you on to her?" I asked.

"Yes," Massey replied, "we'd identified her as a possible suspect. No, more like a strong suspect. The Spanish police have forwarded us surveillance photographs of Billy Crawford with the Columbians and some of them showed him with a blonde woman, we now know is Alison Carlisle. Of course, we didn't identify her at that time, but the intelligence brief that accompanied the photographs identified her as a Scottish woman so we had the Border Agency run their recorded CCTV film from the date of the last photograph, for all flights arriving from Palma at both Glasgow and Edinburgh Airports, just in the off-chance she arrived through there. We got lucky and backtracked her arrival with the passport control scanning system and identified her just two days ago. We were in the process of applying for a warrant for her and her home address to establish the association with Crawford, when we learned Boyle and Spencer employ her. It didn't take a genius to work it out, the connections with the Kilbride's from there," she half shrugged. "What we didn't bank on," she continued, "is that she'd stolen the Kilbride's yacht and was preparing to depart for the Channels Islands and if you ask me, it's unlikely she'd have returned to the UK, not with that amount of money at her availability."

I must have raised my eyes at that, for she explained that a search of the yacht discovered charts with the sea route and tides for Guernsey, mapped out.

"We also found a laptop and that's with our techie guys over at Gartcosh, so I'm pretty confident that we'll be able to obtain the details of this mysterious account with Jackie Dewar's ill-gotten proceeds," she smiled. "We're also preparing to apply for a financial warrant under the Proceeds of Crime Act to recover these ill-gotten monies and I don't for one minute believe Dewar will contest the recovery, do you?"

I smiled at that as a fleeting thought passing through my mind of the rage that Dewar must be experiencing.

"All in all, John," she stood and smoothed at her skirt, "that's the inquiry tied up and though I probably don't approve of your lone wolf method, it's pretty obvious that if you hadn't hared down to Rhu Bay and challenged Alison Carlisle, she'd have been gone for good. She seems to have been a smart and intuitive woman and in my opinion, Alison Carlisle would have disappeared and she'd have become someone else."

"My cousin has a law practice, here in Glasgow," she said, reaching into her handbag, "and Mickey assures me that you're a reliable guy, John. Here's his card. He's always on the lookout for somebody to conduct inquiries on behalf of the office; discreet inquiries, precognition statement taking, that sort of thing, Just if it's of any interest to you. I've had a word with him, if you want to give him a call, when you're able, I mean."

She turned to Mickey.

"I know you guys will want a wee word, so I'll grab a coffee from the machine and get you in the car. Ten minutes?"

"Thanks boss," he replied, as he closed the door behind Massey.

I glanced at the business card and slowly exhaled, pleased that Massey seemed satisfied with my account.

"That was really decent of her, Mickey."

"She's not a bad sort," he replied. "Had her own demons in the past with her ex-husband, shit that he is, but found herself a new guy and seems happy enough now. And don't forget, John, though you've been instrumental in cracking this case and the successful conclusion to it, plus the recovery of all that money, it will reflect well on her profile, too."

"Right," he pushed himself off the wall, "I'll be off then for now, but I'll pop by and see you some time tomorrow."

"Oh, I'll be out by then," I replied with some confidence.

He stared at me for a few seconds, his eyebrows narrowing, and then smiled.

"No, I don't think so, buddy and by the way, when you do get out of here, fancy a wee foursome for a meal?" and closed the door behind him before I could say anything else.

I lay back on the pillow for a few minutes, wondering what Mickey was on about when the door knocked and Alex returned, followed into the room by a tall, sandy-haired skinny guy wearing thin metal framed glasses. He looked a youngish thirty or so and the fair moustache was obviously grown to make him seem older. Under his white lab coat, he wore a khaki coloured shirt, knitted khaki tie and khaki coloured trousers with highly polished black shoes.

"John, this is Mister Dalgleish," said Alex.

He extended his right hand, that I took with my left and smiled, "Paul Dalgleish, Major Dalgleish if you want to be politically correct," in a soft, almost boyish voice. Midlands accent, I guessed.

I was puzzled and it must have shown on my face.

"Let me explain John, may I call you John?"

I nodded and watched as Alex sat in the chair, her face displaying what looked like anxiety while Dalgleish stood with his arms folded.

"I've spoken at length here with Alex," he began, turning and nodding towards her, "and I'm aware of the pain that you are currently suffering. I should explain that I'm here at the SGH Neurological Department for a three-month secondment to the NHS from my parent regiment, the Royal Army Medical Corps. My own discipline is orthopaedics, but I'm here primarily to learn about trauma to the skull and spinal injury. My secondary purpose is to instruct in trauma from violent assault, such as gunshot or explosion, though being Glasgow," he grinned, "there's not a lot of explosions, thankfully. I'm recently returned from my second tour of duty at the medical centre at Camp Bastion in Afghanistan, where you'll be aware from news bulletins, a lot of our guys are on the receiving end of gunshot and blast injuries, mainly from IED's. It doesn't take long when you're out there to develop an expertise dealing with some of the casualties," his face had suddenly turned grim, "but the upshot is that I've become something of an expert in orthopaedics."

"I was the consultant on duty when you were admitted," he continued, "and when we had you stripped on the examination table, I couldn't help but see that you have scarring and suffered some gunshot trauma to the left leg. The surgical work that had been done on your leg seemed to be," he hesitated and seemed to be choosing his words carefully, "interesting."

Now, that's not what I would have called the patchwork quilt of stitching.

"What I'm trying to say, John is that my curiosity had been aroused and, as I seem to have some influence around here," he smiled at his own joke, "I was able to get a scan completed for your leg. Frankly, when I viewed the result, I was appalled. I won't comment on a fellow surgeons work and am unable to envisage how he went about repairing your leg, but suffice to say in a very short time, orthopaedic surgery has come a long way. What I'm saying is that if you are willing, I have spoken with the Chief of Staff here at the SGH and obtained his permission to offer you surgery for the purpose of easing the pain you must undoubtedly be suffering. I also have to inform you that part of the agreement for this surgery is that it will be a tuition exercise for some of the surgeons here at the hospital, but you have my assurance I will undertake the surgery."

I was stunned,

Alex, biting her lower lip, her hands clasped tightly in her lap, stared at me, her eyes meeting mine.

"What…what might be the result if this surgery, if I agree?" I stammered as I turned to look at him.

Dalgleish thrust his hands into his lab coat pockets.

"If you should agree, it's my intention to break the leg and re-knit the bones, but properly this time. As you'd expect, there will be post-operative pain, but that will be managed by a standard morphine drip during your stay here at the SGH. I'm guessing you will be with us for no longer than six or seven days. Thereafter," he shrugged his shoulders slightly, "once you've demonstrated that you are capable of using crutches, perhaps six to eight weeks on the crutches, depending on your recovery rate and then I'm pretty confident, it's goodbye to your stick. I won't offer any false hope. It's not a complete restoration of your left leg and after further surgical stitching, your leg won't be very pretty. You will never be fully able-bodied and will likely retain a slight limp. Nor will you be running any marathons, but if my prognosis based on the scan result is correct, you will be

able to bend and support yourself on the leg. Any pain will be so slight as to be negligible and can likely be dealt with by the occasional Paracetamol."
I was taken aback, completely overwhelmed and could only nod to him.
Alex must have seen how shocked I was and stood up, reaching past him to take my hand in hers.
"Yes," was all I could say, "Yes?"

CHAPTER 15

It's been seven weeks since Major Dalgleish operated on my leg. The first few weeks with initial discomfort rather than pain and that's eased daily. I'm still using a crutch, but more to support myself than to actually walk, because it's a bit of a psychological thing. Even though I know I can walk without the crutch, I'm so used to having my stick I still feel that I need to grasp something in my hand. But I'm getting better, a whole lot better.
Alex, who mocks me that I'm no longer gimpy but limpy, is holding my arm as we're stood here in the cold on this wet drizzly morning.
It's the kind of day that suits funerals and I'm pleased to see that this one for a former colleague has drawn a full police turnout, particularly from the Traffic division.
I wasn't totally surprised when three weeks ago Mickey arrived at my door with a four pack of lager that you'll be surprised to know I declined, simply because I was still on some post-op medication. He was visiting to inform me that Jackie Dewar and his minder Scorcher Lamond were both shot to death.
It seemed Jackie had the foresight to install a CCTV camera that recorded visitors to the front door of his luxury flat in George Square. However, Scorcher unsuspectingly opened the door to a caller dressed in a police hat that hid his face and wearing a yellow fluorescent jacket, who without warning shot Scorcher first in the throat, then in the head.
When alerted by a neighbour, the police arrived some hours later and discovered Jackie Dewar had seemingly tried to crawl into a kitchen cupboard to hide, but the gunman had found him and then shot Jackie three times in the body and once in the head. The place had been ransacked and all the furniture drawers turned out. Whatever the gunman had been searching for wasn't ascertained, though plenty of cash and some cocaine was found lying about the flat, so it apparently wasn't a robbery.
But as Mickey pointed out, Dewar had more enemies than pals and was no sad loss to society, so nobody complained that the inquiry soon ground to a halt.
Alex snuggled closer to me, more because she wanted to, than for warmth.
I felt a tap on the shoulder and turned to find Helen Burns smiling at me and who like us, was similarly dressed sombrely in black and recalled her telling me that

Wally had been her tutor cop.

I introduced her, formally on this occasion, to Alex and we three huddled together under Alex's golf style umbrella as the cortege passed us by, escorted by motorcycle outriders and driving slowly towards the entrance of Dalmuir Crematorium. I recognised a tearful Janice when she got out of the car, supported by a slightly older guy, his arm protectively about her shoulder and whom I presumed must be her Simon. If first impressions are anything to go by, he looked a decent enough man.

The service was mercifully short, for to be honest I'm not comfortable in these kind of places and I looked forward to getting out into the fresh air.

We're planning on meeting Sheila Kilbride in the city for lunch and I suspect Sheila will tell us of her plans. I know she and Alex have met for some impromptu counselling sessions and Sheila confided her intention to take off for a while, sell the yacht and the house and use some of the considerable assets her father bequeathed her to see a bit of the world. I should mention that she used some of these assets, at her insistence you understand, to very generously settle my bill. Being practical me, I didn't refuse and the money will more than comfortably see me through the lean patch till I begin work for Lynn Massey's lawyer cousin, Martin McCormick. I inwardly smiled because I now know that one of Martin's associates specialises in divorce and custody and has given me some hope about access to my son Paul. I glanced sideways at Alex, wondering how she'd deal with meeting the wee guy, but inwardly know she'll be fine.

The organ music droned on and I could hear poor Janice in the front pew, sobbing for her father as the curtains were drawn and, with Alex clutching my hand, I could also hear the faint noise of the motor as it lowered the coffin to the basement furnace.

One thing still puzzles me, though.

Where in the hell did Wally Bartholomew get himself a gun?

Needless to say, this story is a work of fiction.
If you have enjoyed the story, you may wish to visit the author's website at:
www.glasgowcrimefiction.co.uk

The author also welcomes feedback and can be contacted at:
george.donald.books@hotmail.co.uk

Printed in Great Britain
by Amazon.co.uk, Ltd.,
Marston Gate.